What the critics are saying...

5 ANGELS "Lacey Alexander has once again proved to be the master of erotic writing and with SIN CITY she has taken the meaning of erotica to a whole new level. The sexual escapades that Marc and Diana experience are deliciously sinful but written in such a way, it makes you want to shed all your inhibitions and become the bad girl you've always wanted to be. SIN CITY absolutely sizzles and it will ignite the reader's arousal with every turn of the page." ~ *Jennifer A., Fallen Angels Reviews*

5 BLUE RIBBONS "Lacey Alexander's talents are boundless and evident in her spectacular stories! This tale earned every one of its five ribbons, and anyone who reads it will walk away a fan of this author." ~ *Tracy Marsac, Romance Junkies*

"Ms. Alexander is probably one of the most talented, straightforward, imaginative writers in erotic romance today. My recommendation is to get your copy of SIN CITY, grab the ice water, put the AC on high.you may need a fan too.and settle in for the adventure of a lifetime." ~ *Jennifer Ray, The Road to Romance*

"For a truly erotic experience that has no boundaries, I recommend SIN CITY and the other books of the Hot in the City Tril⸻ ⸻ ⸻ *Reviews Today*

4 QUIL⸻ ⸻ wonderful job of weaving th⸻ ⸻s to make a story fans of b⸻ ⸻yself completely immersed in the fast pace of the storytelling as well as the blossoming relationship between Diana and Marc. My only suggestion to the reader is to be sure you leave yourself enough time to enjoy the entire story to the last page." ~ *Sashi Ketsel, Novelspot*

4 ½ "Lacey Alexander's second book started off with bang and never slowed down. Erotic from the first chapter it held me enthralled until the last word. Cheers to Ms. Alexander for writing a book where the highly erotic nature of the book does not detract from the romance between the main characters." ~ *Melissa, Enchanted In Romance*

5 *STARS* "If you are looking for white-hot eroticism, then look no further. From start to finish, this one will have your blood boiling." ~ *Christine, eCataRomance*

SIN CITY
HOT IN THE CITY 2

Lacey Alexander

SIN CITY
An Ellora's Cave Publication, March 2005

Ellora's Cave Publishing, Inc.
1337 Commerce Drive Suite #13
Stow, Ohio 44224

ISBN #1419951696

Edited by: *Heather Osborn*
Cover art by: *Dawn Seewer*

Warning:

The following material contains graphic sexual content meant for mature readers. *Hot in the City 2: Sin City* has been rated *E-rotic* by a minimum of three independent reviewers.

Ellora's Cave Publishing offers three levels of Romantica™ reading entertainment: S (S-ensuous), E (E-rotic), and X (X-treme).

S-ensuous love scenes are explicit and leave nothing to the imagination.

E-rotic love scenes are explicit, leave nothing to the imagination, and are high in volume per the overall word count. In addition, some E-rated titles might contain fantasy material that some readers find objectionable, such as bondage, submission, same sex encounters, forced seductions, etc. E-rated titles are the most graphic titles we carry; it is common, for instance, for an author to use words such as "fucking", "cock", "pussy", etc., within their work of literature.

X-treme titles differ from E-rated titles only in plot premise and storyline execution. Unlike E-rated titles, stories designated with the letter X tend to contain controversial subject matter not for the faint of heart.

Also by Lacey Alexander:

Hot In the City: French Quarter
Hot For Santa!
Hot in the City: Key West

SIN CITY
HOT IN THE CITY 2

Dedication

I'd like to dedicate the Hot in the City trilogy to my husband, with fond memories of hurricanes in New Orleans, daiquiris in Las Vegas, and too much win in Key West.

Prologue

Diana Marsh had just switched off the light next to her bed when the phone rang. She reached out in the darkness and put the receiver to her ear. "Hello?"

"Hey, it's me." Marc Davenport, her work associate and long-distance friend. Or was he more than a friend?

Their office-to-office work calls had gotten longer and more flirtatious recently, and hearing his voice made her smile in the dark. "Hey."

"You sound sleepy—were you asleep? Damn, what time is it there? I totally forgot about the time difference."

"It's…"—she switched on the light and sought out her bedside clock—"…just after eleven, but that's okay. I only went to bed a few minutes ago." In fact, she'd decided to turn in after she'd given up on him calling, thinking maybe he'd decided it was a bad idea.

"Are you sure, sweetheart?"

So simple, one little word—*sweetheart*. Despite herself, just the sound of the endearment, delivered in his rich baritone, made her breasts ache a little, her pussy tingle with a hint of awareness. "Yeah, I'm sure. I want to talk."

It was a first for them—a call outside the office. But the workload had been light today and a phone call to ask her opinion on the wording of an entry in the fall catalog had turned into a phone call about a hundred other things: movies they'd seen lately, music they listened to, Marc's hopes of moving to Europe for a while, and even the guy

Diana was currently seeing—although she'd tried to steer away from that topic quickly. Before they'd finally hung up, Marc had said, "Hey, why don't I call you later tonight? We can talk some more."

She'd agreed, thinking it was safe, harmless. Just a little fun, just talking with a friend—a friend that sent frissons of heat echoing through her veins more and more lately.

But she couldn't think about that—in fact, she had to *stop* those feelings before they got out of control.

Because Diana was done being the black sheep of the family, finished being the Class "A" Bad Girl she'd been her whole life. She was cleaning up her act, playing it safe for a change.

Surely a late night call from a...*friend* wouldn't interfere with that?

"I thought maybe you'd forgotten," she said, "or decided not to call."

"No way, sweetheart—you know I love to hear your pretty voice. I'd have called earlier, but I just got home."

"I hope you weren't at the office all this time." Marc worked at the company's corporate headquarters in Las Vegas, where she calculated the time to be after eight.

"No, nothing like that. I just went out with some guys after work. A long happy hour."

"Sounds fun." Diana didn't *do* happy hour anymore and the pleasure-seeking part of her soul experienced a small bout of envy.

"I wouldn't have called, though, if I'd known you'd already put on your jammies and gotten all tucked in to bed."

She laughed. "I'm not exactly four years old, you know. I don't have a strict bedtime."

"Oh, don't worry, I'm very aware you're not a little girl."

"And just what does *that* mean?" she asked in a playful tone. Despite talking on the phone a couple of times a week for the past year, not to mention sending lots of e-mail—some of it work-related, some of it chatty—she and Marc had never met.

"I've seen your picture on the company website, sweetheart," he admitted. She'd seen his, too, and found him utterly hot—the best-looking thing in a suit and tie she'd ever laid eyes on.

"And?"

"And…" She could almost hear his playful grin. "I liked what I saw. A lot."

"What did you like so much?"

"Your gorgeous brown hair with just a hint of auburn, your hazel eyes and creamy skin, and that sexy pinstripe suit you were wearing."

She let out a small giggle. "You can't even see my suit below the shoulders in that picture. And besides, I didn't know pinstripes were sexy."

"What can I say? Professional women get me hot."

Diana didn't reply, just sat up in bed a little and let *herself* get hot at the knowledge that she wasn't the only one caught up in a bit of lust here.

"Just please tell me," he said, "that the skirt is as short as I like to imagine it is."

She let her voice go a little husky. "Uh, yeah, it is. I'm a short skirt kinda girl."

"Mmm, I like the sound of that."

But I'm a good girl, too, she reminded herself. Marc had the ability to make her forget herself, the self she intended to be from now on.

"So what kind of pajama girl are you? What are you wearing right now?"

She sucked in her breath—this was starting to get steamy. And was about to get even steamier, she had a feeling. "The white baby-doll tank and panty set from the catalog," she said, unduly gratified to know he'd be able to picture the skimpy outfit with ease. They were employed by Adrianna, Inc., a maker of fine lingerie and loungewear, and Marc worked on the team that designed and produced the quarterly catalogs.

"Damn, honey, I need to get one of those cell phones that let you send pictures back and forth."

She laughed. "What makes you think I'd send you one of me in my little nighties?"

His chuckle was rich and full-bodied. "Well, maybe you wouldn't, not yet. But I bet I could talk you into it."

"How?"

"That's for me to know," he said, then shifted the subject back to her baby-doll tank set. "So, tell me, does the ultra-soft cotton we describe in the catalog feel as good against your skin as we promise?"

She smiled to herself. "Mmm hmm. Very soft and silky, just like the copy says."

"And do your nipples show through the white?"

Her breath caught and her cunt turned restless, tickly. "I'll...have to check on that," she said, aware her voice had come out more whispery than she'd intended. Getting up,

12

she walked to her dresser and glanced in the mirror. Two dark, sexy shadows puckered against the fabric; her breasts turned heavy. Returning to the bed, she picked up the phone, bit her lip slightly, then answered. "Yes, quite clearly, in fact."

"Mmm, I bet you've got very pretty breasts."

She wished he could see the come-hither smile she knew she wore. "Well, if I do say so myself…"

He offered a light laugh before getting sexy again. "Are your nipples hard?"

Another quick wave of heat. "Um, yeah. They definitely are."

"And your pubic hair? Does it show through the white cotton, too?"

What a wicked boy, she thought. And what a wicked girl she was, as well. For the moment, she'd given up trying to fight it. "I don't *have* any pubic hair. I keep it waxed off."

A slightly stunned silence met her ear and she enjoyed it immensely. "All of it?"

"Yeah."

"God, sweetheart, you just made my dick hard."

Her voice came breathy, hot. "And you just made my pussy wet."

Another tense silence—but this one was pure heat, shared across a distance of over two thousand miles.

"Touch it for me," he whispered. "Will you do that?"

"On one condition."

"Name it."

"Wrap your hand around your cock for *me*."

A few seconds passed and she imagined him unzipping, reaching in his underwear. She envisioned a big lovely shaft, thick and straight as a pillar of stone. "Okay," he finally said.

"You're doing it? Touching yourself?"

"Yeah. You?"

She hadn't yet. But once she pictured him masturbating, just for her, she couldn't *not* touch herself. Licking her lip slightly, she slid her free hand down into her panties, her fingertips gliding over smooth skin until they dipped into her warm, moist slit. She unwittingly let out a light groan as the wetness met her fingers.

"I'll take that as a yes," he said.

"Good assumption."

"I wish *I* could be the one touching you," he whispered. "Do you know how many times I've thought about that?"

No, she didn't, but she liked the sound of it. "Tell me." She gently stroked her middle finger over her damp clit. Sensation radiated outward.

"I've been thinking about you for months, sweetheart. It started out innocently enough. At first, I just wished we lived closer together, wished I could see you face-to-face, spend time with you. But before I knew it, I was fantasizing about kissing your breasts, fingering your sweet pussy, fucking you hard and deep."

"Speaking of my pussy..." Diana began, going breathless with desire now.

"What, baby? Tell me about your pussy. Tell me all about it."

"It's...so hot. Pulsing."

"Are your panties on or off?"

"On."

"Take them off."

"Wait a minute." Biting her lip, she lay the phone on the covers bunched next to her and pushed the white cotton undies down over her thighs, knees, to her ankles. "Okay, they're gone."

"Now spread your legs."

She did, and a rush of delight flowed through her when the air from the ceiling fan cooled her wet inner flesh.

"Now tell me how it looks. Describe it to me."

Diana lifted her tongue to the roof of her mouth as she glanced downward. "It's very…open," she began, then swallowed, her arousal nearly getting the best of her. She'd done a lot of wild things in her life, but she'd never had phone sex, and something about it felt much more intimate than she would have expected; he seemed so close, right next to her ear. She wished he really *were* there, right beside her in bed.

"What else?"

"Pink," she whispered. "There's a lot of pink, and…my clit…my clit is all swollen, stiffened, wanting to be stimulated."

She heard him let out a heavy breath. "Don't make it suffer, sweetheart. Keep touching it. Glide your pretty middle finger over it. Are you doing it? Stroking it for me?"

She could barely breathe. "Um, yes. Yes."

"Good. I can see it so clearly, baby."

"Are you stroking your cock?"

"Mmm, yeah."

She went quiet for a moment, trying to find enough breath to ask him some of the same things he'd asked her, all the while caressing her pussy and imagining him with his pants undone, his shaft in his fist. "What are you wearing?"

"Suit," he said. "I just walked in the door."

"Good—that's how I was picturing you. Now tell me what your cock looks like."

His breath had turned ragged. "It's so big for you, sweetheart."

"*How* big?"

He laughed amid their heat. "Is this your way of telling me size really does matter?"

She let out her own giggle in return. "Well…" The truth was—she'd been with enough men to know a slightly smaller tool could do the job when well used, but she truly did prefer a cock that was on the larger side of the scale.

"Don't worry, honey, I'll take the pressure off. You'd like my size—you'd like it just fine."

"Confident," she teased, still moving her fingers, in circles now, over her needy clit.

"I've never actually gotten out a ruler or anything," he chuckled, "but I think around…nine would be an accurate measurement."

"Mmm, nice," she said, doubting him just a little, but deciding not to ruin the moment by expressing it. Much better to stick to the fun stuff. "Is there come on the tip?"

"Yeah."

Oh, she was bad—so, so bad. "I wish I was there to lick it off for you."

"Oh God, baby," he groaned. "Much more of that and I'll lose it."

"Do you *want* more?"

His rich laughter sounded over the phone line, even if it was coming a bit more shakily than usual. "How can I say no?"

"Well, if I were there, I'd kneel between your legs and lick the pre-come off the tip of your big, hot cock, and then I'd slide my lips down, way down, putting as much of you in my mouth as I could, and then I'd suck you so, so good, baby."

He groaned deeply and she wondered if he was about to come, but then he said, "Are you still playing with that naked pussy? That pussy that I'd give my right arm to see right now?"

"Uh-huh," she breathed. She touched herself gingerly, trying to control the arousal, not wanting to come until he did.

"I want to lick you so bad, sweetheart."

She leaned her head back, let out a little moan. "I want that, too."

"I want to run my tongue over your clit until you come, and then I want to ram this big cock inside your tight little hole."

Diana gasped, rubbing her clit a little harder. She wouldn't be able to take much more. "God, I want you to," she said, breath ragged, voice urgent. "I want you to fuck me so hard. I want to feel your cock pounding deep in my pussy, deep, deep, deep in my cunt."

"Oh, baby, yeah."

"Deeper and deeper," she repeated. "Deep in my hot wet pussy. Deep inside me. Deep. Deep." Oh. Oh. It was coming—any second now, beyond her to stop it.

"Oh…" he moaned. "Oh God, here I come."

Marc let out a ferocious moan over the phone just as Diana's orgasm broke—hard and furious and all-consuming for a few long, hot seconds of pulsing pleasure. Wave after wave rocked her cunt, seeming to echo outward through her limbs.

When the waves stilled, all was silent until she whispered, "Mmm, yes."

"That was…that was so good, sweetheart," Marc said, sounding just as spent as she felt.

"Yeah." Her voice emerged weak, quiet.

They both went silent for a moment, until he asked, "Regrets?"

She wanted to feel guilty, if for no other reason than because she'd broken her own vow, her promise to herself to be good from now on. But all she felt was the thick, warm pleasure of being bad. "No."

"Good." His voice came tender and sweet. "I'd hate it if I thought I'd taken you somewhere you didn't want to go. I mean, I know you're seeing that guy…"

He sounded sorry to have remembered, and she was sorry to be reminded. "Bradley," she said dully. "But don't worry. I enjoyed this too much to be sorry."

When he said, "Good," this time, he sounded more lighthearted, and she could tell he was ready to resume their usual teasing flirtation. "By the way, I think if we had cell phones with pictures, I'd have talked you into showing me more than just your pajamas by now."

Chapter One

A week later, Diana was still thinking about her phone call with Marc.

She thought about it when she got dressed every morning, concealing her tingling breasts and crotch in a matching bra and panty set from Adrianna, Inc., then putting on a suit and remembering that professional women got him hot.

She thought about it when she lay down at night, reliving their dirty talk on the phone until she couldn't resist reliving another part of it, too—slipping her hand in her panties and rubbing her clit until she reached those few blessed seconds of ecstasy.

And she thought about it at every moment in between.

As she walked up Pratt Street toward her office in Baltimore's business district, a breeze from the nearby harbor lifted her hair and rushed up beneath her narrow skirt, seeming to skim coolly across the lacy crimson thong she'd chosen to wear that day. Her cunt responded, turning predictably tickly and warm. A small smile unfurled across her face, all the more sweet since none of the other suits passing her on the sidewalk knew why she was so happy.

She'd always been a very sexual person—but her phone call with Marc had seemed to renew something inside her, given her just the sort of thrill that had been missing from her life lately. By her choice, of course. *Good girl, good girl*, she whispered inside, *gotta be a good girl.* She clenched her pussy muscles tight as she walked, thinking it would quell the tingling sensations, but instead it only intensified them. Which took her thoughts right back to Marc. How he'd asked her to touch herself for him. How badly he'd wanted to see her bare, smooth cunt.

After they'd both come, they'd talked a while longer and she'd suggested that while at work they not mention what they'd just shared. She'd feared it would be awkward—they were required to talk to each other so frequently. And also because she didn't want to be reminded that she'd been so bad. That she'd *enjoyed* being so bad. That she only wished she could *keep* being that bad.

But once and for all, she had to put those days behind her, no matter how many breezes made her crotch tickle, no matter how tempting it was to ask Marc to call her at home again some night and get her off that same way.

Diana had been a bad girl all her life, and her wild ways had put her parents through a lot of worry and disappointment. She'd lost her virginity, very willingly, at fifteen, in her bedroom, to a college boy from their neighborhood who'd come home for the summer looking as hot as fireworks on the Fourth of July—and her mother had walked in just as they were finishing round two. For the following three years, she'd sneaked out of the house constantly—a necessity when she was grounded—and she'd experimented with more than a few boys in the backseats of their cars. If she was dating a guy, sex just seemed to be a natural progression. She'd never worried about what anyone thought and nothing about her actions had ever felt wrong to her. From puberty on, she'd simply yearned for sex so deeply that she couldn't deny herself the pleasure when it was offered.

Add to that being caught drinking on a number of occasions, and once even being hauled to jail with a group of kids caught with alcohol at an unchaperoned party—not to mention a thousand other little conflicts over too much makeup and skirts that were too short—and Diana knew she'd been a lot to handle.

Now her older sister Liz had broken up her picture-perfect engagement and hooked up with some sexy French Quarter private-eye guy, and though Diana was very happy to see her sister finally come out of her conservative shell and find happiness with a total hunk, she also felt somehow responsible for filling her spot.

Of course, her baby sister, Carrie was engaged to a nice guy the whole family liked, but Carrie and Jon had been engaged for so long that she knew her parents were beginning to fear *none* of their daughters would ever make them happy. At twenty-eight, Diana felt obliged to pick up the slack, to be the one who didn't give them grief for once in her life.

The truth was, she admitted to herself as she pushed through the revolving door of the high-rise building that housed Adrianna, Inc.'s Baltimore offices, she wanted their approval.

She wasn't a bad person—in fact, she thought she was a pretty *nice* person. She tried to treat other people with fairness and consideration, she gave money and even some of her time to a few charities of her choice, and she was the sort of person who stopped to help injured animals on the side of the road. Yet she didn't know if her parents really *knew* she was a good person, and she wanted them to know. She knew they loved her, but she'd reached a point in her adult life where she also wanted them to simply *like* her, too.

And things were finally going pretty well in that arena.

Last year, she'd gotten her job at Adrianna, a well-paying and respectable position—she used her marketing degree to organize East Coast marketing efforts and she also traveled considerably for the company, ensuring that new boutiques were set up to market their wares in the most effective way. Her parents were proud of her for working hard and making a good career for herself.

With that had come the means to buy a lovely restored row house in the trendy, historic Federal Hill area, within walking distance of her office. Her mother had raved over the condo and she'd heard her dad, on more than one occasion, tell a friend or neighbor what a great place she had.

And finally, there was Bradley—the nice man her mother had fixed her up with nearly four months ago. She sighed as the elevator took her toward the 15th floor, all signs of her arousal disappearing as thoughts of her so-called boyfriend entered her head. Bradley was tall and blond and handsome, he worked as a systems analyst for a large, successful company in the suburbs—and he was such a damn gentleman that he had yet to lay a hand on her.

Well, he'd put his arm around her on occasion, and he'd kissed her—pleasant yet sadly spark-free kisses goodnight at the door—but to Diana, a woman who loved pleasure and craved sex, his soft kisses seemed like next to nothing.

She knew Bradley needed a sweet, chaste woman in his life who could appreciate his love of fine wine, his culinary skills, his gentle and respectful manner—and she was trying very hard to *be* that woman, just hoping that whenever they finally got around to fucking he'd be an animal.

She'd even tried to seduce him several times, until he'd eventually explained that he thought it was better to wait, to let their relationship grow, so that when they finally made love, it would be important and meaningful. Diana loved important, meaningful sex as much as the next girl, but she also loved getting-to-know-you sex and we're-attracted-to-each-other-and-I-want-you sex, too.

Of course, if Bradley had succumbed to her attempts at seduction, it would only have been getting-to-know-you sex, not we're-attracted-to-each-other sex, because as it stood, she simply didn't feel that hot, fun, wild sort of chemistry that sometimes made it so hard for her to keep her hands off a guy.

But she'd also known men with whom attraction really had changed and grown over time, and given how perfect Bradley was in so many ways, and how happy her parents had been since they'd been dating, she was sticking with him, convinced she'd become more enamored with him as time passed. She could be a good little wife who knew how to "make love" to her man, and how to be content and happy with one guy for the rest of her life. Women the world over succeeded at this—so could she.

Still and all, when wind blew up her skirt and made her pussy tingle, it took her a minute to remember that she probably shouldn't revel so heedlessly in the sensation if she actually expected to be the good girl her family made her want to be. And although she'd let herself off the guilt hook regarding her oh-so-naughty phone conversation with Marc—deciding it was only a slip-up because she was frustrated from no sex—her new habit of thinking about him all day and masturbating at night with him in mind simply had to stop. As did the fact that her panties got wet every time she talked to him now. Her desires were out of her control, but she simply had to ignore them and hope they would go away over time, like finally breaking a bad habit.

Of course, it was a hard thing to *truly* hope for, because it felt so delicious and good and naughty, but she still tried.

After all, she was here, and Marc was far away, in Las Vegas.

And she would probably marry Bradley one of these days and make everyone very happy.

Except maybe you, a voice whispered inside her as she made her way to the office break room to pour her morning coffee. She needed to ignore that, too.

Diana slid behind the desk in her small office, ready to get her mind off her worries—and Marc—and onto Adrianna, Inc. Mock-ups for the print ads publicizing the new Atlanta and Miami boutiques were due in a few days and needed her close attention. As did a hundred little details that should keep her good and busy all day.

"Ouch, girlfriend, look at that cleavage."

Diana's office friend, Shyla, appeared in her doorway. A beautiful woman with skin the color of café au lait, she wore a striking suit of orange—a shade only Shyla could pull off. Shyla had shown Diana around the office on her first day and they'd become fast friends. Shyla was always quick to notice things like cleavage or short skirts or sexy shoes, and she was always very free about touching, so much so that Diana sometimes wondered if Shyla might be bisexual. Diana wasn't into that scene, so if Shyla ever made a move on her, she'd have to turn her down in such a way that they could remain friends. But even if she wasn't into other girls, Diana never minded hearing she looked hot.

In response to Shyla's comment, she glanced down at her chest. She hadn't really planned it or even noticed, but indeed, the low cut of her new black suit, along with the superb support of her Adrianna bra, showed off her breasts to considerable advantage.

Returning her gaze to Shyla, she laughed. "Believe it or not, I didn't even realize."

Now it was Shyla's turn to let out a near-cackle. "As a matter of fact, I *don't* believe it. I know you too well."

Diana and Shyla had been out dancing and drinking together before—well, back before Bradley and her quest to clean up her act—and they'd had lots of occasions to discuss sex. Diana seldom felt a need for secrets, so she'd filled Shyla in on her past and her nearly constant hunger for pleasure.

"Come on, now, you know I'm trying to change my ways." She'd filled Shyla in on that, too, much to her girlfriend's consternation.

"My granddaddy always used to say—you can take the feathers off a chicken, but it's still a chicken."

Diana just blinked, then squinted. "What?"

Shyla grinned. "Girl, you can try to change your ways, but you're still the same *you* inside." She gave her head a knowing tilt. "And the you *I* know was born to be naughty."

Diana cast a playful smirk and decided to change the subject. "So did you just come in here to ogle and harass me, or did you actually have a purpose for your visit?"

"It so happens, I do have a purpose, Miss Cleavage." She raised her eyebrows. "Richard wants to see you in his office. Asked me to let you know as soon as you got here."

Diana's curiosity instantly piqued; this sounded important. "No idea what he wants?" Richard was their boss, an Adrianna's VP.

"No, sugar, but I suspect he'll enjoy lookin' at those pretty breasts as much as I am." With that, she winked and disappeared from the doorway.

Diana just laughed and shook her head, then picked up her coffee cup and made her way down the hall to Richard's office. She leaned around the doorway to peek inside, knocking on his open door; he looked up and smiled. "Diana, come on in. Have a seat."

Richard was a very attractive man in his mid-thirties who the old Diana would probably have pursued, except that he was married with kids. Even so, she wondered if Shyla was right, if he'd notice her boobs. Which, she thought immediately, should make her feel guilty. But it didn't. Damn, what if Shyla was right about feathers and chickens?

Diana sat down in the leather chair across from his desk and crossed her legs, her skirt rising a little higher on her thighs. "Shyla said you wanted to see me?"

Richard tilted his head, looking like he had bad news. "I know you're not fond of last minute travel," he began slowly.

He was right. They'd discussed it many times. Diana loved traveling for her job, but she liked a little notice, and didn't always get it, due to store openings being pushed up or held back. She simply nodded and waited, already feeling tense. He was going to tell her she had to get on a plane tomorrow or the next day, leaving her no chance to wrap up or delegate the important items on her desk at the moment.

"Well, unfortunately, this particular edict comes down from Adrianna herself."

Adrianna Kline, founder, CEO, and namesake of the company. Diana sat up a little straighter.

"She wants you in Vegas, Diana." The corporate office. "Seems that ever since Kelly Winston left marketing, the catalog team is suffering from a lack of female input. Given that we market *to* females, it makes sense to have you there."

Diana nodded. "I *have* gotten more calls than usual from them lately." From Marc, she meant. Every day in the past two weeks, in fact—although she'd thought some of them might be fabricated just because he wanted to talk to her. "But still, why me?"

"They've been interviewing, unsuccessfully, for the position since Kelly left. As of right now, they need help putting the fall catalog to bed. They're a week late already. Adrianna tells me the guys on the team are great at what they do, but they really need a woman in the mix, to bounce ideas off of, to steer them in a direction that's feminine and sexy."

Diana shook her head. "That still doesn't answer my question. Why me?"

Richard tilted his head and smiled. "It's a compliment. She's seen your marketing skills pull our East Coast advertising together, making it strong, cohesive, and effective. She's also seen what you do in the boutiques to make sure they're each unique while at the same time unmistakably Adrianna's. You know district sales have risen since you arrived, and Adrianna thinks you're part of the reason why. She sees you as a woman who's smart, savvy, and knows what appeals to other women."

A rush of fulfillment washed through Diana's body. Adrianna had noticed her work. Before this moment, Diana had never even imagined she was on Adrianna's radar screen. She didn't try to hide her smile. "That's extremely satisfying to hear."

Richard returned the grin. "I thought you'd think so. So…you won't be too angry with me when I tell you she'd like you out there ASAP? As in flying out tomorrow and starting work with the catalog team the next day?"

Diana took a deep breath. Richard, of course, had no way of knowing the ramifications of this request. He had no idea she'd been flirting with a member of the catalog team for months, or that they'd recently had dirty phone sex. He also had no idea that her cunt was throbbing now, at the very idea of meeting Marc, of having a chance to…

A tremor of pure longing echoed through her body, and she only hoped Richard hadn't seen it. Damn it, she couldn't think about what might happen between her and Marc right now; she had to answer her boss.

"No, Richard," she said with an indulgent smile, "I won't be mad at you. So long as you take responsibility for anything important on my desk that I can't deal with by day's end, you can tell Adrianna I'll be at the office first thing Wednesday morning."

"No problem, just e-mail me with a list of issues and I'll deal with them," he replied, clearly pleased she hadn't put up a fuss. "Eileen will have a travel itinerary to you by five."

Diana got to her feet, her mind and body humming with the suddenness of this new plan and all it might entail. As she made her way to the door, Richard stopped her. "Diana."

She turned to find him leaning back in his chair, twirling a pencil absently between his fingers and wearing an almost mischievous grin. "What?" she asked.

"I hope you won't think this is out of line, but...that suit does very fine things for you."

"Thank you," she said as a naughty little thrill zipped through her—turned out Shyla was right, at least about Richard enjoying the view of her boobs she'd unwittingly provided. It was gratifying to know she could get to even a conservative guy like her boss.

As she made her way back down the hall, though, she also had to wonder again if Shyla was right about her still being naughty, no matter how she tried to change. Well, one thing was for sure. She'd likely find out on her little trip to Las Vegas. If any place on earth could make her misbehave, it was probably Sin City.

* * * * *

Marc sat at the table in the conference room, gaping at the screen of his laptop. Then he felt a dirty little smile edge its way onto his face. He read the e-mail again.

Guess what? Adrianna has asked me to come to Vegas. Seems you boys in catalog need a woman to keep you in line, and I'm just the girl for the job. :) I'm flying out tomorrow—am waiting for my itinerary right now, after which I'm headed home to pack. Looks like we'll be trading in the phone for real face-to-face contact. See you then. D

Damn, even in e-mail, she made him hot. He needed a woman to keep him in line, all right, and she *was* just the girl for the job. Adrianna had told the catalog team she was bringing in outside help, but she hadn't yet decided who—that had been this morning and they'd heard nothing about it since. Well, he'd have to commend the lady boss on her choice. His dick was perking to life in his pants already.

Of course, the truth was, he didn't know if Diana would be interested in taking their sexy phone talk further now that they'd really have the chance. Phone sex was fun, but real sex was definitely a different event altogether. And although she seemed to be as naughty a girl as he could possibly want, she was dating that guy—Bradley. She didn't always sound happy about it, but he knew she kept seeing him, so it was hard to know what to expect from her visit.

Besides which, they had work to do, and a lot of it. Adrianna had informed him and the three other guys on the team that she expected them to work weekends until the fall catalog was ready to go to print. Fortunately, despite such talk, their boss wasn't a slave driver—he knew her well enough to know she wouldn't expect them to work around the clock or anything totally exhausting, but she did expect them to treat Saturday and Sunday as nine-to-five days until the task was complete.

All of which meant he could look forward to spending a lot of time with Diana, but he had no idea how much of it, if any, would be social. And damn, he wanted to get social with her. He wanted to get downright intimate, if only she'd let him.

As of right now, though, she was a mystery woman. He knew she was smart, capable, flirtatious, and gave good phone sex, but he had no idea how she would be in person. In fact, for all he knew, she'd be embarrassed about how dirty they'd gotten with each other on the phone that hot, hot night. Of course, she didn't *seem* embarrassed in her e-mail message, but...well, he'd just have to feel her out a little.

Pulling up the reply screen, he typed.

Am looking forward to ditching the phone for the real you. Yes, Adrianna complains I lack the proper discipline. That's right, I've been a very bad boy...but maybe you can teach me...to write catalog copy that will appeal to the demographics. The bad news: boss lady has announced we'll be working weekends 'til the catalog's done. The good: our nights will be free. Give me a call at the office after you get settled at your hotel and we'll make plans to get together tomorrow night—I'll show you Sin City in style, sweetheart. M

The heat of anticipation rippled through him as he hit Send. The message contained nothing more teasing and flirtatious than usual between them, but it would be her response that mattered.

He checked his watch. A little after two, and after five in Baltimore. Damn, he'd have to hope she got it before she left, or that she'd check her e-mail tomorrow at some point while traveling. Still, he wanted her to get the message *now*, so he wouldn't have to wait and wonder, agonizing over what her answer would be.

To kill a couple of minutes before he started checking for a reply, he accessed the company website, clicking on the appropriate links until he reached her professional profile — and her picture. He hadn't been lying that night — the woman made pinstripes sexy.

Now he only hoped he'd be lucky enough to get to run his hands through those long, lovely locks, a tawny shade mixed with just a hint of red. He hoped he'd get to kiss those silky lips, get to reach past the lapels of her jacket and massage what he suspected would be an outstanding pair of breasts. As she'd recently pointed out to him, that's where the photo stopped, but it didn't take a lot of imagination to let his mind travel lower, to hope he got to push up her skirt and see that smoothly waxed pussy she'd so kindly fingered for him that night on the phone.

His cock stood at full attention now, damn it. Just what he needed with three hours of work left. Then again, this wasn't new — at Diana's request, he'd resisted the temptation to allude to their phone sex, but ever since their conversation, he'd been battling a near-constant hard-on.

Dave, Rick, and Blaine were all in the break room right now, having claimed they could brainstorm a layout for the stockings page better if they were munching on candy bars from the snack machine. He'd told them he'd be right behind them as soon as he finished inputting the tentative copy he'd written for Adrianna's Lush Velvet collection, but then he'd gotten Diana's e-mail, and the only stockings he could think about right now were on *her* legs.

Did she wear stockings? The kind with lace on top? Did she use a garter belt with them, or did she wear Adrianna's patented "Snug-n-Lacies", that stayed up by themselves?

Studying her picture, a hot little fantasy rose to his mind.

The guys all sat around the conference room table when Diana came marching in, wearing a conservative suit and stern, black-framed glasses, her hair pulled back in a severe bun.

Her eyes narrowed on him. "You've been a very bad boy, Mr. Davenport. Your Lush Velvet copy sucks. Present your hand."

He held it out, palm up, and she slapped it with a ruler.

The sting reverberated through his body, right down to his cock.

Oh yeah. As Marc sat as his desk fantasizing, his dick got harder and harder. With another glance at the doorway, he grabbed up some tissues for later, then unzipped his pants and reached inside, taking his shaft in his hand.

But in the fantasy, it was *her* hand.

She was dragging him by it now, roughly, up to the head of the table, saying she was going to make an example of him. Releasing him from her grasp, she reached down for the hem of her skirt in a very crisp, businesslike manner, then lifted it to her hips, revealing pretty lace top stockings with a white garter belt, and no panties — only a pretty, bare pussy, a hot little slit that spread slightly to expose a sweet pink clit, just as she'd described to him on the phone. "Lick my cunt," she demanded.

Of course, he obeyed, sinking his tongue into her warm, salty moisture, savoring the taste and smell of her while his co-workers watched.

"Harder!" she demanded. "You need to work harder on your writing and harder on my clit."

So he went at her like a man who hadn't eaten in a week, licking and lapping and sucking, burying his face in that wet, pink paradise until her juice was all over his face.

"Harder, you bad boy! Lick it!"

She said it over and over, demanding he obey, and he delivered, working his tongue and lips on her cunt like never before.

At his desk, he stroked his cock in rhythm with his imaginary licks, closing his eyes as the blood gathered hotter and hotter in his groin, sinking deeper into his fantasy. This wasn't his normal sort of sexual daydream—he was usually more into dominance than submission—but something about Diana gave him an anything goes sort of feeling, so when the thought had come to mind, he'd just gone with it.

Now she knelt in front of him, her face down by his stiff rod. "You've learned to work hard, you naughty boy, but now you're going to learn to take what you're given and like it."

"Okay," he said.

Somewhere in the fantasy, his pants had dropped, so she reached around and slapped his bare ass with the flat of her hand, hard. "Did I tell you to speak?"

He almost said no, but then just shook his head.

"You will speak when I tell you to speak and only then. Now, tell me you want me to suck your cock, bad boy."

He looked down into those lovely hazel green eyes, intense and punishing and hot. "I want you to suck my cock."

"I'm going to suck you 'til you come," she said. "You might want me to stop, you might be tempted to beg me, because it's so fantastic you can't stand it, or because you don't want to come yet, but if you say a single word, I'll stop for good, understand? So be a good boy and be very quiet, except for one last thing. Tell me you want to come in my mouth."

Mmm, yeah. "I want to come in your mouth."

As his schoolteacher-type dominatrix lowered her lips over his shaft, taking him all the way to her throat, he stroked himself harder. He prayed he was still alone, but he wasn't about to open his eyes and find out—it would break the fantasy and he was in too deep to let that happen. In his mind, his hand was Diana's wet mouth, sliding up and down his hard cock, sucking him in, sucking, sucking, all the while looking up at him with her forceful dom eyes behind those austere yet sexy glasses.

Before he quite expected it, he was biting his lip to stifle his moan, and his come went shooting into the tissues he'd placed there to catch it, his body jolting with hard twitches of pleasure.

"Damn," he whispered, not quite able to believe he'd just jerked off in a conference room where anyone could have caught him.

He opened his eyes and was—thank God—alone. He had no way to know, of course, if anyone might have happened into the room, then exited when they'd seen what he was doing, but no point in worrying about it.

The only thing he was really worried about at the moment was his fantasy girl's reply to his e-mail. He clicked the button to check, and sure enough, a message from her waited in his inbox. Blood ran hot through his veins as he clicked to open it.

Am wondering if I'll be able to resist all the sin in Sin City. Will call you tomorrow afternoon and we'll find out. D

Jackpot, he thought, pulling back the arm of an imaginary slot machine. If it was up to Marc, Diana was going to sink so deep into sin here that she wouldn't ever want to crawl out.

Chapter Two

Diana's room at The Venetian bordered on luxurious. She hadn't expected the company to put her up at one of the expensive hotels on the strip, but she certainly thought it would make her visit to Vegas seem…more like a visit to Vegas. Already, the lush atmosphere was beginning to intoxicate her a little.

Her suite featured a king-size bed with elegant fabric draped on the wall above the headboard to form a faux canopy, and a sunken living room area divided from the bed space with a wrought iron half-rail. The pale walls contrasted against the rich shades of burgundies and reds in the fabrics.

After unpacking her suitcase and ordering a late lunch from room service, she picked up the phone and dialed Adrianna, Inc.'s corporate line.

"Adrianna, Inc., where all your lingerie dreams come true," answered the receptionist in her usual perky tone.

"Hi Holly, it's Diana. Can you put me through to Marc?"

"Sure thing. Hey, are you here?"

Diana laughed. "Yep, I'm hanging out in my lovely room at the Venetian."

"Plush, I bet."

"Very. I'm surprised we provide such accommodations for ourselves," she said on a light giggle.

"Well, you know Adrianna. She likes only the best."

Even though Diana didn't actually *know* Adrianna, she supposed she *did* know that much about her.

A moment later, Marc picked up the phone. Knowing he was only a few miles away made him sound all the sexier. Diana's pussy actually quivered when he said, "I'm glad you're here."

They discussed the usual—her flight, her room—until finally she said, "So, are we on for tonight?"

"Absolutely, sweetheart, and I've got quite an evening planned for us."

"Oh?"

"I'll be picking you up at your hotel in a stretch limo, then we have tickets to a show."

Diana's jaw dropped. "A limo?"

On the other end of the line, Marc chuckled. "It just so happens a friend of mine had already rented the limo and bought show tickets, but a work conflict came up and he had to cancel the hot date he had planned. He offered it all to me, so now *his* hot date is *our* hot date. Sound good?"

It had been so long since Diana had been on anything remotely resembling a hot date that it sounded positively yummy, but she restrained herself and simply said, "Sounds great."

After they hung up, she took a nap to help acclimate her to the time change, watched a little TV, then took a shower since it was almost time for Marc to pick her up. To her surprise, she actually felt a little nervous, an emotion she wasn't used to. She figured it had to do with her lingering uncertainty over what would take place between them while she was here.

She'd meant what she'd said in her e-mail message yesterday—she truly wondered if she'd be able to resist him, and sin. She had to try, though. She had to try to follow through, purge the bad girl once and for all, show herself that the good girl could win. In fact, if she succeeded in resisting both Marc and Sin City's decadent charms, she could go home to Baltimore knowing for sure she could settle down and be a good little wife to Bradley; she could give her parents the grandchildren they'd always wanted and be the daughter they'd always wished she could be.

But just in case the good girl *didn't* win, she'd made an awkward phone call to Bradley last night—telling him she wanted to take a break from their relationship. He'd sounded just as unhappy about it as she'd expected, but she'd had to do it. She did a lot of things, but she didn't cheat. Of course, she didn't tell Bradley she was sorely tempted to have sex with one of her colleagues—she'd said she wanted to think about their relationship, where they were headed, and decide if they should move forward. It had sounded a lot like a business transaction, but it had also been the truth. She had doubts, and she figured this trip would make it clear to her if she could really, truly settle down and marry him.

Maybe she could. Maybe, at worst, this would turn into one last fling—something she'd be honest about with Bradley afterward.

But if she was lucky, it wouldn't even be *that*. If she was lucky—and strong—it would be a matter of good company, some laughs, and nothing more.

Although when it came time to select a dress from her closet, she found temptation awaiting her already. She studied the one semi-conservative cocktail dress she owned—bought to attend her father's retirement party a few months ago—and told herself it would be an appropriate choice for a night out with a man she hardly knew. But then she reached for the red dress she'd bought six months back yet had never worn. She remembered spotting it in a store window — something about its simple yet risqué lines had spoken to her. At the time, she'd thought she was buying it for some especially sexy occasion that would eventually reveal itself to her, and the bad girl inside her was currently whispering, "This is it." She *shouldn't* wear it, but...she took it off the hanger and put it on anyway.

The gathered crinkly fabric caressed her skin wherever it touched her — most notably at her breasts. The short length showed plenty of leg and the halter-style top of the dress dipped ultra-low, to a spot not far above her navel. The result was a v-neck that revealed the full inner curves of both breasts and the valley between. Indeed, as she looked at herself in the mirror, she knew this was a dress made for sin, pure and simple, and she loved the way she looked in it.

Checking her watch, she scooped up the small evening purse she'd filled with her room key and a couple of makeup items, then departed to meet Marc in the lobby.

The anticipation of the long-awaited meeting with her phone lover had her skin prickling with a combination of nervousness and excitement. When she stepped onto the elevator with two men who immediately let their gazes wander over her admiringly, her pussy began to feel achy and hot.

But it's just a dress, she reminded herself. *It doesn't mean you're going to do anything you shouldn't. It doesn't mean you can't be a good girl tonight.*

The moment she spotted Marc across the lobby, she knew she was doomed. He looked even better than the picture she'd seen online. His dark hair and olive complexion gave him an exotic air, and he looked crisp and handsome in a black suit that appeared tailor-made for his body. Even within the confines of the suit, she could tell he possessed broad shoulders and a muscled chest, and—when he turned to face the opposite direction, not yet having spotted her—a very nice ass.

If all that wasn't bad enough, the nail in her coffin came when their eyes met across the room. His were chocolaty-brown, deep, rich, and they cast a sexual glimmer the camera had failed to capture.

The bad girl inside Diana instantly knew this was going to be trouble—trouble of the very best, most delicious kind.

* * * * *

Marc thought he shouldn't have been surprised at how damn sexy she looked, but he still was. Her pinstriped suit had turned him on, but when it came to arousal, the dress she'd chosen for this evening was on an entirely different plane. From what he could see of her breasts—which was a lot—they looked firm and full and even more delectable than he'd imagined.

"You look...fabulous," he said as they approached each other in the busy, ornate lobby.

Her smile was half-modest, half-seductive. "Thank you." Her voice came out more whispery than he'd ever heard it on the phone, ratcheting his lust up another notch.

He gave her a light hug, careful not to let his crotch bump up against her—a little soon for that. But not too soon to feel those superb breasts brush his chest through their clothes, nearly making him let out a little moan.

When they climbed into the plush confines of the limo, she sat close to him, despite the large bench seat. She crossed her legs, letting her already short skirt reveal still more shapely thigh, and that quickly, Marc formed a theory. She might be dating that Bradley guy, but tonight he suspected she was all his.

It was a short drive up the strip to the hotel where their show was, and they spent it talking about the heat, the limo, and the action on the strip, which he assured her would become far busier as the night progressed and darkness fell. It was a chance for them to get used to being together, face-to-face—something that felt strange after so many phone conversations, but only for a minute or two. By the time the limo driver opened the door to let them out, Marc already felt comfortable with her, and he suspected that would only grow as the evening continued.

Over dinner in an elegant restaurant in the hotel, conversation deepened. Across a small candlelit table for two, they started out talking about work, but soon edged into Marc's hopes for leaving the company soon. He hadn't told anyone, only Diana, but he was currently doing a series of phone interviews with Briolet International, a company in Paris that made snow skis and accompanying gear. They needed someone to head up their North American marketing efforts and they wanted it to be an American.

"I'm not sure I'd want to move *that* far away," Diana said. "Don't get me wrong, I'm hardly a homebody, but for your average middle-class American, it takes a certain daring to put a whole ocean between you and everything you know."

He grinned. "Maybe that's why I want to go. I've always been an adventure-seeker. I guess that's what brought me to Vegas a few years back—it seemed like an exciting place to live and work."

"And isn't it?" She raised her eyebrows.

He tilted his head and flashed a small smile. "Sure it is, but...I've been there, done that now. I'm ready for a *new* kind of excitement, and living in Europe for awhile seems like it fits the bill."

She gave her head a coquettish tilt. "I guess it's a good thing I got here *now*. Just think, if you'd gotten that job before I had occasion to travel to Vegas, we'd never have met. And so far..." The smile that formed on her lush red lips was filled with seduction. "I'm finding this a real pleasure, getting together outside of the office, off the phone."

Her words were simple, but that sinful little smile said so much more. He wondered just how predatory he looked when he replied, "I am, too. But the night's very young, sweetheart. We're just getting started and I've got a whole lot more pleasure in store for you."

"I can't wait," she cooed across the table.

His cock tightened a little more in his pants. *Neither can I, baby, neither can I.*

* * * * *

The show, Diana learned when they arrived at the theater, was called "Girls Just Wanna Have Fun". Although nearly as many well-dressed women as men were seated around them, she got the distinct impression from the pictures next to the box office that this was a gentleman's show.

Apparently Marc got that idea, too, because once they were seated in their private booth facing the stage, he leaned over and said, "Uh, this might be a pretty racy show, sweetheart. I didn't even ask my friend, Dan, what kind of show it was, but...I hope it won't embarrass you or turn you off."

Diana bit her lip. She'd never been to any sort of strip club or men's show, and the truth was, she found herself curious. "No worries. I'm sure I'll find it entertaining, whatever it turns out to be."

His small smile said he liked her style, and the truth was, she *expected* a Vegas show to be racy.

When the lights went down and the curtain lifted, a dozen busty women appeared, decked out in short black vinyl dresses cut to reveal their breasts, all firm and round with pointed pink nipples. They began to dance in unison to hot, steamy music and before Diana knew it, many of them were stripping down to only black vinyl g-strings. Others disappeared from the stage and came back for the next number, this time decked out in shimmering transparent bodysuits and enormous feather boas, which they cleverly used to reveal tantalizing views of their breasts and crotches in time with the burlesque-type music that played.

Just sitting next to Marc as they both watched the sexy women on display for their viewing pleasure seemed intimate and sensual. Diana drank the wine Marc had ordered, leaned a little closer to him without quite planning it, and continued to enjoy the show.

The acts grew more erotic as the performance continued. One dance featured two of the curvy women stripping each other out of glittery costumes before caressing each other's arms, hips, breasts. The two eventually mounted a small set of steps to climb into an enormous champagne glass filled with soapy water, where they moved sensually together, washing each other's bodies in time to the music.

Diana had been aware of the arousal slowly escalating inside her, but this particularly hot number had her pussy pulsing in her panties and her breasts feeling heavy and hot. She found herself wishing she could reach inside her dress and caress her own breasts, tease her nipples. *You shouldn't want this*, the good girl inside her warned. But she did. And as always, when desire found Diana, it took over, making it so little else mattered besides acting on her wants.

Since she couldn't quite find the courage to fondle herself, despite the darkness of the room, she automatically leaned farther into Marc, lightly rubbing the side of her breast against his arm. He turned to gaze down at her in the low-lit room and she saw the same arousal swimming in his eyes. She licked her lip, looked up at him, and hoped he read the longing there.

Mmm, yes, he did. She knew because it was at that precise moment he slid his hand onto her thigh. Diana's cunt burned for his touch as she watched the next act—six girls working stripper poles, each dressed in a hot getup she suspected you might find in a men's club. One girl wore a white leather vest, a white thong, a cowboy hat, and little white boots. Another looked like a biker babe, with a black leather cap and jacket, and black fishnet stockings held up with a garter belt. A third wore the filmy costume of a harem girl.

As she might have predicted, each of the six sensual girls stripped down to tiny, barely there g-strings, all the while still spinning and shimmying around their pole. A few catcalls came from men in the audience as the dancing got steamier and steamier, a couple of the girls even beginning to touch themselves. The cowgirl, still in boots, hat, and g-string, molded her big breasts in her hands, twirling hard nipples between her fingers. The biker chick—fishnet still intact over a tiny black thong—even reached inside the stretchy fabric covering her pussy.

If Diana had wanted to touch herself a little while ago, it was nothing compared to now. Marc's large hand caressed her inner thigh, but he'd been moving very slowly—not even to the top of her stocking yet. She didn't want to be here anymore; she wanted to be someplace where she could rip his clothes off and have her way with him. She wanted his hands all over her, his cock inside her. She knew it was wrong, and wished like hell she didn't feel that way, but to deny it would only be lying to herself. *Good girl, where are you?* Nowhere near the Vegas Strip, clearly. Her pussy felt so full of arousal that she wondered if it were possible to have some kind of spontaneous orgasm, without even being touched there.

As the action on the stage got hotter and hotter, the crowd reacted, as well. Around them, Diana heard more whistles, and a few men muttering things like, "Oh yeah," and "Keep goin', baby." On the stage, two girls had taken to one pole now, and as they shimmied and swayed around it, they also ran their hands over each other's hips and breasts, and engaged in painstakingly slow, sensual kisses.

The sight set Diana's cunt even more ablaze. She'd had occasion to watch the occasional porn movie with past boyfriends, and she'd seen some girl-girl scenes, but witnessing these two lovely women just feet away from her, making out so tenderly, lips touching like butterfly wings, aroused something new in her, some untapped heat she'd never quite felt before. She had a split-second urge to be up there with them, getting naked, kissing and touching, having her aching breasts caressed by the lovely dancers. This was easily the most erotic thing she'd ever watched.

It was then that the tempo of the music suddenly changed—getting faster, taking on a driving beat. The showgirls responded accordingly, changing their slow, tantalizing dances into something faster, hotter, more demanding. The girls worked their poles harder, performing athletic moves and death-defying spins, until finally they each took their spot back behind their own pole and began moving in unison, thrusting their pelvises forward in time with the hard beat, effectively fucking the poles. Their breasts jiggled with each thrust and the whole room filled with hot, lashing sexual energy, raw and reckless.

Touch me, Diana thought. It was all she could do not to drive her own pelvis forward into Marc's hand, which now caressed her thigh in a hard, intense massage. God, sometimes it was hell being so bad.

As both of them watched the women on the stage pump against the thick, shiny poles, Diana thought she'd die of lust. For the women, and for Marc. And just when she thought his hand was easing closer to her soaking wet slit, the music stopped; the dancing came to a dramatic conclusion with one final thrust punctuated by all the girls letting out a well-timed groan, and the curtain closed.

Applause and whistles permeated the air as the lights slowly came up, seeming to transport them all back to reality. Marc gazed down into Diana's eyes and she looked back, letting the heat she saw in his brown depths radiate through her chest and downward. His hand was gone from her thigh—he'd needed it to applaud—but suddenly,

Diana didn't mind. The show was over, and their limousine was only steps away. Out there, they wouldn't have to stop *and* they wouldn't have any interruptions.

His look grew tentative, however, as if he wanted to make sure they were on the same page. "So...what did you think? Too racy for you?"

She shook her head and boldly met his gaze. "Not at all. I *loved* it."

Fresh new heat flared in his eyes.

"I do have a question, though," she added as other patrons exited the theater around them.

He slid his arm comfortably around her shoulder. "What's that, sweetheart?"

She bit her lip, cast him her sexiest look, and spoke just loudly enough for him to hear. "Why didn't you touch me during the show?"

He raised his eyebrows, clearly surprised, which she liked. "I *did*. Because I couldn't help myself. I was afraid you'd slap my hand away."

She shook her head. "I meant..." She stopped, sighed, then spoke lower. "Why didn't you touch my pussy?"

She watched him draw in his breath and hoped she wasn't coming on too strong—but the bad girl in her was clearly alive and well and on vacation in Sin City.

"I was aching for you to touch it," she went on, "and I kept thinking you would, but..." She let out a sigh, her body still wracked with frustration.

"Truth?" he asked with a smile.

"Of course."

He leaned a little closer to her face. "I was *dying* to touch that sweet little pussy of yours, but...technically, we just met. I wasn't sure you'd go for it here, in the theater. And I didn't want to risk trying something you might not want. Didn't want you to think I'm some kind of pushy asshole."

His answer was earnest, and also moving, because it meant he really cared how she felt about him, but it still struck her a bit funny. "Marc, does something about me say prim? Have I ever done *anything* to make you think I wouldn't welcome your advances?"

He gave his head a knowing tilt. "Well, you *are* dating another guy. Maybe that felt like a pretty big reason not to touch you, too. I feel bad enough just having put my hand on your leg."

She let her eyes fall shut for a second at the unpleasant reminder. Talk about crushing her arousal. And she hadn't planned to tell Marc this, since it could only encourage him and make her less and less likely to resist, but... "Actually, I sort of broke up with Bradley last night."

He blinked. "Really?"

"I...don't know that it's totally over, he and I, but...I had a feeling I couldn't come out here without wanting to get intimate with you. So I told him I was having doubts about our relationship, which is very true, and that I needed some time off from it." The further truth was, right now she was sorry she'd ever met Bradley.

And she was also sorry that no matter what happened with Marc, she would probably still go back to Baltimore when this was over and continue trying to be the woman her family wanted her to be. Why couldn't *this* guy live in Baltimore and have her parents' blessing?

Finally, she lifted her gaze to his. "Tell me something. What kind of girl do you like exactly? Do you go for someone who's prim and proper?"

He grinned. "You really have to ask, sweetheart? I'd think you'd have figured me out by now."

She *did* suspect she knew the answer, but something in her had to make sure first, before she let go completely of that woman who dated Bradley and wore conservative dresses and repressed her sexual urges—let go of her just for tonight, anyway. "I just need you to tell me. I need to hear it."

She watched as he took a deep breath, clearly not quite sure what she was after, what she wanted him to say. "Truth?" he asked again.

She nodded.

He let out a sigh of concession. "Okay. The truth is, the girls I *really* go for are the ones who aren't afraid to shed their inhibitions. I love a girl who likes to get really, really wild."

His words revived a little of the heat between her thighs as she flashed a sly smile up at him.

"Well?" he said, leaning slightly forward. "Did I give the right answer or the wrong one? In the big spectrum of females, where exactly do you fall, Diana Marsh?"

She tilted her head and told him *her* truth. The truth that felt so good on her tongue, and in her body. "In the big spectrum of females, I fall right where you want me to. So despite my best efforts to change my evil ways, it looks like this is going to be your lucky night."

* * * * *

When they reached the street, the Las Vegas strip had become a neon jungle. Desert heat still scorched the air, driving them toward the comfort of the limo, but Diana stopped walking for a moment anyway, pulling back on Marc's arm, just so she could look around for a moment and take it all in. Sensing her fascination with the place, he whispered in her ear, his voice smoky and hot. "Welcome to Vegas, baby."

She cast a sexy smile, hoping he could read in it how very ready she was for some Sin City action. After the erotic show they'd just watched together, and given that, for the first time in months, she was spending the evening with a man who wanted her to get wild, she was relieved to have given up the attempt to be a good girl—for now anyway.

As she entered the limo, Marc told their driver to cruise the strip for awhile. "It's the lady's first visit here," he explained. "I want her to see the strip in all its glory." She hoped that really meant, *I want to have my way with her in the back of the limo.*

Once they were both closed inside the plush, cool car with the privacy window raised between them and the driver, Marc opened the mini-fridge, pulled out a bottle of wine, and uncorked it. After turning on some music and pouring two glasses of Chardonnay, they toasted. "To tonight," he said, "and whatever it may hold."

Diana swallowed a long drink of the light, fruity wine, then took both their glasses and set them aside. Pointing at Marc, she curled her finger forward as if to silently say, *Come here.* As he began to move toward her, she shifted to her knees and reached up to open the car's sunroof. The sights and sounds of Vegas seemed to spill in upon them, but that wasn't enough—she wanted to feel herself sinking into this place, absorbing it, with Marc.

Balancing on her heels on the plush seat, she poked her head up through the roof and let the hot wind blow through her hair. Easing up through the opening to stand behind her, Marc wrapped one arm around her waist to keep her steady. Mmm, this was more like it, she thought. A sexy man holding her close as they whisked through one of the most decadent cities on earth.

Turning slightly, she reached one arm up behind his neck and pulled him down for a sensual kiss. She practically purred as his warm tongue eased into her mouth—he kissed just as good as she could have imagined, and this first kiss with Marc was far more electrifying than any kiss she'd ever shared with Bradley.

Their kisses continued, growing more sensual and hot with each passing moment as the limo eased up Las Vegas Boulevard, a million lights from grand hotels and casinos surrounding them on either side. When his cock grew hard against her ass, Diana couldn't resist wiggling against it. "You feel so good," she said, her voice nearly getting lost in the hot wind whipping above the moving vehicle.

As she looked over her shoulder into his eyes, his hands eased upward from her waist onto her breasts. She released a slight moan at finally being touched by him in one of her most sensitive, achy places.

"Is this okay?" he asked softly near her ear. "I mean, considering the Bradley situation."

She turned her head toward him again, practically purring her answer. "I told you, we're not together right now. And the reason is...you. I want you so much more than I've ever wanted him, Marc. I wish I didn't feel that way, but I can't help it—I do."

Behind her, she heard him pull in his breath at her reply. "I'm so glad. And, mmm, you feel good, sweetheart. These lovely breasts feel just as gorgeous as they look in that hot little dress."

Still peering over her shoulder, she let her tongue slide sensuously over her upper lip and said, "Squeeze them."

At this, his big, capable hands molded her deliciously. Diana didn't care that anyone on the street or in other cars on the massive ten-lane boulevard could see him caressing her—she simply arched her needy breasts into his hot palms and drank in the sensations as his shaft grew still bigger, harder, like a column of steel at the crack of her ass. It felt so right, so natural, that it was amazing to her they'd just met face-to-face tonight. Clearly, you really *could* get to know someone through only phone calls and e-mail.

"Woohoo! Yeah, baby!" a guy yelled on the street when they were stopped at a red light.

Marc growled in her ear. "I think he likes watching me play with your pretty breasts."

She wiggled her ass against him in response, and the guy on the street, who was part of a sizable crowd dressed to party, yelled, "Flash us, honey!"

Diana didn't know whether it was the wine, the arousal, the city, or the fact that it had been far too long since she'd felt this free and open with a guy, but without hesitation, she placed her hands over Marc's on her breasts, slipped her fingertips inside the halter top of the dress, and pulled back both sides to reveal herself to the crowd on the street.

An array of cheers and hollers—from both men and women—rose up as she shimmied her boobs back and forth for the spectators, and their response made her cream her panties a little more. Only as the light changed and the limo started forward again did she put her dress back into place, laughing at her own crazy wantonness. Marc still wrapped around her from behind, now chuckling, too. "Damn, sweetheart, I knew you'd be fun, but…"

She turned to him with a playful smile. "I can't believe I just did that!"

He grinned. "Well, believe *this*—it totally turned me on. Not that I needed any help in that area." He leaned into her again from behind, reminding her.

She flashed her sexiest look. "Did you like them?"

"I didn't even get to see them," he said, looking at once frustrated and amused. "But the fact that you're wild enough to have that kind of fun makes me think you and I are more alike than I realized."

"Well, maybe you'll get to see them later," she tormented him, turning back to face the warm breeze.

The fountains of the Bellagio danced next to them on the right side of the car, and the mock Eiffel Tower of the Paris Hotel towered on the left. Overhead walkways and trees rising from the sidewalk added to the ambience and made her feel utterly surrounded by this town. Behind her, Marc's cock felt bigger and bigger as his hands lowered to the front of her thighs, slowly easing up under her dress.

"Are you sure you're only nine inches?" she asked above the sounds of the street and the wind. She was teasing, but she was also beginning to think maybe he hadn't lied.

He laughed. "Only?"

"Okay, color me impressed. You feel incredibly huge."

In reply, he slid the delightfully hard shaft against her, easing it deeper into the valley of her ass, at the same time pressing his fingers over her miniscule panties. She let out a pleased gasp as his touch echoed through her needy pussy. "Mmm, baby," she said, and began to move her cunt against him.

His voice came low, heated, in her ear as they undulated against each other. "You're so hot."

"Mmm," she purred in reply, still rocking her body, rubbing against him, front and back, delicious. "Rub my pussy. Rub my sweet little cunt."

Her dirty words elicited another hot growl from him as the car eased to a stop at another red light. "Do you know how badly I want you, sweetheart?"

"Why don't you tell me about it?"

"I want to thrust this big, hot cock so deep in—"

"Davenport!" a guy suddenly yelled from the street.

Both of them stopped moving, in shock, and Marc muttered, "Shit," under his breath as both of them looked toward the voice.

"Who is it?" she asked.

"You won't believe this, but it's Dan, the guy who gave me the show tickets and the limo." He lifted a wave to his friend and Diana looked over to find two guys in nice suits—one dark-haired and classically handsome, but looking just a bit rough around the edges; the other blondish, tan, and cute, with broad shoulders beneath his suit jacket.

"See you're having a good time in the limo," Dan said on a laugh, and Diana wasn't sure if he was referring to the fact that they were both poking their heads through the sunroof or that Marc was with *her*, a girl in a sexy dress who probably had "hot and ready" written all over her face.

"Dan, Craig, this is Diana Marsh." Marc looked back to her. "I used to work with these guys at Brookner Advertising before I joined Adrianna. Speaking of which…" Again he glanced to the two good-looking guys. "I thought you had a late presentation tonight and that's why you couldn't use the car and the tickets."

A triumphant smile spread across Dan's face, making him appear just a little predatory. "Just got the biggest account of our careers, dude."

By this time, the limo driver had pulled the car to the side, realizing his passengers were talking to someone on the street.

"We were just on our way to celebrate," Craig said, "but, uh, looks like the rest of our group just disappeared into the crowd without us."

Dan peered up at them, head tilted. "So, is this a private party or is there room for two more?"

On one hand, Diana wanted to be alone with Marc, but on the other, his friends seemed nice enough, and Dan *had* given them the limo. Not wanting Marc to feel put on the spot, she answered. "There's plenty of room. Come on in." Then she turned to Marc and said quietly, "If that's all right with you."

He wore a small, knowing smile and spoke softly, as well. "I was just about to put my hand inside your panties, but I want whatever *you* want."

The two guys were already moving toward the car, so they didn't hear when Diana whispered, "I'm not sure I could say no, even now," just before ducking back through the roof.

Marc followed suit, dropping back down into the car next to Diana, trying to absorb what she'd just said. Did she mean...? Did she want him to touch her even though they had company now? He'd meant exactly what he'd said about going for girls who liked to get wild, so the skin around his cock stretched a little tighter at the notion.

Despite their dirty phone call, he'd been concerned with making sure she would welcome his advances, afraid she wouldn't be into watching what had turned out to be a strip show and figuring old Bradley would keep them apart. He liked her too much to risk letting anything ruin their relationship.

He knew nothing *serious* would ever grow between them—for more reasons than he could name. They lived two thousand miles apart, he hoped to be moving to Europe soon, and despite her attraction to him and her breakup with Bradley, she seemed to feel some obligation to the guy. But no matter what happened while she was here, he'd wanted to make sure that in the end they'd still like each other, still be able to work together in that easy way they'd developed, a way that made work seem an awfully lot like play.

Because of that—hell, if she'd shown up wanting to do nothing more with him than watch a movie or share a pizza, he'd have happily done it. His dick would've been none too pleased, but he liked her enough to just want to be around her, whatever the activity.

Now, though, she'd finally convinced him that she was indeed as playful as the girl he'd been flirting with for months, and as naughty as the girl who he'd masturbated with on the phone. And the boyfriend hindrance had disappeared, at least for the time being. So even though he'd have settled for pizza, he and his cock were both a hell of a lot happier waiting to see exactly how wild she was willing to get in this limo—alone, or with his two friends along for the ride.

Once inside, Dan and Craig settled back in the plush bench seat across from them and Dan reached for the open bottle of wine and two more glasses. Diana cuddled up to Marc, locking her arms around one of his, pulling her legs up in the seat beside her so that her warm thigh pressed against him. Her breasts, half-exposed from the deep, open neckline, rubbed against his arm through his suit jacket.

Dan took a sip of his wine and narrowed his gaze on Diana. "Where'd you find this beautiful woman, dude?" he asked Marc.

In an effort to say, *Whatever happens here, she's mine*, he slid his hand between her thighs, midway between knee and crotch. "Diana and I are sort of…" He gave her a playful glance. "…e-mail pen pals. And now she's here on business."

"And pleasure, too, looks like," Craig chimed in with a grin.

"By the way, how'd you enjoy the show, Diana?" Dan inquired, wearing a suggestive smile.

She didn't even blush when she said, "It was fun. You missed some very hot women, Dan."

The two guys across from them chuckled at her sexy candor and Marc was impressed as hell with her sensual confidence. "I'll bet," Dan said.

"So…your first time in Sin City?" Craig asked before taking a sip of wine.

She nodded. "And although the show was very sexy, I'm…still looking for some serious sin."

Chapter Three

Over the next hour, they drained two more bottles of wine and cruised the strip. As they passed the mega-resort casinos, Craig gave Diana his opinion on the best places to gamble, and Dan, conversely, seemed to have seen every show in town. "Not just because there are mostly naked women in them, either," he claimed with a laugh.

"No," Marc said, chuckling, "couldn't be that. It's because you're such a connoisseur of fine song and dance."

As they passed the towering pyramid of the Luxor, Diana asked Craig how the gambling was there.

"There? It sucks," he said softly, offering a sad sort of smile.

She raised her eyebrows and took a drink of her wine, waiting for an explanation.

"Blackjack dealer who works at the Luxor broke his heart," Dan explained.

She blinked. "Really?" She was always interested to hear about people's romances—failures or successes. She might have few inhibitions when it came to sex, but inside, she held the notion of true romance dear.

"Sad but true," Craig confirmed. "Won two hundred bucks at her table the night we met, and she refused to go out with me, saying she'd get in trouble for dating a customer. But I kept coming back, so many times that I wasn't a customer anymore—"

"More like an annoyance," Dan injected, making them all laugh lightly.

"And finally," Craig went on, "she went out with me."

"*What* was her name?" Marc asked as if trying to remember. "Marlene or something?"

"Marla," Craig said before switching his gaze back to Diana. "It got serious fast. I was crazy about her."

"What happened?" Diana asked.

Craig shook his head regretfully. "Old boyfriend re-entered the picture. Eventually she went back to him. Left me high and dry four months ago."

"And he hasn't gotten laid since," Dan added.

Craig arched one irritated eyebrow at his friend. "Thanks for adding that part." He looked at Diana once more. "Truth is, I've had a hard time getting over her."

She cast a gentle smile. "Well, if you ask me, she made a stupid decision. You seem like a great guy." She wasn't even sugar-coating it. Craig struck her as the perfect masculine-but-slightly-sensitive guy-next-door, and she liked how he'd shared his story with her.

"You've got a very nice girl here, Marc," he said, but then he rolled his eyes, looking a bit sheepish before returning his gaze to Diana. "Although I have no idea what possessed me to spill my guts to you."

"Uh, the wine, I'm guessing," Marc said.

From there, the conversation turned to sex, and Dan tossed out a question at random. "What's the wildest sex you've ever had?"

Craig supplied an answer. "Easy. Once Marla and I did it on her dad's pool table—while he was upstairs."

Diana raised her eyebrows, laughing, and the guys shared easy high fives. "Dan?" she asked. "What about you?"

"Hmm," he replied, thinking it over. "I guess I'd have to say it was on the fifty-yard line of the Sun Devil Stadium."

This got even more of a response. After the gasps and laughter, he went on.

"I used to live in Phoenix, and a girl I was dating worked at the stadium. She had a fantasy about doing it on the field, so one night we snuck in. *I* wanted to turn on all the lights, but she was afraid it would blow our cover," he added with a wink.

"Marc, what about you, dude?" Craig asked.

"Uh…" he said, grinning as if he'd been caught doing something naughty already, "let's not go there."

Diana turned to him with an inquisitive smile. "Why not?"

"Keeping secrets from the lady, Marc?" Dan joked.

He shrugged, still wearing a guilty grin as he glanced at Diana. "Well, maybe I *do* want to keep a secret or two…for your benefit."

"Hmm," she said, "intriguing."

Across from them, Dan was narrowing his eyes on Marc. "I wouldn't put up with that crap, Diana. In fact, I think you should dump his ass and go out with *me*." He winked.

"Tempting," she said, "but I'm wondering exactly what I have to do to find out Mr. Davenport's naughty little secrets." Casting Marc a sexy smile, she leaned provocatively up against him, rubbing her breasts against his arm as she'd first done back at the show. Setting her wineglass aside, she slid one hand up his thigh. "What's it gonna take, hmm?"

He gave her a playful look of warning. "You'd…better tread carefully there, sweetheart. I'm already beyond frustrated."

"Still?"

"What do you mean, still?" Craig asked.

Marc leaned back his head and rolled his eyes. "Truth is, you guys sort of showed up at…an inopportune moment."

"Shit," Dan said. "Why didn't you tell us to take a hike?"

Marc glanced down at her with a reproachful smile. "Because Diana is too polite."

"I wasn't just being polite—I really wanted to hang out with your friends, get to know them a little."

"Well, I'd say you've accomplished that," Marc said on a laugh. And indeed, Diana did feel she'd gotten to know Craig and Dan as they'd cruised the neon strip together, joking and sharing stories. But she also suffered from the same frustration Marc did, and she wanted to ease it, for both of them.

"Hey, Diana," Craig said, "that reminds me, you didn't answer the question. What was the wildest sex you've ever had?"

Sitting snuggled up to Marc, her breasts aching and her cunt tingling with desire, she found herself having a very unorthodox urge and feeling very tempted to indulge it.

Maybe it was the wine.

Maybe it was the city.

Or maybe it was an impulse to show Marc exactly how wild she could be.

Glancing back and forth between Marc and the other two guys, she said, "I can't quite believe this, but...I think I'm about to have it right now."

With those words, she looped her arms around Marc's neck and kissed him—one of those hot, slow tongue kisses he'd already discovered she was so good at delivering. If a mere kiss from this woman set off tremors inside him... Damn, what would happen when she took things further?

He'd decided a while ago that he'd misread her when he'd suspected she wanted to fool around while his friends watched, but now his thoughts turned that way again. And he sure as hell couldn't resist her kiss, or the notion of watching Diana set herself free. Still, he had no idea how far she wanted to go in front of Dan and Craig, so he would leave it to her to set the pace.

Her tongue twined warm and wet around his and he was dying to touch her—her breasts, her pussy—but *she'd* have to let him know if that was okay.

As if reading his mind, her hand slid up his thigh and directly onto his hard cock. "Ah..." he breathed at the sweet sensation of her delicate palm stroking his erection through his pants.

She massaged his super-stiff shaft in a rhythm that urged him to thrust it up into her hand. Push...push...push... "Mmm, sweetheart, that's so fucking good," he said, his voice coming out raspy.

Across the car, Dan and Craig looked completely awed—not to mention envious—and Marc couldn't blame them. It had been clear that Diana had built a quick rapport with them and that they considered him damn lucky to have her on his arm — now he knew instinctively that they were appreciating her sensual generosity as much as he was.

"Is this okay?" she murmured to him between kisses. "Here, like this?"

He could barely catch his breath to answer her in a low whisper just between the two of them. "It's *very* okay. As long as *you're* sure it's okay."

Her eyes looked glassy with passion. "I want to excite you. And your friends seem nice."

He nodded, still whispering. "They're good guys. And…trust me, this excites me…maybe more than anything in my entire life."

As she continued to knead his dick, he reached for her breasts, letting his hands fall into the same hot rhythm she was using on him, molding her sweet mounds through the crinkly fabric of her dress. His thumbs lay across the exposed inner curves, so he gently stroked them upward, liking the way her breath turned heavy at his touch.

Their kisses continued, but soon degenerated into hot, sharp little collisions of their mouths, hard and hungry. Marc couldn't wait another second to push that red fabric aside, and once he'd bared her breasts, he stopped kissing to look down. A sound of sheer amazement rose from his throat at the sight of them — large and round and tan with lovely dark, rosy nipples that stood taut and hard.

"Just as gorgeous as I imagined," he said on a rough breath, stroking the pads of his thumbs across the beaded nipples, making her let out a hot little cry. "So damn pretty, baby," he whispered, taking in every smooth, inviting curve with both his hands and his eyes. "So damn pretty."

She watched him caress her, slowly dragging her tongue across her upper lip, which only got him hotter. Push...push...push...against her hand, which was wrapped around him through his pants now, holding his cock firm and tight.

When he curved his hands around the outer edges of her breasts, then dropped to graze his tongue across one stiffened nipple, she released a sigh and let her head fall back, as if submitting, offering her lovely mounds up for his consumption. He sucked first on one, then the other, going back and forth between the two pink buds which were clearly in need of his attention. He kneaded her breasts as he laved them and nursed at them and reveled in the hot little sounds of delight that kept escaping her.

Her breasts were so beautiful he thought he could touch and kiss them all night—never get enough of their pretty, round firmness, the perfectly distended nipples that felt so good on his tongue.

But finally she pushed him back, off of her, and he saw that her chest was big enough to hold back the sides of the dress of their own accord. He loved nothing more than the sight of a woman in a state of passionate disarray—her clothes half-on, half-off.

On the opposite seat, his friends still watched in thrilled, silent pleasure. "Look," he said softly to Diana. "Look at how they're watching you, sweetheart."

Diana followed his lead, glancing over to the guys, her eyes shining with the wonder of true excitement.

"You're a beautiful woman, Diana," Dan offered, his voice coming thick and deep.

She smiled at the compliment, saying, "I've never done anything like this before."

Craig released a sigh of pleasure. "Don't stop. You're amazing."

As if the guys' assurances had prodded her, she turned back to Marc, smiled sexily into his eyes, and leaned over to begin working at his belt buckle. He pulled in his breath, watching. Unzipping his suit pants, she grabbed the top band of his underwear and pulled it down, all the way, hooking it beneath his balls, a sensation that added considerably to his arousal.

She licked her lips as she studied his full length; his shaft lay hard and flat against his abdomen, reaching past his navel, and her hot little sigh told him she liked what he had to offer. Women usually did. Reaching down, she wrapped her fist full around it, pulling it up from his stomach, her touch electrifying.

When she bent to delicately lick the drop of white fluid from the tip, his whole body shuddered from that one touch of her tongue. He only hoped he could survive the rest—he had a feeling Diana was going to be an expert at this.

Flashing him the look of a hungry vixen, she leaned over and ran her tongue all the way around the head, twice. He let out a moan and had the urge to close his eyes and drop his head back to the plush headrest behind him, but he didn't want to miss watching her ministrations.

Next, she went lower, and licked a path of wet heat from the base of his shaft all the way to the end, where she let her lips close over him and slide down, down, taking in as much as she could handle. A groan rose from inside him, deep from his gut—he felt the caress of her sweet, warm lips *everywhere*.

Still pinning him with her hungry gaze, she began to move up and down on his length with her pretty mouth—slow at first, then picking up speed. Her lips stretched tight and wide around him, her mouth like a wet, deep glove.

"Suck me, sweetheart," he urged her in a low voice. "Suck my cock."

As she worked him over, he began to fuck her mouth, just a little—both because he couldn't restrain himself from the urge and because he sensed Diana was the type of woman who liked to be fucked in a lot of different ways.

So he made small thrusts between her soft, dainty lips, watching with awe as she slowly took him in a little deeper, then a little more, until she was sucking more than half his length.

She was perched beside him, her knees planted next to his thigh, her ass in the air. So he reached around, finding the back of one leg, sliding his hand up past the top of her stocking and onto her ass, bringing the red fabric with him.

He squeezed and caressed her round bottom as she continued sucking him. Sinking his fingers into the crevice, he found the thin band of her thong panties and let his touch slide down onto the soft fabric covering her cunt. She flinched a little at the touch and he said, "Easy, baby, just gonna rub your pretty pussy while you suck me."

He used his first two fingers, moving them in little circles over the small mound of flesh hidden beneath her panties. She began undulating against his touch, and when he reached farther between her legs to stroke her clit, she moaned against his shaft.

Across from him, Dan and Craig both had their cocks out now, working them with their hands as they watched Diana's skilled mouth slide up and down his rock-hard column.

Marc curled his fingertips around the soft fabric of her thong, pulling it away from her mound, finally letting his fingers explore her bare pussy. Damn—he'd never felt softer, smoother skin in his life. He caressed her outer lips, liking the feel of her tender skin on his fingers, then sank his touch into her wet center, stroking. She was soaked, instantly drenching all four of his fingers as he glided them through the soft folds and ridges of her open cunt, making him even hotter as she laved his cock.

When she finally rose up off of him, he immediately noticed how swollen her mouth looked. Still fingering her pussy, he used his free hand to draw her to him for a hard kiss, needing to feel those bee-stung lips on his.

She kissed him while squirming against his touch, but her panties kept intruding, the elastic closing over his fingers. Finally, he muttered, "I need to get these damn panties off you."

With that, she rose up on her knees, reached slowly up under her dress, and began to peel down what turned out to be a thong of red mesh. She wiggled her ass and made a grand show of removing it, stopping when it reached the bottom of her thighs. After easing back to the seat, her sexy red heels planted on the floor, her dress settled around her hips so that her pretty, naked pussy was on display, she lowered herself onto all fours and did a slow, sensuous crawl across the car until she finally sat down between Dan and Craig. She held her legs out straight before her, the panties still at her knees, and flashed Marc a wicked smile. "Come take them off."

He was totally absorbed in her now, loved what a dirty girl she was being—far more than he'd even dared to dream. Following her command, he eased down onto his knees and slowly drew the tiny panties down over her calves and ankles, watching as she pulled out one red heel, then the other.

Tossing the damp panties over his shoulder, he looked into those wild eyes of hazel and said, "Now, sweetheart, I've *got* to take a good long look at this hot little pussy."

In response, she spread her legs wide and her pussy opened with them—gaping and swollen.

"Oh, honey," Dan groaned, and Marc saw from his peripheral vision that his friends were still stroking their dicks as they leaned forward to study her cunt, as well.

Her soft pink flesh glistened beneath the stream of Vegas nightlight admitted through the sunroof. Her clit protruded, a hard little mountain of need.

He planned to lick and kiss and suck every inch of her beautifully engorged pussy, but as he'd told her, first he just wanted to take a long, slow perusal. He wanted to smell her tangy sweet aroma, wanted to feel her smooth outer lips, wanted to memorize her from her erect clit to her little round hole.

As Marc ran his fingertips painstakingly around the outer edge of her pussy, Diana couldn't help fondling her breasts, massaging the round globes, lightly pinching her firm nipples. This moment was making her feel more alive, more sexually vital, than anything ever had. She couldn't quite believe she was doing this, yet somehow it had come easy. She'd always thought she was a wild child, but up to now, she'd always kept sex between her and one other guy. Indeed, the combination of Sin City and Marc Davenport was inspiring her to new heights of sexual gratification.

As Marc's friends watched him so intimately exploring her cunt—mmm, now he was gently stroking his thumbs from top to bottom in her wet pink flesh—she took the opportunity to look back and forth between the two handsome men, scrutinizing their cocks. Neither was quite as long as Marc's glorious and unexaggerated nine inches—which had both challenged and thrilled her to suck it—but they were still very fine. She liked the way they looked being held and stroked by masculine hands. Dan's possessed a bright pink head that sported a little come, while Craig's had a slight curve and was intriguingly thick.

Looking at both shafts made her yearn to see Marc's again—it was so big and hard she thought she'd never get enough of it.

But at the moment, she was experiencing a whole *new* temptation.

Only if it pleased Marc, though. That's all she wanted. She'd already discovered that pleasing this man was more than half the thrill for her.

She leaned down, taking his face between her hands, and whispered quietly. "Tell me what else you want."

His dark eyes looked consumed by desire. "I want a lot of things."

Somehow she had a feeling he wanted the same thing she was suddenly so very tempted to do. One of them had to say it. She spoke even lower. "Do you want to share me?"

His breath came heavy, his answer without hesitation. "Yes." Yet his eyebrows instantly knit. "But only if you want that, too. Only if you're a hundred percent into it."

She smiled, ever the bad girl. It flowed through her veins, part of her blood.

She kissed him, hard, quick, then sat back up, shocked at her desire, stunned by her daring, and ready to thrill them all anew.

She glanced back and forth between Dan and Craig, then let herself indulge in a long-time fantasy. "Do you boys want to kiss my pretty breasts?"

She had just enough time to catch the awe and excitement on each guy's face before they both bent to her chest. And just as they each took a nipple into their mouth, Marc went down on her, raking his tongue over her clit. She let out a pleasured sigh, then leaned back a little deeper in the plush seat and spread her legs farther apart.

Diana had never experienced such brazen ecstasy. Having three men suck on her at once filled her with an indescribable pleasure she'd only dreamed about. She loved looking down to see all three of them mouthing her and delighted in the way each felt different. Dan sucked her nipple hard, making her feel the pull deep within her breast. Craig, conversely, delivered hot little licks across her other pearl-hard peak, to leave it looking prettily wet in between his ministrations. When he changed to sucking, she could tell he ran the tip of his tongue around her nipple even as he gently pulled on it with his lips.

Below, Marc delivered the greatest joy of all. Each stroke of his warm tongue was like a trail of fire racing across her cunt. "Mmm, yes, baby," she purred, peering down at him overtop Craig's and Dan's heads. With his mouth still buried between the widespread lips of her cunt, Marc peered up at her, eyes glassy—he looked drunk on her, which was just what she wanted. She wanted them all to be totally intoxicated with each other.

Out the tinted windows, the sparkling lights of Vegas shimmered around them, and above her, through the open sunroof, the illumination of a million bulbs shone down bright enough that she had a lovely view of the three men pleasuring her with their wet mouths. She thrust her cunt at Marc, panting, knowing she would come soon. Intense pleasure rose within her, making her pussy feel light and heavy at the same time, making her feel so lost to it that she mindlessly pumped her body at all the glorious male mouths. The sounds of wet suckling filled the big car, along with Diana's moans, coming low in her throat, growing louder and louder as she neared her climax.

"A little more, baby," she whimpered. "Keep licking me. Keep licking." The command seemed to inspire them all to work a little harder, suck a little deeper.

As Diana neared orgasm, she had the strange sensation that her nipples were longer and harder than they'd ever been before, that her clit was bigger and more rigid than ever in her life. She closed her eyes, basked in the forbidden delights, thought again how incredible it was to have three perfect mouths pleasuring her body, then she tipped over the edge.

Deep, rough waves of satiation rolled through her as she cried out, "Yes! Yes! Yes!" with each one. "Oh! Oh! God! Yes!" She'd never come so intensely.

Her three lovers each continued working at their tasks until she went completely still beneath their mouths, then they finally released her spent flesh.

She opened her eyes to see Marc smiling up at her as he dropped a soft kiss just below her belly button. "How was that, baby?" His hands slid up to cup the outer curves of her breasts.

She hoped he saw the deep heat swimming in her eyes. "You have *no* idea." Still recovering from the climax of a lifetime, she let her head fall back as she laughed, and murmured, "So, so good."

Her eyes were shut, but she felt Marc place another kiss on her stomach. "Mmm." And without quite thinking about it, she reached out to either side of her until she was curling her hands around Dan's and Craig's cocks.

"Unh…" Craig moaned next to her.

"Oh, baby," Dan muttered.

She opened her eyes and flashed a sexy, playful smile at her three companions. "It was so good that I feel I must show my gratitude."

Craig let out a deep, excited laugh as she began sliding her fists firmly up and down the two pleasantly hard shafts.

"Damn, sweetheart," Marc crooned, still caressing her breasts, his chin resting on her abdomen, "I keep thinking you can't get me any more excited, but…"

"Then you don't mind if I make your friends feel good?" she asked with a sinful little grin.

"It's arousing the hell out of me."

"I want to arouse you even more."

At that, Diana released the two nice-sized cocks from her grip and got to her knees on the floor, positioning herself between Dan's legs. Smiling up at him, but mainly thinking of Marc's eyes on her, she closed her hand around the base of his shaft, then lowered her mouth onto his cock.

The taste of pre-come met her tongue, sweet and gooey, making her hungry for more. She went as far down on him as she could without straining herself. With Marc, she had strained and stretched and worked to relax her throat so she could take him in deeper—because there was so much to take in and because she wanted so profoundly to pleasure him—but with Dan and Craig she only planned to go as far as what came naturally.

"Oh baby, that's very nice," Dan whispered. She hoped desperately that Marc was watching her mouth slide up and down this shaft just as it had on his a little while ago. She liked the way Dan's hard-on filled her mouth, but she'd *loved* the way Marc's had. It had made her want to suck him dry, but she'd resisted in order to keep him hot and ready for more.

When she felt hands on her breasts, at first she didn't know whether they belonged to Marc or Craig, which excited her. Looking slightly to the right, though, she spotted Craig down on the floor with her, reaching under her to play with her dangling nipples.

That meant the hands currently caressing her hips and ass belonged to Marc—mmm, yes. She did her best to thrust her pussy out toward him, and he rewarded her by stroking it.

Beneath her, Craig fondled her, pinching her nipples, and behind her—oh God! Marc had just inserted a finger into her hot little hole. He moved it in and out in time with her ministrations to Dan, then inserted another, maybe a third—she couldn't tell.

She fucked Marc's fingers, releasing needy whimpers, and when that ceased, giving way to a light, rustling sound, she glanced over her shoulder to see him rolling on a condom. Finally, his hands molded to both her hips, his glorious cock poised to enter her aching pussy.

She pushed against the thick pressure and it sank in, warm, deep, in one long slow stroke that demonstrated for her just how ready she was. "Unh!" she cried around Dan's width. Normally, she might have to ease onto nine inches a little at a time, but her cunt had accepted Marc's enormous rod like a snug little glove closing around a hand.

She instantly loved the sensation of being filled from both ends. Craig's touches and nips at her breasts made the experience even more spectacular.

Deciding she needed to give him some special pleasures, too, she let Dan slip from her mouth, and turned to find Craig. He lay stretched out on the floor, his head beneath her elevated stomach, so she shifted herself over him into a sixty-nine.

As she slid her lips down over his cock, she felt the thickness of his shaft fill her in a whole new way. It still didn't stir her in the same intense manner as sucking on Marc had, but she'd never had such a thick cock in her mouth and taking him in stretched her lips pleasantly. Marc had shifted with her as she straddled Craig's body, and he fucked her in smooth, hard strokes that made her cry out against Craig's shaft, which curled naturally toward her throat and aided her in adjusting to his width.

Marc's hard fucking grew more powerful until she thought the entire lower portion of her body might split apart from the incredible thrusts. And when she least expected it, a tongue, Craig's, began to lap at her clit. *Oh yes, yes, yes*, she whispered inside as she continued to give him the same oral attention. It was the perfect titillation added to the pounding of Marc's cock. She cried out as he drove into her, the sound vibrating around Craig's shaft, which seemed to increase the intensity of his licking. It came hard and wet until she felt as much like she was fucking his mouth as she was fucking Marc's big rod.

That's when it broke—like an explosion of fireworks, like hot sparks shattering into a million pieces to fall across her body. This orgasm was longer, sweeter, something she was able to ride out, wrenching every drop of pleasure from it before it ended.

Only then did she realize she'd released the cock from her mouth in order to scream her release. When she finally went still, she collapsed next to Craig on the floor. He reached out to rub her leg. "You're an incredible woman," he told her with a smile. "Thank you."

Unbelievably, the simple compliment made her cunt quiver, even after all that little piece of flesh had already been through. In response, she lifted her head onto the fabric covering his thigh, reaching out her tongue to give his erection another little lick. She offered him an easy, sensual smile and hoped this night might help him move on after his breakup with Marla.

Marc lounged on the floor with them, too, now. He situated himself between her legs to gently stroke her outer lip with his thumb. "Tell me, sweetheart, can this sweet pussy of yours take anymore?"

She laughed softly. To her surprise, her cunt was still hungry, still hot. "Well, you have an incredible cock, baby, and you use it *very* well...but yeah, I can take more. I *want* more."

Their gazes met. "What exactly do you want?"

"I want you to fuck me until you come."

Marc's eyes seemed to glaze over at her words.

She grew vaguely aware that the car was moving in a different direction than the last time she'd looked; she caught sight of the MGM Grand, its walls changing from one electric color to the next. Other cars passed them by on the busy boulevard. If they only knew what was going on inside *this* car, she thought, they'd beg to watch.

As she looked around her at her three handsome men, all wearing their suits, and all with their nice hard cocks exposed, she still couldn't quite believe the pleasure she'd let herself indulge in tonight, and she was ready for more.

To make sure they all had a good view of her ass and slit, she rose on all fours and crawled slowly to the other seat, where she and Marc had started the evening. Once there, she leaned over it, resting the upper half of her body on the plush fabric, which felt scintillatingly soft on her bare breasts.

"Come and get me," she cooed to Marc, then reached behind her and used her first two fingers to spread open her lips and give them all another enticing glimpse of pink.

She looked over her shoulder at him, bit her lip. "Come on," she said softly, casting a sexy smile. "I'm waiting for you."

He returned the grin and got in position behind her, but didn't enter her hungry cunt.

Finally, she got impatient. "Why aren't you in me?"

She heard his rich chuckle just as he dropped a little kiss high on her ass. "I'm looking," he said. "I'm looking at your hot little hole. It's all nice and open, and I'm enjoying the view."

When she again glanced over her shoulder, she found Craig and Dan had returned to their seats, clearly sensing that her focus had narrowed to Marc again. "Is it wet?" she asked.

Marc audibly pulled in his breath at the question. "Mmm, very. And there's a pretty little trail of juice leaking out."

Her patience was growing short again, and he sensed it.

"You want my cock in you, sweetheart?"

She nodded. "Badly."

"All right. Here it comes."

And then his colossal erection was sliding slowly into her again—deep, deeper, deepest, making her groan. "So big," she whimpered. "Fuck me."

As before, his thrusts were thoroughly intense, filling her to the brim and making her scream with each stroke. And as he fucked her, she realized there was more than just the sensation of a huge cock—there were fingers playing about her ass, passing gently over the tiny fissure. He caressed her, rubbing her asshole, gently prodding at the opening.

She let out a moan and drank it all in: the cock inside her, the sweet stimulation of her anus. Wetness—he was rubbing her with wet fingers now, which he must have slid through her arousal to lubricate her.

Hot little circular caresses on her asshole soon led to pushing, easing into it, and another oh-so-pleasant intrusion. She heard herself sob.

She'd had guys play with her ass a little, rubbing the tiny gap and getting her hot, but this was the first time she'd actually been fucked there, even just with fingers, and it was incredible, especially with Marc's continued driving thrusts into her pussy. Her whimpers turned desperate and needy. Her control over her body felt lost. So many sensations, hard and soft, fast and slow...oh God, she couldn't take much more.

She hadn't thought she could come again, but she'd also never had her asshole stimulated quite so thoroughly while an enormous cock filled her. She reached up under herself, between her legs, and pressed three fingers over her slit. Finding her clitoris, she rubbed around it in hot little circles. It took only seconds to reach her third and most intense orgasm of the night. She screamed out—hard, loud cries that surely alerted anyone within hearing distance on the street that a woman was having her brains fucked out in the limo.

Behind her, Marc knew he couldn't last much longer. He thought it was a miracle that he'd managed to keep from shooting his load before now.

Damn, to think that a few hours ago he was worried about offending her by coming on too strong, by touching her back in the theater. He'd hoped Diana would want to get wild with him, but he'd had no idea his flirtatious little friend would be open to something as hot and out-of-bounds as what they were doing right now. It had him nearly out of his mind with lust and he was going to explode any minute.

Even so, he wanted to hold off a little longer, so he eased back, pulled his cock out of her. But when he looked down and—shit—saw how open *both* of her passages were, the sight alone was nearly enough to push him over the edge. He couldn't keep himself from slipping his cock back into her just a little—just enough to tease.

"Are you all gonna come soon?" she asked them over her shoulder.

"Oh yeah," Dan said, half-growling.

"Mmm, good," she purred.

Marc delivered almost-painful-now mini-thrusts, aware both guys were stroking their cocks behind him, getting close. It seemed a safe enough time for him to ram back into her, fuck her hard. He did, and she cried out, arching her back.

He pounded into her fast and furious, gave her everything he had, and when he finally heard his friends let out the moans that came with orgasm, first Dan, then Craig, he finally let himself go inside her, moaning his last.

Chapter Four

Marc barely slept that night. He was too keyed up by the wild evening he'd spent with Diana. First, they'd dropped Dan and Craig at the Brookner office downtown so they could pick up their cars, after which he'd instructed the driver—a guy in his thirties who had surely heard the racket and known exactly what was happening—to take them to the Venetian.

Sitting in the back of the limo, he'd kissed Diana with all the passion he had left inside him after spending so damn much of it through the evening. "Well," he'd said softly, his hands buried in her hair, "looks like you found that sin you were looking for."

She'd misunderstood his intent. "Did I just...mess things up with you by doing what I did tonight? Make you...not like me as much as before? Do you think I'm a slut?"

"God, no, sweetheart," he whispered. The truth was, before tonight, he'd liked her—a lot. Now...he was crazy about her. "I *loved* what you did tonight. And I *love* how sexually free you are. I promise."

She peered up into his eyes. "I did it mostly because I wanted to please *you*."

He knew that. She'd asked him before she'd done it, of course, but he'd also somehow sensed that it had more to do with him than with Dan and Craig. "And I love that."

Stepping out of the car with her, he'd kissed her once more and watched her walk away, into the hotel, in that sexy dress, thinking how much *more* sexy she was underneath it.

Now, it was morning, and he feared it would be strange to see her in the office. What if she had regrets? What if fooling around with all three of them had seemed fun at the time because she was in Las Vegas and had been drinking and had just seen a very arousing show, but she had awakened thinking, *What the hell did I do?* He'd known girls before—back in college and even since then—who'd let themselves get wild when they'd been drinking or high, but who felt used and ashamed the next day.

And to think they had to walk into the corporate offices of Adrianna, Inc. this morning and go straight to work like nothing had happened.

He was passing through the crisp, contemporary lobby when she stepped off the elevator, looking exactly like the professional woman on the website—but also somehow like the hot, sexy vixen he'd partied with so decadently just hours ago.

Like him, she was a little early, so Holly wasn't at her desk yet, and they were alone. He closed the distance between them.

When he spoke, his voice came low and was filled with earnest concern. "How are you?"

"I'm fine," she said with a confident smile.

He blinked, then grabbed her arm and pulled her into the stairwell next to the elevators, where no one would happen upon them.

She seemed surprised, peering up at him with expectant eyes.

"No, I mean—*how are you*? How are you *really*? After last night?"

She tilted her head and gave an indulgent smile. "Well, my pussy is a little sore, but other than that, I'm completely fine. Did you think I'd have regrets or something?"

He let out a quick sigh. "Well, I thought you might. I mean...you said you'd never done anything like that before."

She spoke matter-of-factly. "No. But I thoroughly enjoyed it."

Okay, so he was being an idiot here. Worrying needlessly over this woman who he...well, who he...damn it, just as he'd realized upon parting with her last night, he was pretty damn wild about her. He let a sheepish smile form. "Good. So did I."

With that, he molded his hands to her hips through her jacket. Her crisp, sexy suit was a sensual shade that bordered between blue and black—darker than the silk blouse of midnight blue she wore underneath. He leaned in close and, now that he knew she was truly okay, let a little of the natural animal in him come out. He practically growled his words. "Do you know how fucking hot you were last night?"

Her laugh was full-bodied and sexy.

He laughed, too. "I still can't quite get over it."

"So had *you* ever done anything like that before?" She splayed her hands across his crisp white shirt on either side of his tie, lightly kneading his chest through the starched fabric.

"Um, yeah, actually."

She looked aroused. "Is that one of those secrets you were keeping?"

"Let's just say I knew some pretty crazy girls in college. And there was another time a couple of years ago—one of my friend's girlfriends decided to invite a few of us into a bedroom at a party. And…"

Her eyebrows lifted. "Still more?"

He was back to feeling sheepish. "Yeah, some other times. What can I say? I've been a…sexually experimental guy," he concluded with a grin.

"Well, now that I've experienced it, I can say with authority that it all sounds like a lot of fun," she replied with a light, pretty laugh, and he nodded.

It *had* been fun. Every single time, he'd felt like the luckiest guy on earth to be living out something most men only fantasized about. But now, well…all the other times had been fun, all right, but they'd been nothing like last night for him. Last night his heart had pounded in his chest, and his cock had felt like it was going to explode over and over again. Watching her commit such hot, sensual acts with such bold flair and confidence had made him think she was fucking amazing.

He let his hands slide around to cup her ass through her skirt, which was, he'd noticed immediately, nice and short as she'd promised him that night on the phone. He leaned into her, pressing his hard-on against the front of her cunt.

"Mmm," she said, pulling him down for a kiss.

He whispered in her ear. "Do you know how much I'd love to fuck you right here in the stairwell, sweetheart?"

She licked her lip in that sexy way of hers. "I'd love it, too, but my pussy really *is* sore. We need to give it a short rest, I think."

Letting his hands descend from her ripe ass, he used one to gather her skirt and slid the other down to finger her through her panties, which he could tell was another sexy thong. He wasted no time pushing the lacy fabric aside and inserting his middle finger up into her moist center.

"Mmm, nice," she breathed, moving on it, and against his cock, just a little.

"Not too sore for a little finger-fucking, huh?"

"Apparently not." She was getting into it now, working her wet cunt up and down.

A floor above, a door opened—someone else coming into the stairwell. He immediately withdrew his finger and separated from her. "All right," he said, no longer speaking quietly. "I'll see you in a little while for our first brainstorming session."

"Okay, see you then."

As footsteps descended the tile stairs, getting closer, Marc—with his back toward whoever approached—stuck his middle finger in his mouth and sucked it clean while she watched, then exited the stairwell back out into the lobby, his cock hard as granite.

* * * * *

Diana began to climb the stairs after Marc's quick exit, hiding the naughty smile that wanted to leak out. Only after passing a nondescript man and waiting for his footfalls to fade somewhere below her did she return back to the 5th floor of the high-rise building—one of several levels which housed the Adrianna corporate offices.

Since Holly still wasn't at her desk, she took a seat on the lavish sofa provided in the waiting area, her pussy still tingling from Marc's little stairwell assault.

She didn't know why he kept thinking she was a good girl, the kind of girl who would wake up in tears of remorse after a wild night out, but she couldn't help thinking it was sweet of him to care.

The truth was, she'd been overwhelmed by the sexual pleasure a woman could find with multiple partners. For years, she'd fantasized about such a situation, maybe even wished for it—she'd once dated a football player in college with a lot of hunky, sexy friends, and she'd almost hoped he would invite her to do him and one of his friends at the same time, but he never had. And only *doing* had made her truly understand the hot, forbidden delights to be experienced with more than one man.

And as for the good girl she was supposed to be *trying* to be, well—she'd known as soon as she'd laid eyes on Marc, the moment she'd felt the hot chemistry between them, that it was a lost cause. For now, anyway.

As for the rest of the trip...well, if she could get her lust for Marc under control, maybe she'd be strong enough to cool things down with him a little.

And if not, then—as she'd decided once before—this would probably be...a last hot fling. Her last chance to get in all the hot sex and illicit experiences a good girl couldn't have. Maybe after *that*, she'd at last be able to embrace the part of herself that really did want to be nice and sweet and respectable...for her parents' sake.

The ding of the elevator made her look up. A young, pretty blonde, petite and shapely in a short pink skirt and clingy stretch top, stepped off. "Good morning," she said to Diana. "Can I help you?"

Diana smiled, recognizing the voice she'd only heard on the phone until now. "Holly?" She pressed one hand to her chest. "I'm Diana."

Holly's pale blue eyes lit up. "Diana!" She held out her arms and Diana rose to give her a hug. She and Holly had always gotten along famously and Diana felt like she knew her, as often as they spoke on the phone. The hug was short but warm, and as the two women's breasts pressed briefly together, Diana noted the sexy scent of Holly's perfume. Funny, Holly was so sweet and fun-loving on the phone that Diana had never pictured her being so attractive.

Holly asked about her flight and then about her first night in Vegas. Without a plan in mind, Diana simply replied, "Marc was kind enough to take me out to dinner and a show."

"Which one did you see?"

"I...forget the name," she said, laughing and thinking how unlikely that sounded, so she rushed on quickly. "Lots of lights and feathers and sequins and dancing, though."

"Ah. Probably Jubilee or Folies Bergere." Holly tilted her head, putting on a playful, hesitant smile. "You know, I hope this isn't totally out of line, but...I think Marc likes you...you know, romantically. And I think you two would sort of just...fit together really well, know what I mean?"

Diana smiled, thinking—*oh, Holly, if you only knew how well Marc and I fit together.* "Well, that might be true, but I'm...sort of seeing someone back in Baltimore."

Holly looked crestfallen. "Sort of? Is it serious?"

"Well, I should explain. We're broken up right now—I told him I wanted some time on my own before things get any deeper between us. But...I think if I can just get a few things worked out in my head that...he may be the one."

Holly tried to smile. "Well, that's great, Diana. Really! He's a lucky guy."

"Marc knows," she added, feeling the need to put Holly at ease about the situation.

Holly nodded, then changed gears. "Listen, I need to tell Adrianna you've arrived. She'll want to come out and say hello before you get started with the guys."

"Oh, she's here already?"

It still wasn't quite eight and Diana had always pictured the queen of Adrianna, Inc. coming in a bit later than the rest of the staff, enjoying the perks of being boss.

Holly nodded emphatically. "She's a workaholic. In by seven most days. Makes the rest of us look lazy."

"Hmm," Diana replied, thinking she'd obviously pegged Adrianna wrong.

Taking a seat behind her desk, Holly picked up the phone and relayed that Diana was in the lobby.

A moment later, a statuesque woman of striking beauty joined them. Her creamy skin made her long raven hair—pulled conservatively back in a clip—all the more dramatic. Her classic business suit of heather gray hugged a figure worthy of the lingerie she designed. "Good morning, Miss Marsh, I'm Adrianna Kline. It's a pleasure to meet you." The slender hand she extended sported an impeccable manicure.

As Diana shook her hand, she couldn't help being somehow taken aback by the woman before her. "It's truly a pleasure for *me* to meet the woman behind Adrianna, Inc."

A thin smile found Adrianna's rosy lips. "I appreciate you coming to our aid on such short notice."

"I'm happy to help however I can. I just hope I can live up to your expectations."

"As I'm sure Richard told you, I've seen your work and I've been very impressed. I suspect your creativity and flair for the feminine is just what our boys in catalog need to get them back on track."

"I'll do my best," she promised, aware that she felt strangely submissive in Adrianna's presence, as if she'd do whatever the woman asked, not only because it could boost her career, but also as if there was something deeper at work.

Adrianna turned to Holly. "Show Miss Marsh to the conference room where she'll be working with the catalog team." Then she shifted her gaze back to Diana. "If you need anything at all, don't hesitate to call on Holly." With that, she whisked back out of the lobby, her heels clicking across the floor as the other two women watched her go.

Tentatively, Diana turned to Holly and forced a small laugh. "Don't worry, if I need anything, I'll get Marc's help with it." She felt odd to have Adrianna pledge Holly's help so emphatically.

But Holly only smiled. "Oh no—I'm truly glad to help out with anything you need. It's my job." She gave a merry shrug, jiggling her pert breasts slightly. "And I know she may seem bossy toward me, but I *love* working for Adrianna. Whatever she wants me to do, I'm happy to."

Sounded like Holly had that same your-wish-is-my-command reaction to their boss that Diana had just experienced. "There's something about her..." Diana began uncertainly.

Holly's smile stayed in place. "I know, she has a very strong personality. It's a little jarring when you first meet her, but you'll get used to it quickly. It's just her way. She's frank, honest, and lets you know what she thinks, whether good or bad. She treats all her employees well, though, and I guess it works for her. We have a very low turnover here in the corporate office."

Interesting, Diana thought as Holly showed her to the conference room, where she found Marc and his co-workers waiting for her. He introduced her to Rick, Dave, and Blaine, all pleasant-seeming men whose ages probably spanned from twenty-five to thirty-five. They were all pleasant-*looking*, as well, and she began to wonder if every man in Las Vegas was handsome.

Diana took a seat and tried to forget that Marc was right next to her with that big, beautiful cock in his pants, or that he'd been fingering her pussy only a few minutes ago. She had to concentrate on work, after all.

Together, the guys explained to her the sort of trouble they were having, although they didn't seem to completely understand the problem.

"Adrianna says we don't *get* females," Blaine, the youngest, cutest of the team said. "Myself," he went on with a typically male grin, "I get females all the time, so I think I'm doing just fine."

Everyone laughed, Diana included.

"She says we don't understand the nuances of what draws a woman in and makes her want to buy a particular piece of lingerie," the oldest guy, Dave, offered. His dark hair needed a trim and his sleeves were already pushed to his elbows at eight a.m., but he looked comfortable and confident in himself.

Rick added, "She says we have no sense of feminine language, whatever that means." Like Marc, Rick was thirtyish, but much lighter in coloring—he was the fair-haired boy of the bunch.

Diana laughed and said, "Well, luckily, I know *exactly* what she means. We're in the business of seduction, gentlemen. Adrianna seduces women with her lingerie designs, the colors, the cuts, the fabrics. But *we* have to seduce women with our *words*. We have to know where romance becomes sex and where sex becomes something dirty. We have to tell them how our bras and panties will make them feel—on their bodies, in their minds. We have to find the phrases that make them feel sexy and that also make them understand feeling sexy is okay. Remember, we're not marketing only to the Gen-Xers here—our clientele spans the age range. We have to make them think that putting on a piece of Adrianna's lingerie will change them, will change their lives. We have to let them know our products will make them into sexual beings for their man, but at the same time make them into *sensual* beings, for *themselves*. It's all a mind game, gentleman," she concluded, pointing to her head. "Now, show me what you're working on right now."

Next to her, Marc slid over a magnetic board containing a mock-up of a two-page spread for Adrianna's racy leather line, called Sinsuous. She studied the pictures, held in place by small magnets, then read the headlines and copy they'd created. She turned it around and began pointing out their errors which, to her, were obvious.

"These shots of the garments," she said pointing to particular pictures, "are fine, even good, but for these others we'll want to pick softer poses. Not all women are comfortable with the concept of buying leather through the mail, so we need to keep this soft, need to use primarily photos that say classy and sexy instead of down and dirty. Do we have other shots to choose from?"

"Um, yeah," Blaine said. "A lot of them. We just picked the ones that appealed to us the most."

She laughed. "There's our problem. You're *guys*, guys. We're not producing Playboy here. We're trying to find that fine line between sexual and romantic that will appeal to *women*."

The men around the table all began to nod, some looking like they got it, a couple looking like they were still trying to wrap their minds around the concept that not all things appealed to all people in exactly the same way.

"And speaking of down and dirty, you guys have serious language problems. Use of the word 'dirty,' for instance. And 'hot,' and this mention of 'S&M fantasies'?" She shook her head. "For some women, these images totally gel, but it will have others flinging our catalog against the wall and demanding to be taken off our mailing list. As I just explained, not all words appeal to all females, not even all females who might decide they want to add a piece of leather to their lingerie drawer."

"Do you have any suggestions?" Marc asked. She suspected he was hiding a smile, likely thinking that he knew dirty words certainly worked for *her*. And now that her mind was back on *that*, on him, on them, she had to resist the temptation to pin him in place with a sexy gaze.

Refocusing on the task at hand, she thought for a moment, got up, and walked to the blackboard that stood on an easel at the end of the table. She picked up the chalk and drew two connected rectangles to represent a two-page layout, then wrote headlines:

Sinsuous = Sensuous.

And on the adjoining page:

For the darker side of seduction.

"Your copy could start with something like, 'Fulfill your secret fantasies in your favorite item from our Sinsuous leather collection'. After that, work on how it will feel on their bodies, how it will feel in their *brains*, and only *then* how it might please their man. At the absolute worst, you might get away with using the word naughty, but if so, keep it light and playful, or have the corresponding photo show a woman who's happy, laughing, in her Sinsuous leather."

By lunchtime, Diana had helped the guys revamp six key layouts in the catalog, and she thought they even seemed to be catching on by the last couple, pointing out what was wrong and providing the answers before she did. She'd wondered why *she'd* been the person asked to do this job, but she suddenly felt invigorated by the task, and she understood that Adrianna had somehow known she'd be the right choice.

Marc and Blaine took her to lunch at a local pub near the downtown office. The dark setting might have been a perfect place to attempt a little more of what she and her lover had tried that morning in the stairwell, but not with Blaine along.

When Blaine excused himself to the restroom, though, Marc leaned over the table. "I've been wondering, sweetheart, do *you* own any Sinsuous leather?"

She tilted her head and flashed her coquette smile. "As a man once said to me before embarking on hot phone sex — that's for me to know."

He eased back and grinned, crossing his arms. "And me to find out?"

"If you dare," she said, getting up and heading to the bathroom herself, making certain to wiggle her ass on the way.

* * * * *

As the trio stepped off the elevator after lunch, Holly said, "Diana, Adrianna would like to see you in her office."

She couldn't help being surprised by the request. The woman's greeting this morning had given Diana the idea that Adrianna didn't plan to provide any direction on how to handle her assignment, and this would be a bit too soon to request a progress report. "Did she say why?"

Holly shook her head, pretty blonde locks bouncing on her shoulders. "But it's probably just a get-to-know-you sort of thing. She generally does that with new people."

"Oh." Hmm. Well, it sounded easy enough. And given how oddly she'd felt herself wanting to please Adrianna when they'd met that morning, Diana didn't mind the idea of spending a little more time with the woman. Even if she did strike Diana as something of an enigma.

Holly led Diana down a short hallway with one door at the end. She instantly got the idea that—whereas the other side of the office, where she'd worked this morning, was busy and buzzing with people and activity—this smaller, quieter side was perhaps Adrianna's private domain. Holly knocked lightly on the mahogany door that stood partially open.

"Yes?"

The pretty blonde peeked inside. "Diana's back from lunch."

"Ah, good. Show Miss Marsh in."

Holly opened the door and Diana stepped inside, noting that Holly closed it behind her.

"Have a seat, Miss Marsh." Adrianna motioned to the deep leather chairs across from her desk, which was also made of rich mahogany. Even the walls, Diana realized, were covered with majestic wood panels, punctuated with tall, ornate bookshelves and framed pieces of sedate art—paintings of girls in long dresses and bows in their hair walking through fields, or picnicking on blankets beneath large trees. The entire wall to Diana's right featured large windows with deep sills and ornate burgundy drapes held back with gold ties.

Once she took in the dark, warm room softened only by the natural sunlight spilling in, she quickly found herself refocusing on Adrianna. Even with the other woman seated behind her desk, Diana became aware of her regal air, her stately posture. Her flawless complexion looked smooth and touchable.

Adrianna lifted a stemmed glass to her thin but pretty lips. "Join me for a glass of wine?"

Diana realized an open bottle jutted from an ice bucket on the credenza behind her boss. Another glass waited there, as well. "Yes. Thank you."

Adrianna poured the wine and passed it across the desk to Diana, their fingers touching during the exchange. As soon as Diana took a sip, she knew she was tasting a very expensive and elegant Riesling. The sweet wine nearly tickled going down.

Her boss cast a polite smile. "I wanted the opportunity to spend a little private time getting to know you."

Diana wasn't sure what to say, so she simply nodded.

"Tell me about Baltimore," the elegant woman said.

Taking another sip of wine, Diana made the requisite small talk, filling Adrianna in on having been raised in a suburb, her refurbished home in the city where she liked the hustle and bustle, and concluding with how much she enjoyed traveling for Adrianna, Inc., since it gave her the opportunity to get a taste of so many other places. "And now I can add Las Vegas to my list," she ended with a smile.

"So you're enjoying our little gambling den?" Adrianna asked with a light laugh.

"Very much," she replied, and just the thought of Marc and how much she'd enjoyed him and his friends last night set her pussy to tingling again, unbidden.

"May I ask you a question that could be deemed personal, Miss Marsh?"

Diana sat up a bit straighter in her chair, surprised. "Um, sure. Certainly."

"Do you wear our Adrianna products?"

She nodded. "Yes, I do."

"And are you wearing them now?"

Another nod. "Yes."

Adrianna gave her head a slight tilt. "May I ask which ones?"

Diana drew in her breath slightly. "Um, a bra and thong set from the Starlight Collection — in smoky indigo."

"Lovely choice. May I see?"

Diana flinched. Had she heard that correctly?

In response, a sly little cat's smile spread across Adrianna's thin, pretty face. "My apologies, Miss Marsh — I can see I've caught you off guard, which was not my intention." She shook her head, still looking as relaxed and pleasant as if they were discussing the weather. "I understand completely if my request made you uncomfortable. You're certainly not obligated in any way to comply." She gave her head a surprisingly friendly tilt. "It was unorthodox, and even out of line. I suppose I'm simply interested in which of my designs women choose, and why. It educates me to see my products on different body types. Very unprofessional behavior, though." She held up her wine. "Clearly, I've had one too many after-lunch glasses of wine today. Forgive me."

Diana was ninety-five percent sure the beautiful, elegant Adrianna had just attempted to seduce her. Her chest went hollow. "Nothing to forgive," she said lightly. "And I can understand how it would be gratifying to see your lingerie on various women."

Adrianna's small smile somehow continued to seduce and intimidate Diana at the same time. "This company is my life, Miss Marsh. I'm thirty-four years old and I've spent the last twelve of those years building Adrianna, Inc.

into what it is today. Hopefully you can understand if I appear a bit overzealous about it."

"Of course," Diana said, pushing up from her chair, suddenly uncomfortable making eye contact with her superior—it seemed too intimate. She took a few steps to one of the wide windows that overlooked downtown and Las Vegas Boulevard in the distance, biting her lip uncertainly, wondering what it would be like to be with a woman.

Certainly if she were attracted to women, Adrianna was a lovely female specimen with her long legs, high breasts, her smooth complexion, and those wide eyes with their long, black lashes. In fact, as she tried to envision what it would be like to fool around with Adrianna, her cunt went hot. And when she wondered how *Marc* would react to the idea, she felt herself swelling against her panties.

Still looking cool and sophisticated, Adrianna rose from her desk and approached Diana near the window. The woman stood close enough that Diana picked up a scent of musky perfume. She found herself wondering exactly which Adrianna, Inc. garments Adrianna wore under *her* prim suit.

"Is it too soon to ask how your work is going?" Adrianna inquired easily.

Diana was both unsettled and slightly aroused by her nearness. "No, actually. It's going quite well. I think the guys are catching on about what appeals to women."

"I'm sure you're explaining to them that each woman is her own animal, with her own unique set of urges and desires."

"Yes," she said.

A part of Diana was tempted to ask if Adrianna still wanted to see her lingerie. She found herself wondering what it might feel like to kiss another woman, to press against a woman's curves, to rake her tongue over a woman's nipple.

Since when are you so curious about those things? she couldn't help asking herself.

If she was honest, it had started last night, at the show, with Marc. It had been wholly erotic to find herself aroused by the same things that aroused a man—and to share it with him without feeling shy or confused.

But if she was *completely* honest, any vision she might form of herself getting intimate with Adrianna didn't feel complete—or even all that appealing—without Marc involved. It was just like last night in the limo. Being with Dan and Craig had been like being with Marc, just in another way. She'd understood that it would excite him and she'd wanted that more than anything. If Marc were here and if he wanted her to experiment with Adrianna, she thought she probably would. In fact, she probably wouldn't be able to resist. But Marc *wasn't* here. And that made her decision easy.

"Speaking of the catalog," Diana said, smiling politely up at her boss, "I should probably get back to work with the guys. Unless there was anything else you wished to discuss."

Adrianna gave an acceptant and respectful smile. Her eyes seemed to say they both understood that Diana was turning her down, but that it was okay. "No, nothing else," the other woman said. "I just wanted to get to know you a bit better, and make sure you know that we're glad you're here with us."

Diana returned the smile. "I'm truly glad to be here."

Adrianna walked with her to the door, and as Diana placed her hand on the doorknob, Adrianna took a step closer, as close as she'd stood at the window. "Perhaps we'll have the opportunity to get together socially before you return to Baltimore."

Perhaps," Diana said, curious if *socially* meant *sexually*—and did she *want* that? Did *Marc*? She couldn't help wondering just how far she was willing to take her overwhelming desire to please and excite him in whatever way she could.

Chapter Five

"How's your pussy?" Marc asked when she stepped into the conference room to find him alone there.

The question made her flinch. "Why?" Did he somehow know what had just transpired in Adrianna's office?

He laughed, looking confused. "Because you said it was sore this morning and I was hoping it was feeling better."

She looked around the room. "Where are the other guys?"

"Brainstorming in the break room. They like a change of scenery. I can go get them if you're ready to get back to work. By the way, what did, uh, Adrianna want?"

She felt breathless. "That's why I wondered if we were alone. You won't *believe* what just happened to me."

He cocked a small smile in her direction. "Did Adrianna try to seduce you in her office?"

Diana gasped, then shut the conference room door to ensure their privacy. "How did you know?"

He shrugged. "I know Adrianna really well. I've known her since long before I started working for her, in fact. And I just had this feeling, you're her type.

She sucked in her breath. "Does she only like women?"

He shook his head. "No, she's an equal opportunity seductress. The way she looks at it is like this. She's not planning to ever get married or have kids—she's married to Adrianna, Inc. She doesn't feel she has time for relationships, and I don't think she's even interested in having one. But she still has physical needs, and she's pretty happy to fulfill them with men *or* women, whoever's available that she's attracted to."

A peculiar inkling made Diana say, "You?"

He gave her a frank look. "A long time ago. Before I worked here. Since then, well…we occasionally run into each other socially, but we've made it a point not to even act like we know each other, let alone do anything together. Makes it a lot easier to work together, you know?"

"I'll admit I'm relieved that *you and I* seem to be able to work together okay, even given…you know." She smiled.

He replied with a nod. "I had the same worry, but it's going amazingly smoothly, isn't it?"

She tilted her head, wondering something else now. "Has Adrianna seduced anyone else—I mean anyone *here*?"

Another shrug, a soft smile. "Holly."

"*Holly*?"

He laughed at her wide-eyed shock. "Just between you and me, I think she and Holly are a pretty regular thing. Holly once told me over too many drinks at happy hour."

"But Holly's so…sweet."

"Doesn't preclude her from being sexual. I don't think they have anything emotional going on or anything—I think they just make each other feel good and move on. It's easy for them to spend a lot of time in Adrianna's office with the door closed since Holly's her secretary as well as the receptionist."

She shook her head, trying to clear it.

Marc's expression turned sympathetic. "I thought about warning you, but I wasn't sure she'd really make a pass. And…I also wasn't sure how you'd respond."

Diana plopped back into a chair, still stunned. "Well, I'm beginning to see why people need help getting things done around here. Instead of working on Adrianna, Inc. business, everybody's fucking Adrianna."

Marc just laughed. "Not really. Only Holly."

She cast an amused smile. "And you."

"Ancient history."

"And nearly me."

He raised his eyebrows, and she could see his instant arousal. "*Really* now. You were tempted?"

She cast an uncertain look. "I don't know. Not really. But I found myself wondering…well, wondering what *you* would want if *you* were there."

He smiled, looking pleased. "You would do that just to get me off?"

"Maybe." She grinned flirtatiously. "As you know, that's certainly part of what drove me to do what I did last night."

He continued to look satisfied, even moved. "I'm not sure if this makes me a selfish pig, but I like hearing that."

"Well, now you know *exactly* how you affect me, as if it wasn't perfectly obvious before," she said teasingly. "I was a bad girl before I got here, but something about you makes me want to be a *very, very* bad girl."

He leaned against the table next to where she sat. "Have you ever done another woman before?"

She shook her head.

"But now you're interested?"

She grinned at his enthusiasm. "I said *maybe*," she reminded him. "And like I said, it would probably depend upon *your* level of interest."

"Oh, I'm interested, all right, sweetheart. No need to doubt *that*."

"You know, I used to think I was pretty wild before I came out here, but I'm beginning to feel naïve."

He flashed a look of doubt. "You? No way. I saw the way you were last night—nothing naïve about you, baby." He slid his hand onto her thigh, up under her skirt. "Speaking of which, do you want to come over to my place tonight? A little dinner, a little playing? Can I tempt you with *that*?"

Diana smiled. "Now that's a temptation I can't resist. I would love to come to your place tonight."

He leaned in for a slow tongue kiss, his hot, masculine mouth on hers making her forget about Adrianna entirely. "Good. Because as much as I like watching you with others, I also get a little possessive sometimes, and I'm really looking forward to having you all to myself."

Diana's heart fluttered a little. She was beginning to think he was perfect. And if she didn't have Bradley or her parents to worry about, not to mention the fact that she lived on the other side of the continent, well…she couldn't help thinking that it was like Holly had said this morning—Marc seemed like a perfect fit for her.

* * * * *

Marc drove toward the strip to pick Diana up for dinner at his place, as planned. After that, he was going to get naked with her and make sure they both had a very good time.

What an initiation she'd had to Sin City already, he thought, chuckling to himself. And yet, she was still up for another night of passion in his bed. God, with each passing hour he liked this woman better and better.

And not only was she hot and beautiful, not only was she a daring, adventure-seeking lover, but he also found her brilliant. He knew she thought everything she'd taught his team today about marketing Adrianna, Inc. was simple and obvious, but she'd made him understand that they truly did need a woman's input if they intended to market items to women. He'd found her sense of authority rather sexy, too — it reminded him a little of Adrianna.

The thought of the boss lady made him shake his head lightly. Even though nothing had happened between them, ever since Diana had told him about Adrianna's seduction attempt, he'd had visions in his mind of those two beautiful females pleasuring each other in Adrianna's office.

Tonight Diana was all his, though. Even if he thought it odd that he was starting to feel a little possessive, as he'd told her back at work. That sort of emotion didn't usually set in with a woman for a good long while. And yet, here he was, feeling selfish about someone he'd just met.

But they *hadn't* just met, he reminded himself as he turned onto Las Vegas Boulevard. They'd gotten to know each other plenty before ever meeting in person. And she'd turned out to be…well, perfect. He sometimes ran with a fast crowd and it seemed unbelievable, incredible, to discover she *liked* the kind of crowd he ran with, that she fit so easily in his world. He'd always thought he'd have a hell of a time finding a woman who accepted and even enjoyed his lifestyle, and who was also smart enough and funny enough and sweet enough for him to want to be with in a long-term way, but...

What the fuck was he thinking? She wasn't a long-term prospect, even if he wished she was. She might not be with good old Bradley in a technical sense at the moment, but he knew the guy remained in the picture for some reason. What type of man was he and how did he keep a woman like Diana happy? And even if Bradley *wasn't* in the picture, well...he would soon be going to Paris if he got the job with Briolet. There was nothing here holding him back.

When he pulled up outside The Venetian, Diana stood waiting, looking as gorgeous as ever. It was the most casual he'd seen her — she wore a sexy white miniskirt and a tight fitting, multicolored pullover top. The brightly hued top hugged her beautiful breasts and was cut low enough to give him lots of cleavage to salivate over until he could get those two firm mounds of flesh in his hands and mouth. The white ultra-high-heeled shoes she wore were equally hot, and made her legs look even better than the last two times he'd had the pleasure of perusing them.

On the way back to his apartment, she filled him in on the shopping she'd done after work, the great new shoes she'd bought, and how she wanted to take one of the gondola rides offered at The Venetian before her stay there was through.

"I'll gladly take you on a gondola built for two," he told her, leaning over to kiss her just before they pulled away from a stoplight.

As they talked more about the sexcapades—or attempts at them—which had surrounded her since her arrival, he couldn't help laughing, thinking that up until that moment in their visit, no one would've ever suspected the woman next to him was a total sex kitten on the prowl and that she'd been finding lots of interested alley cats since her arrival only a day earlier. He liked how easy it was for her to meld those two personalities into one—how she could be concerned with shoes and gondolas one minute and telling him how it had felt to be with three guys the next.

"I never could have imagined how it would feel to have three different men's mouths on me, but I can't deny that I loved it," she told him.

He couldn't help teasing her. "As much as you love sucking cock?"

She lowered her chin and gave him a playful look. "I enjoyed what I did with Dan and Craig, but you must have been able to tell last night that I loved your cock the best."

Speaking of cocks, his was growing rapidly. He cast her a grin. "What's so special about mine?"

She smiled, then spoke frankly. "Mmm, it's so nice and big and straight, perfectly proportioned, and it fills my mouth so very well."

He glanced down at the bulge in his blue jeans, which was starting to become painful. His zipper strained. "Damn, sweetheart, I need you to suck me right now. You just got me rock solid."

She licked her lips, looking so sexy he thought it should probably be illegal. "Want me to?"

Did he ever. But he was also a sensible guy. "It's still light out. If we pass any trucks or vans, they might see."

"Do I seem like a girl who would let something as little as that stop her?"

God, she was fabulous. He smiled and leaned back slightly in his seat. "Then come and get me, baby."

Diana bent over the console, working at his belt buckle and the button on his jeans. Even that much pressure near his straining cock was getting him hotter than he'd been just a minute earlier. He loved her eagerness, loved how she wasn't afraid of any sexual situation thrown at her. Even if she'd been shocked by Adrianna today, he knew fear had nothing to do with her reaction. He also loved how easy this felt—how it somehow seemed like they'd known each other for a very long time.

After unzipping his jeans, she instantly pulled out his throbbing shaft and went down on him. "Oh, fuck yes," he breathed and wondered how the hell he'd be able to drive the car now.

Getting a blowjob behind the wheel was one thing he'd never done, and he relished glancing down to see Diana's head in his lap, working up and down; her warm little mouth felt like a slice of heaven. She sucked on him as if his cock were a giant straw, her lips wet and hot. The vibrations of the car added only slightly to the sensations, but enough that, at moments, her ministrations felt electrical.

"Oh baby, suck me with that sweet mouth," he whispered. He nearly missed a red light, the quick stop jostling them both, but he reached down one hand to hold her head steady, and used the time to devote his full attention to watching her without the distraction of driving. He couldn't resist lifting slightly toward her in the slow, heated rhythm she'd set. When a delivery truck pulled to a stop next to them, he didn't look up, but wondered if the guys inside saw what a lucky man he was.

"Just three blocks left, sweetheart," he whispered when he made a turn near home. "But just a little more and...oh yeah."

His sweet little Diana kept sucking him and just as he pulled into the parking lot of his condo complex, he said, "God, *now*, sweetheart! Here I come!" and he shot into her mouth, nearly wrecking the car. He pulled himself back from the pleasure just in time to steer between the vehicles parked on each side of his space.

And he knew it shouldn't surprise him when she kept her pretty lips wrapped around him and sucked him completely dry, but it still did.

* * * * *

As far as Diana was concerned, they'd started their evening off right. Now that she'd accepted her inability to say no to anything that involved this sexy man in this sexy city of sin, she wanted to soak up every bit of passion she could. Because whenever she went back to Baltimore, that was it—it would be like turning off a light switch. No more wild Diana. No more fun, exciting sexual experiences. And no more Marc.

That last part made her cringe a little, so she pushed it out of her mind. Right now, she was all about fun, and having sucked Marc's big beautiful cock to orgasm before they even reached his place made her exit the car wearing a smile.

That was when she came face to face with a guy wearing old khaki pants that had been cut off into shorts, an open shirt with the sleeves ripped out, and a pair of untied work boots. He was big, dirty, sweaty—and handsome. "Hello," he said. He had longish, messy dark hair, big green eyes, and a smattering of dark curls on his chest spanning downward and narrowing into a line that disappeared into his pants.

"Hey, Carter," Marc said, approaching from the other side of the car. "How's it goin', dude?"

"Too damn hot out here," Carter said with a grin.

"You eastern boys are pussies," Marc said with a teasing laugh. "Out here, we like the heat. Hell, even Diana here isn't complaining, and she's from Baltimore."

Carter shrugged. "Gets pretty damn hot down there, too. I'm from way up in Maine," he said, smiling at Diana with crystal clear eyes.

"What brought you to Vegas?" she asked.

"Work," he said. Then he pointed at the Weed Eater he held. "This glamorous job is only something I do on the side. By day I help construct those fancy hotels on Las Vegas Boulevard."

"Diana is staying at The Venetian," Marc informed his friend.

Carter grinned in recognition. "Ah, my first job on the strip."

After a few more minutes of small talk, in which she learned that Carter lived in the condo next door to Marc's, the couple excused themselves. "Or I'll never get dinner made for this lovely lady," Marc said.

"Can't have that," Carter replied. "I'd better get back to work, too, or I'll be sweeping up grass clippings by moonlight."

The moment they stepped in Marc's door, he gave her a knowing grin. "So…what do you think of Carter?"

She smiled playfully. She didn't usually go for the grimy type, but… "Hot," she said, "if you want the truth." Then she winked. "But not as hot as you."

He laughed. "Carter's a good guy, and chicks go for him, so don't worry, I'm not hurt." He narrowed his gaze, still looking amused. "So long as you keep reminding me I'm better."

"After what I just did to you in the car, you shouldn't have any doubts."

Cupping her cheek in his hand, Marc replied by leaning in for a warm kiss. He could still taste the remains of his climax on her lips, and that brought her lovely ministrations back even clearer than her words did. "That was the most magnificent blowjob I've ever had, sweetheart."

Licking her lip in a way that nearly turned him hard again, Diana sensually cupped his crotch and grinned. "I was inspired by my subject. I had a lot to work with."

His chest tightened with fresh desire as he kissed her once more. "You drive me wild," he purred in her ear.

Diana helped Marc with the simple dinner of spaghetti, meat sauce, and garlic bread he put together. "Sorry I can't do anything fancier. I'm not a gourmet kind of guy," he said as he dropped the spaghetti in boiling water.

"I love a good spaghetti dinner, and besides, I'm not exactly handy around the kitchen, either. None of us Marsh girls were blessed with that particular skill."

He closed his arms around her. "That's okay. You were blessed with *other*, much more *important* skills."

"Now, Bradley, on the other hand, is a great cook," she told him without thinking.

"Figures." He leaned back against the counter.

She laughed. "If I didn't know better, I'd think you were jealous."

"Don't worry, sweetheart, I know that—broken up right now or not—you've got a guy waiting at home for you." He crossed his arms and gave her a probing look. "So, do you do the kind of stuff with Bradley that you've been doing with me? Does he know what a hot little firecracker he's got in you?"

As if, Diana thought. Bradley would be positively horrified if he could see the extracurricular activities she'd indulged in here. "Uh, no."

He gave his head a disparaging shake. "You're wasted on him, sweetheart. Fucking wasted."

Although she tried not to let it show, Marc's words bothered her. It was so unusual to find a man who really thought her sexual freeness was a true plus, something you'd look for in a real, lasting relationship. Was he right? Was she wasting herself? Was her willingness to indulge her sexual whims truly something to value? *She'd* always liked herself and her actions just fine, but the people around her—her parents, the "serious" boyfriends she'd had here and there along the way, her counselors in high school and college—had certainly seemed to feel she was a problem child.

Before she and Marc sat down to dinner a few minutes later, he turned the lights low, lit candles, and poured two glasses of wine. Taking a seat across from her at the table, he held up his glass and grinned. "Same toast as last night. To tonight and whatever it may hold."

She smiled and clinked her glass against his, and found herself wishing her relationship with this man wasn't a temporary thing.

"Tell me about this Bradley guy," he said when she least expected it. "I know he's a great cook and that you seem attached to him, but I also know you're out here having a damn good time with *me*. What's it all about, sweetheart?" The tilt of his head and the care in his voice kept his question from sounding like prying. Further, it inspired her to answer truthfully.

She told Marc everything—about the bad girl she'd always been, about the good girl she aspired to be, about wanting to please everyone she knew and particularly her parents, about just wanting to be what *they* wanted her to be.

When she was done, Marc took a sip of wine and looked her in the eye. "Are you really gonna waste your life that way, Diana?"

She took a bite of garlic bread, chewing carefully, considering her answer. "How is it a waste to make people happy?"

"The only people *I* care about are the people who accept me as I am. Those are the only people I give a damn about making happy."

He sounded so…well-adjusted. She'd always thought *she* was well-adjusted, too, thought it was enough to like *herself*—but suddenly she wondered if she were going about life all wrong with this plan to be a good girl. "I wish it were that simple for me."

"So do I. I mean, I'm not trying to throw a crimp in your plan, but...I care about you, sweetheart, and I want you to be happy." He reached across the table to graze the tip of one finger across her hand where it fiddled with the stem of her wineglass.

Just that one little touch made her pussy feel achy. And *that* made her want to forget all about the discussion they were having. It was easy to doubt her plan *now*, sure—having her hot, sexy lover tell her it was okay to do exactly *what* she wanted, any *time* she wanted. But once she got back home and he was no longer around, she'd realize her plan was the right one to follow. Wouldn't she?

"Don't worry, I *will* be happy. No doubts about that. Now, tell me about you. And Paris. Tell me why you want to go."

He gave her the lazy grin of a sexy playboy. "Just the next adventure on the road of life, that's all. I came to Vegas looking for fun and I've had a lot of it. And I've built my career. Europe seems like...something a single guy should do, that's all. The next step."

She laughed. "Marc does Paris. Sounds like a porn movie. Of course, I think they're much freer about sex over there than the average American, so you should be able to find lots of pretty models to keep your bed warm and your social life interesting." As she spoke, an unexpected pang of jealousy pulled on her heart. She had the nerve to let the idea of him with other girls bother her? She was surprised, but couldn't stop the feeling.

He shrugged, grinned. "Hopefully. But girls seem too skinny over there. At least the models. No curves, you know?"

She laughed. "You like a curvy woman, huh?"

"Oh yeah." His sexy eyes were planted squarely on her cleavage. "I like *your* curves—a lot, sweetheart."

Her breasts tingled a bit and she found herself eating a little faster, because talking with him was very pleasant, but fucking him was even better.

"Tell me about your neighbor, Carter," she said. For some reason, thoughts of sex had turned her mind back to Marc's earlier intuition about her finding his neighbor attractive.

"Like I told you, he's a good guy. We've become close friends. He's been kind of down lately, though. He'd been seeing a showgirl for a few months—I think he had it bad for her. She broke up with him a few weeks ago, and besides moping about her, all he does is complain about missing the sex."

Diana couldn't help laughing. "Seems like *all* your friends are heartbroken and sexless. But hey, tell him to come to the Adrianna offices—I'm sure Adrianna would be willing to take care of his frustrations."

He grinned, tilting his head to give her a speculative look. "Or...right here, next door, huh?" He raised his eyebrows, teasing her.

She smiled boldly. "What are you suggesting, lover?"

He still looked playful, aroused. "Uh, just wondering how much your pussy would tingle if I decided to call him up and ask him to join us for a little party."

"For your information, my pussy is *already* tingling, just sitting across from you."

She loved watching the excitement pool in his dark eyes. As their gazes connected, his bare foot nudged her knees apart beneath the table. She spread her legs obligingly and he caressed her inner thigh with his soft, cool toes. "Just me, huh? I'm all you want right now?"

She gave her head a sexy tilt. "It's like I keep telling you. I want *you*. And I want whatever *you* want. Whatever gets you hot."

He smiled. "I never would have pegged you for the submissive, Diana."

She shrugged. "Me neither, so it's a surprise to us both. Does *that* turn you on, me being submissive?"

He thought it over, then replied. "So far, everything *about* you turns me on. I love how bold you are, baby," he said across the candlelit table. "You have no idea how much it thrilled me to see you with those other guys last night while I watched."

Diana bit her lip, felt her nipples harden within the tight lace of her bra. "You like to watch, huh?"

He nodded, still caressing her thigh. "*Oh* yeah. In fact, I'm surprised you're just now figuring that out. Truth is, I consider it kind of a weakness, but I can't seem to change it."

"Doesn't have to be a weakness. Some people might even see it as a strength." *Me. Now.* After last night. After imagining Marc watching her fool around with Adrianna earlier today. She'd never wanted such things up to now, but he was showing her parts of her sexuality she'd never seen before.

"Glad you see it that way."

Partially because he couldn't reach her pussy with his toes and partially because she wanted more of him than just his foot anyway, Diana pushed back her chair and got to her feet.

Marc did the same and before she could even come toward him, he backed her up against a wall. His dark expression was at once paralyzing and stimulating.

She locked her gaze on his. "You make me wet with just a look."

"Imagine how wet you'll get when I do *other* things." With that, he buried one hand in her hair and kissed her — a slow, sensuous meeting of tongues that nearly drove her out of her mind. His other hand skimmed up from her waist to caress her breast through her clingy top. She moaned into his mouth when he pinched her nipple through her clothes, before pressing his knee between her thighs. She instinctively moved against it, rubbing against his leg. He had the ability to get her so, so hot, so, so quick. This was more than just needing sex — this man had *power* over her, *sexual power*. And she loved it.

A big part of her wanted desperately to be alone with him tonight, as they'd planned. She wanted to let him ravish her body in every way known to man, wanted to see exactly how crazy he could make her all by himself.

Yet another part was almost frightened by the idea of being alone with him too much. Frightened he'd do too many wonderful things to her, give her too many of those dark, hot, sexy looks, say too many things that warmed her inside and made her never want to go back to Baltimore.

And besides, he liked to watch.

And what Marc liked, she liked. What Marc wanted, she felt compelled to give.

She was surprised it had taken her this long to figure it out, too. She'd known *she'd* liked *being* watched by him, but she'd just now come to realize how deeply that worked both ways.

"If you think," she began, almost breathless, "your friend Carter would be interested, why don't you invite him over?"

Predictably, he flashed another of those dark smiles. "Are you sure?"

She nodded vigorously. "I mean, if *you* are. I know we planned a night alone."

He looked speculative for a moment, then laughed. "We'll have time for other nights alone. But if you're in the mood for a double dip, sweetheart, well then, I'm your ice-cream man."

Chapter Six

Diana had no idea what exactly Marc told Carter on the phone, but when he showed up at the door in a clean t-shirt and shorts, his hair still damp from the shower, his eyes pinned her in place immediately. His gaze said he knew what he was here for, that Marc hadn't been subtle.

She sat on Marc's sofa, one leg curled under her. Carter joined her there as Marc opened another bottle of wine and retrieved an additional glass from the kitchen. By the time Carter took the stemmed glass from Marc's hand, Diana was feeling anxious to get know Carter a little better. "Maine, huh?" she asked.

He smiled. "It's a world away from Vegas."

"I'm starting to think *anyplace* is a world away from Vegas," she replied with a laugh. "There's something in the air here, some aura of…"

"Excitement?" Marc asked, eyebrows raised.

She nodded. "Something about being here makes me feel like I can do anything, like there aren't any rules."

Marc grinned. "There aren't."

She looked to Carter, half-smiling. Wine and anticipation was turning her giddy and sexy and uninhibited. "What do *you* like about Las Vegas, Carter?"

He chuckled easily. "I might complain about the heat, but I don't miss the cold winters. And I think there's a feeling of…" He looked thoughtful, and she immediately decided there was more to him than just a lot of hard, sexy muscle. "A feeling of possibility here," he said. "A lot of people come here when they need a new start. The city swallows some of them whole and spits them back out. But other people find exactly what they need."

"Which is?" she asked, intrigued.

"Freedom, I guess."

She laughed.

Carter arched his eyebrows, wearing a small grin. "Something funny about that?"

"I was just thinking that before I got here, I thought I knew about being free—but I'm finding a whole new kind of freedom I never even thought about before." She glanced at Marc and they exchanged a smile as her pussy spasmed softly beneath her skirt.

Her breasts felt heavy, needful, and she was ready to pursue more of this Sin City freedom she'd found. "So, have you two ever done this together before?"

Marc cast a slightly surprised smile, as if he wondered exactly how bold she would be. "Done what before, sweetheart?"

She ran her tongue sensuously across her upper lip before answering. "Shared a woman."

Both guys laughed. "Truth?" Marc asked.

"Of course." She took a sip of her wine as Marc settled into an easy chair a few feet away.

Marc glanced at Carter, then at her. "We've talked about it. Always thought we might have a three-way with Carter's old girlfriend. But…" Marc laughed, "…Carter was afraid he'd regret it, be too jealous."

"I was…you know…pretty serious about her," Carter said.

She nodded in understanding.

"So…no, sweetheart. You're the first."

She smiled. "Good."

Fortunately, just being around the two men made Diana forget the worries and emotions she'd been experiencing a few minutes earlier. Her pussy was hot and her breasts achy, and she was feeling aggressive and very ready to proceed. Marc's eyes *made* her ready. She so wanted to thrill him as she had last night.

Crossing her arms over her waist, she peeled her top off over her head, revealing a bra of pale pink lace that just barely held her breasts in at the prettily scalloped edges.

Marc grinned. "Adrianna's 'Delicate and Dainty' Collection."

She nodded.

"You wear it well, sweetheart."

Marc left his chair and moved in, hovering over her. Bracing his hands on the back of the sofa on either side of her, he lowered a hot, lingering kiss to her hungry mouth, then one small kiss to the high curve of her right breast, and the left, before sinking to his knees between her legs. Without hesitation, he reached up under her skirt and found the elastic band to her matching thong. She lifted her ass slightly, allowing him to peel it down, down, down. Her pussy felt positively free and wild beneath the thin little skirt.

Tossing her panties aside, Marc was back at her thighs, running his strong hands up under the skirt again, this time cupping her ass, and lifting the skirt high enough around her hips to reveal her aching cunt. "So fucking pretty," he said. "I keep forgetting. Then I see it and go wild inside." With that, he sank his tongue into her slit and she let out a hot little cry, parting her legs. She began to utter a series of breathy moans as he ate her, glancing over to Carter, whose eyes met hers in between watching Marc mouth her naked pussy.

"Come here," she said to Carter, opening her arms to him. The easy invitation was all it took to bring him across the length of the couch, shucking his t-shirt on the way. His kiss was surprisingly gentle for a man so big and muscular, and Diana let her arms fall around his broad shoulders. She buried one hand in his mane of thick, dark hair and used the other to explore his sinewy back, arms, and chest in a sensuous caress. Below, Marc continued to lick her where she was the most needy and hot as she undulated her hips against his generous mouth.

Carter's hands found her breasts, squeezing, kneading, then quickly lowering the cups of the bra to free her. He groaned at the sight, before taking one stiffened nipple into his mouth.

Her breath was ragged watching him suckle her breast while Marc simultaneously sucked her clit between his lips. "Oh yes, oh yes," she whispered between small moans of delight.

Carter moved from one breast to the other, sucking, licking and mouthing them in an almost leisurely fashion that pleasured her sensitive nipples beyond belief.

After a blissfully long interlude, they all shifted to a new position, letting Diana guide them. "Carter, will you lick my pussy now?" she asked him sweetly.

"Anything you want." His earnest reply let her know he was sincerely interested in their mutual pleasure, not just his own.

"And *you*," she said softly to Marc as she stretched out on the couch, "bring me that big hard cock. Right here." She pointed to her open mouth and Marc practically growled as he ripped his shirt off over his head, revealing a tan, muscled chest before hurriedly opening his pants. Diana loved the way his cock popped free—it had clearly been tightly constrained and was anxious for some attention.

Lying on her side, she lifted one leg up to the back of the couch, giving Carter easy access to her pussy, which was wet and pink and pleasantly swollen. Marc knelt on the floor next to her, so that his erection stood at just the right height to reach her hungry mouth.

Taking it in was just as pleasurable as Diana remembered. He was so big, so incredibly hard—going down on him was a challenge she thoroughly enjoyed. Carter's easy, relaxed licks up and across her gaping, needy cunt added the perfect heat to keep her at an intense level of arousal as she concentrated on getting as much of that massive cock in her mouth as she could.

Marc caressed her breasts, still held partially captive in the tight lace that had hid them earlier. "That's right, baby," he crooned, low and hot. "Take me deep in your throat. Do it slow. Easy. Take it all in between those pretty lips."

His coaxing helped—she worked to relax her throat muscles, to lull herself into a near-hypnotic state that would allow her to pull him down deep, to give him the best blowjob of his life, even better than in the car. Finally, lost in the slow movements, in the tender lust enveloping their threesome, she realized she had most of him inside her mouth. His width stretched her lips wide, his length reached impossible depths. She'd never felt so full, so absorbed in any kind of sex. Above, he was leaning his head back, moaning, whispering, "So good, baby, so good."

She loved pleasuring this man more than any other she'd ever been with, so she wanted it to continue, wanted to suck him deep into her for as long as she could. When he looked down, watching her work, he seemed amazed, stirred, touched. "You're so perfect, sweetheart. You love my cock in your pretty mouth, I can tell. You suck me so good, you've got me all the way in. Damn, I'm about to explode just watching you swallow me this way."

Even then, she didn't let up. If he wanted to come like this, she would let him. Whatever he wanted, whatever would make him feel the best.

Finally, it was him who pulled away, extracting all of those hard, beautiful inches from between her lips. "Don't want to come yet, baby," he breathed. She instantly missed having him there, though, and he seemed to sense that. He slid his fingers between her lips and she sucked on them as he bent to kiss her breasts.

Below, Carter's ministrations were languid and intoxicating. She credited his slow mouthing as part of what had simultaneously lulled and excited her enough to take Marc's whole length down her throat.

Somewhere along the way, Carter had slid two fingers into her moist passage, and as Marc delivered soft, light licks to her nipples, just catching the hard beads on the tip of his tongue for a pleasant snapping, rippling sensation, she realized Carter was starting to slip one finger into her ass, too. "Ah, God! Yes," she murmured.

"You like that?" Carter asked, his voice soft but confident. "You like my finger in your tight little asshole?"

"Mmm, yeah. Please fuck me with it," she whispered, because his finger was all the way in now and she couldn't believe how much she craved sensation in that sensitive opening.

While dragging his tongue in lazy strokes across her clit, he fucked her pussy with the fingers of one hand, her ass with the finger of the other. "Unnnhhhh…" she gasped. "Yeah…that's it."

She thrust herself against him now, against his big, strong mouth and work-roughened fingers. He was providing the perfect stimulation to all her special places as Marc sucked her breasts. She held them up for him, cupping her hands on their outer curves.

"Oh, will you fuck them?" she begged as she got hotter and hotter below. "I want you to fuck my breasts with that beautiful cock."

Marc's eyes filled with fire. "Oh, baby, yes." With that, he straddled her waist on the couch and his erection dropped into the valley of her cleavage.

"Oooh, yeah," she breathed, her voice ragged with excitement as she pressed her breasts around his length and he began to slide his shaft back and forth to create a hot, delicious friction.

Now it was complete. All her sensitive places were being fucked in some way. She undulated her whole body to soak up the hot, consuming sensations. The room became a symphony of heated moans and panting breaths as the three of them moved in slow, sensual rhythm.

"Oh, God," she whispered when the first hint of orgasm flared in her pussy.

After that, it tore through her like a freight train, coming on so fast that she screamed with each wave of ecstasy that shook her body. Long and intense, it left her weak and more sated than she thought she'd ever been.

They rested that way a little while; Marc reached down to touch her face and she kissed the back of his hand.

When she began to come back to herself, she wanted Carter. She wanted to show him her sincere appreciation for his sweet and oh-so-thorough affection. "Carter," she whispered.

He lowered a last gentle kiss to the soft outer flesh of her cunt. "Yeah?"

"Come here. Take your shorts off and come kneel next to my face."

The little groan he exhaled in response sent a rush of hot air over her pussy. She gasped at the sensation, anxiously awaiting his arrival as Marc gently caressed her breasts while sliding his still-erect shaft slowly back and forth in her soft, malleable flesh.

They both watched Carter drop his shorts, then his white boxer briefs, to reveal a beautiful cock to go with the rest of his hot body. Nearly as long and pretty as Marc's, his rod jutted upward from a thatch of dark hair and the very sight made Diana even hungrier.

She bit her lip, studying his lovely dick as he brought it down beside her.

Glancing up at Marc to find him watching her as carefully as she watched Carter's cock added infinitely to her excitement as she turned her head sideways and reached out one hand, wrapping it around the thick, solid shaft and drawing it to her waiting lips.

First, she licked the tip, tasting the white drop of pre-come gathered there, relishing the feel of having both men's eyes watch her perform this intimate act. Swirling her tongue about the pink head and drawing that first rounded inch into her mouth, she looked up at them both and made sure they saw the joy on her face, that they knew how much she loved what she was doing. After that, though, pure hunger took over and she drew more of his cock in, as much as she could easily take, and she sucked on him, enjoying the sensation when he began to move with her, gently fucking her mouth.

Marc fucked her breasts harder then, too, and even if her pussy was a little lonely, she had no complaints with two big, lovely cocks at her disposal.

Marc's warm thrusts brought the tip of his erection up near her mouth, and soon she couldn't resist leaving Carter's shaft for Marc's, then moving back again, taking turns on the two big shafts she couldn't seem to get enough of.

Finally, when her needy cunt begged for more attention, the guys allowed her to again shift them into a new position.

"Condom?" she whispered to Marc.

He hurriedly pulled his wallet from his shorts and she watched anxiously as he ripped open the packet and rolled it on.

Pushing his shoulders, she sat him up on the couch and straddled him, wanting his enormous cock inside her wet, empty channel. Situating her pussy directly atop the broad head, she slowly impaled herself on it in one long, filling stroke that reverberated through her whole body and sent a little moan echoing from her throat.

"Tight," Marc whispered with a wicked smile.

She looked into his dark eyes and licked her upper lip in response.

"Sore?" he whispered.

She'd forgotten. "No, not at all," she said, pleased that she'd recovered from last night's pummeling.

Carter now sat next to them on the couch and she reached down, taking his erection in her hand as if to lead him by it. "Bring it up here and let me suck it some more," she said.

"Wait," he told her, then walked around to the back of the couch, which brought his cock to the perfect height. She grabbed onto it, pulling it toward her, and—placing it between herself and Marc—she was able to close her lips around it.

Carter let out a thick sigh of pleasure as she began to work him over, and Marc lifted his head to look, only a couple of inches away from Carter's cock.

As she moved up and down on Marc's incredible shaft—mmm, it felt even bigger and more powerful in this position, with all her weight on it—having him so very close as she sucked another man got her even hotter and wetter, until she could *hear* his dick moving through the slick juice of her pussy.

She used her tongue, her hands, and every part of her mouth to bring Carter pleasure as Marc got a close-up view of her work. Stopping once to flick her tongue over the end of Carter's long shaft, she then thrust her tongue into Marc's mouth for a hard French kiss. She repeated the action several times, sucking on Carter, then kissing Marc, drawing Carter's cock closer and closer to Marc's mouth until finally she found the daring to kiss Marc *around* the head of Carter's erection. Neither man protested, although

Carter's groans deepened as Diana and Marc licked at each other's tongues, simultaneously delivering licks to his cock, as well.

Diana watched Marc's eyes overtop of the hard phallus that stretched between them. He met her gaze, unapologetic, clearly as deep into the heated encounter as she was, until they were no longer reaching for each other's mouths at all, just staring glassily into each other's eyes as they delivered sensual licks to Carter's hard cock.

Above them echoed Carter's low, guttural moans. Below, Diana's pussy felt more deliciously filled than it ever had before. Marc's hands, which had for a while cupped her ass, had now moved inward, inch by inch, until the tips of his middle fingers together worked in unison to rub the hot little fissure there.

When he finally eased the tip of one finger inside, where Carter's had so recently been, she let out a long low cry, still licking on Carter's cock with Marc's help. When the lovely finger began to move in and out, it made her fuck him harder, harder.

"You want more in your tight little ass, sweetheart?" Marc asked around his friend's erection.

She nodded vigorously. "Unh…"

Marc pushed his finger deeper inside, making her cry out again.

She resumed sucking Carter's cock out of pure instinct and need—wanting all the holes of her body filled. Marc eased a second finger into her ass and she cried out again, taking it in, feeling the unusual way that mysterious opening was reacting, widening, convulsing around his fingers in almost the same way her pussy did. "Mmm, oh God, oh yes." A nearly nonsensical string of exclamations left her as the pleasure in her ass began to spread outward, through her pussy, through her whole supercharged body.

She was so into the grand fucking she was receiving that she didn't even wonder where Carter was going when he pulled away and left the back of the couch. But a moment later he was behind her, his hands molding and exploring. They roamed her ass, up past the twisted skirt at her hips and around to her breasts, squeezing and caressing, letting the nipples get delightfully pinched between his big, kneading fingers. She missed his cock in her mouth, but replaced it with Marc's kiss, his tongue.

"Lie down," Carter said, his voice low and surprisingly demanding. "Stay like you are," he clarified, "but stretch out on the couch."

Despite having called all the delicious shots so far, Diana felt no inclination to argue, interested to see what this strong, sweet, sexy man had in mind for them next. With Marc's huge cock still inside her, they shifted so that he was lying lengthwise on the couch and she continued riding him. Her pussy had adjusted to his size and now it was easy to fuck him, fast or slow, gentle undulations or wild bounces.

"Let me suck your nipples," Marc said, and she bent over so they dangled above his face. He nipped at one, then shifted, taking the other into his mouth for a hard, pulling suck.

Behind her, Carter continued his caresses—his hands explored her belly, her back, her thighs, her ass. She found herself lifting her butt as much as she could without losing Marc's cock, to give Carter better access.

When she felt him lick the hungry, tiny fissure of her ass, she let out a hot gasp. And from that moment on, she was lost to the sensation.

The sensation of his tongue, licking, licking, then pressing, seeking entry, poking at the tight little hole.

The sensation of his fingers, gently prodding, stroking, pushing, dipping inside.

He was ever-so-slowly spreading her asshole wider and wider until her moans were emanating from deep inside her, and he said, "Three fingers," and she knew he meant that's what he had inside her ass.

She fucked those fingers as she fucked Marc's wondrous cock, wondering how much pleasure she could take—and admittedly, wondering how much more her ass could take, too. It felt pleasantly stretched, as if much more would be impossible.

But his fingers were so wet as he gently moved them in and out, and his lazy rhythm somehow made her relax, enjoy, simply sink into the pleasure so deeply that she forgot about the possibility of pain.

When his fingers departed and she heard another small packet being ripped open, she tensed slightly. And when she felt his cock prodding the tight little hole, she was sure it would never go in without splitting her apart, and she almost asked him to stop. But the little part of her that wanted him in her ass so badly she could taste it kept her quiet, kept her patient, kept her lulled into submission.

When the head slipped in, she screamed out in what she was certain sounded like pain, but was definitely pleasure. "Good," she added breathlessly, so that the two suddenly tense forms would know Carter wasn't hurting her, but instead taking her to yet another whole new sexual place.

His thrusts were slow, gentle, in the same easy, tentative rhythm she'd assumed with Marc since this exploration of her ass had begun. Each soft drive inward took him a little deeper, until she could feel that second hole filled up with him, filled nearly to bursting, and yet, it was so good, so incredible, that she never wanted it to end.

A part of her thought it seemed unnatural to have a cock in that part of her body, yet perhaps that was exactly why it felt so delicious. Her whole being felt stretched to its limits, fucked in a more complete way than she'd ever dreamed possible.

She leaned down to whisper in Marc's ear. "He's all the way in my ass."

Marc nibbled her earlobe. "Do you like it, bad girl?"

"I can't believe I can take you both like this at the same time, but...mmm, God, yes, it's good."

Except for small, rolling movements, they'd gone almost still, and for the first time in awhile, Marc thrust a little harder into her. With Carter wedged in tight behind him, she felt Marc's movement so much more, and she let out a little scream of pleasure.

Carter followed with a thrust of his own—firm, deep, but not forceful. He was clearly trying to make sure he didn't hurt her, and was doing an excellent job. She moaned at this thrust, as well, so deep in her anus that it produced sensations she'd never before experienced.

They took turns, each man gently driving himself into her, each move eliciting a response from deep inside her. Soon they both fell into a new rhythm, picking up speed, the thrusts coming harder, the pistoning cocks moving farther in and out of her two hot openings. She was screaming throughout, because the alternating thrusts left no fraction of time without the deep plunges that threatened to tear her apart, yet filled her with a pleasure so profound it felt delightfully obscene.

Marc licked and sucked her breasts and Diana lost herself completely in the sensations that were so powerful they left both body and mind overwhelmed. She screamed and cried and let them fuck her deep—pussy, ass, pussy, ass, pussy, ass.

And then it hit hard, a strange, shattering orgasm that had her screeching, crying out, as their thrusts continued to echo through her core and intensify the hard, fast, brutal waves of pleasure/pain that consumed her.

"Aw, God, here I come," Carter said behind her.

He was packed so tight inside her that she felt the spasms of his cock—another nearly overwhelming sensation that made her cry and beg, saying, "Please, please!" without even understanding what she was begging for.

"I'm coming, too," Marc yelled on a tremendous groan and he thrust up harder inside her than he had through the whole encounter, and she reveled in the knowledge that he was spilling his come for her.

When Carter pulled out a few seconds later, her ass was left feeling open, gaping. He kissed the back of her shoulder and asked, "You okay?"

She couldn't speak, but nodded. "Mmm."

She rose off of Marc and fell back onto the other end of the couch, her body spent and still racked with aftershocks of the intense orgasm.

Within an instant, he was with her again, stretching out beside her, taking her in his arms, and whispering in her ear. "You never did *that* before, either, did you, sweetheart?"

She shook her head.

He kissed her cheek. "Did you like it?"

"Mmm. Oh, yes." A little of her strength was returning. "I don't think I could do it every day or anything, but it was…the most intense sexual experience I've ever had."

He smiled, chuckling to himself.

"What?" she asked, forming a small grin of her own.

"Talk about a double dip," he said. "I had no idea how literally that would turn out."

* * * * *

Marc didn't want to take her home that night; he wanted her to stay with him, sleep in his bed. But she insisted, pointing out what a drag it was to wake up in the place your clothes were not, then have to rush back and get ready for work. He'd been in that position before, so he knew what she was talking about, but he was still disappointed.

Even so, Carter had gone home after lying in Marc's bed with them for a little while, snuggling, drinking wine, listening to music, and it left Marc a little time to enjoy her by himself.

He'd have thought after the last two nights he'd be sated, but the next morning, he woke up with a raging hard-on. Damn, seemed Diana had taken him to The Land of Perpetual Arousal.

By the time he got to work, he could think of nothing but fucking her again. Alone this time. He'd truly enjoyed sharing her with Carter last night, but that possessive streak inside him was beginning to get a little bigger now. Yes, he got off on watching, and sharing, and he loved giving her these new experiences. But he also wanted to give her every possible pleasure *alone*, too. He supposed maybe it was some crazy unconscious attempt to show her he could be all the man she'd ever need.

But on the other hand, maybe that didn't matter. She'd made her intentions about Bradley clear last night.

He thought she was making a huge mistake, hooking up with a guy who didn't make her see fireworks, but Diana was such a confident, competent, determined woman that he didn't think he had a chance in hell of making her change her mind.

He let out a sigh that came out sounding more like a little grumble. *But hey, it's none of my business if she wants to ruin her life.* If all she wanted from him was sex—well, hell, he loved sex and he loved it with Diana, so that was just fine.

And he'd be sorry when it was over, that was for damn sure, but he'd recover. He'd go to Europe as planned—and if this job came through, he'd be going sooner rather than later. So if, God forbid, he suffered any heartache after she returned to her other life in Baltimore, well, he'd be too busy starting a *new* life to let it bother him very much.

When he walked in the conference room, the last to arrive, Diana was already busy at work—she stood at the head of the table saying to the rest of the guys, "No, we don't want to tell our customers the stockings 'are great for sex', Blaine. They can figure that out on their own, and the pictures certainly speak for themselves. So our copy should be subtle. We want to stress things like 'cool comfort,' and 'at work or at play'. 'Under your favorite slinky dress at the cocktail party, and for whatever comes next.' *Subtle* suggestions, gentlemen."

She smiled at Marc as he closed the door, and by the time he'd taken a seat, she was moving on to a discussion about panty styles. She looked stunning in a candy apple red suit with another short skirt. The jacket hugged her curves and the white silk blouse beneath showed just enough shadowy cleavage to remind him how beautiful her breasts were, how she loved to have them sucked and fucked.

The first time the group took a break, he pulled her aside. "Take a ride with me," he said.

She looked confused. "Huh?"

"Come on." He grabbed her hand and began to pull her from the room and up the hallway, dropping his grip only when a couple of people from another department appeared in their path. Once in the lobby, he said to Holly, "We'll be back in a few minutes if anyone asks."

"All right," she said as he pushed the button to summon the elevator.

"Where are we going?" Diana asked under her breath.

"Like I said, we're taking a ride."

She gave him a curious smile.

When the elevator arrived, it was blessedly empty. The moment the doors closed, he pressed the button for the top floor, twenty stories up, then reached for her, pulling her into a long, hard kiss as his palms closed over her round ass.

"What are we—?"

He cut her off with another plunge of his tongue into her mouth, then answered. "You keep me hard day and night. I'm suffering already. Speaking of which, is your pussy sore again today?"

She shook her head with a small smile. "Doesn't seem to be. It must be getting acclimated to Sin City."

"Good," he said, dropping his fingers from her ass down to her sweet little cunt, rubbing the back of her mound.

She squirmed against his hand with a cute little "Mmm" sound, and lifted her hands to his chest.

"How about your lovely little ass? How does *it* feel?"

She laughed a bit, even as she moved against his caresses. "*That* part of me could probably use a break."

He grinned. "I thought so. Don't worry—no more ass play 'til you're good and ready for it. Meanwhile, though…"

She tilted her head. "Yes?"

"I'm gonna fuck you so good," he promised, low and hot.

She purred her reply. "I can't wait."

"You don't have to. It's gonna be right here, right now."

She raised her eyebrows. "On the elevator?"

He gave a quick, solemn nod before turning her to face the mirrored wall—reaching around to take her hands and plant them on the shiny surface—then opening his zipper. Pushing her red skirt up, he found the elastic at either hip and pulled her panties down onto her thighs. Then he plunged himself into that sweet, warm flesh.

"Oh!" she cried out, looking over her shoulder at him. "Oooh."

He let out a moan of his own as her lovely cunt took his whole cock, wrapping around it like a velvet sheath and sending waves of pleasure through his chest, thighs.

"What'll we do..." she murmured, clearly breathless, "...if the elevator stops...before we're done?"

"We'll cross that bridge when we come to it," he said, pounding hard into her wet heat. "I just...had to have you...now."

As if on cue, the elevator sounded with a ding and slowed to a stop. With adrenaline pumping like wildfire through his veins, Marc quickly withdrew, but knowing he didn't have time to zip up, he just yanked the hem of Diana's skirt down, backed into a corner, and pulled her in front of him, to cover his bared shaft.

When the door opened, a group of people in business attire similar to their own stepped on—two men and three women. One of the men pushed the button for a floor almost all the way to the top, which meant they'd be there for a while.

His cock stayed thoroughly erect through the ride, jutting hard into the back of Diana's red skirt. The thought of her panties being halfway down her thighs as they rode made him even more impatient than before and he shifted slightly, so that his cock lay just over the crack of her ass. She backed up slightly against him, helping them both feel it more. It was all he could do not to push up her skirt and drive it back into her hot pussy right in front of these people.

Glancing down as the floors slowly ticked by, he saw the little vent-like slit in the back of her skirt, and given that the skirt was short anyway…

Reaching down, he grabbed hold of his dick and lowered it, slipping it into the vent. When he let go, it made her skirt rise a little, but their elevator companions were busily chatting about some presentation they were giving and seemed not to notice. When she shifted in front of him, the head of his shaft grazed her inner thighs and made him stifle a groan. And when she backed up a little farther, getting more and more daring, his cock settled right at her pussy, the top ridge of it pressing against her slit. He let out a sigh.

In front of him, Diana moved again, just slightly, subtly lifting her ass toward him. It was all he could do not to tremble—not only from the profound lust they were sharing, but also from the risk they were silently indulging in. Reaching down, he positioned himself for entry, nudging lightly.

She let out a breathy sigh, but covered it by clearing her throat.

The other passengers still seemed oblivious, so he eased into her, just a little. Ah, God, she was slick and warm.

She leaned back, taking him deeper by an inch, maybe two. He wanted to growl his pleasure and the accompanying frustration. Damn slow elevator. But on the other hand, their silent daring added to his excitement.

He pushed farther into her moisture, perhaps another inch.

She let out a small sound, but covered it with a cough—which vibrated throughout his cock, nearly making him come. He closed his eyes and tried to breathe slowly. He counted to ten. He wished like hell he could see the look on her face because he was very glad he had *her* to shield *his*. He probably looked just as lusty as he felt.

Finally, just when Marc thought he was going to explode, the elevator dinged again, came to a stop, and let the group of five out. As the doors slid closed, Diana turned to face him. Her expression looked almost feral as she dropped to her knees and took his massive erection in her mouth.

Wrapping her hand around the base, she sucked on him furiously, giving him a beautifully decadent view of her lips — painted red today to match her suit — wrapped around the big cock jutting from his suit pants.

He pumped into her hungry little mouth until the ding announced that they'd arrived on the top floor, which only housed one quiet office, so hopefully there would be no one there waiting for this particular elevator.

By the time the doors opened, Diana was back on her feet, shielding him from view again, but blessedly, there was no one waiting to get on. Stepping around her, he pushed the button for their floor. As soon as the elevator took off, though, he pushed the Emergency Stop button, bringing the car to a jarring halt.

She instantly turned to the wall again, lifting her skirt up over her ass and bracing herself against the mirror. "Fuck me. Hurry." She sounded as excited and breathless as he felt.

Noting for the first time just what a lovely view the shiny, mirrored walls provided, Marc looked to the back of the elevator, watching them in profile as he reinserted his cock into that sweet pussy that was always so anxious to welcome him.

She arched her ass to give him easier entry and he reached around and fingered her swollen clit as he drove into her wet, tight hole. Together, they moved against one another in a perfect pounding motion and just as he said, "Oh, baby, this won't take long," he was there, on the brink, ready to come.

"Hold your skirt up, way up," he warned as he pulled his cock out.

She followed his instructions and bent over, understanding what he was going to do. Holding his erection, pointing it at her gorgeous ass, he shot his come onto her, moaning and groaning as the pleasure racked him hard. She whimpered and cooed at the sensation, letting out a long, deep "Mmm," when he took his hands and began to rub it in, moving his palms in big wide circles.

"Thought this might be easier," he said, his voice raspy. "Didn't want you to have come dripping down your legs when we get off the elevator. And I was too impatient for a condom." In between her sighs of pleasure, he continued working the white semen into her skin.

Just then, the phone in the elevator rang. It was right next to Diana, so she snatched it up, even as he continued rubbing her moist ass.

"Yes, we're fine," she said into the phone, smiling over her shoulder at him.

On impulse, Marc reached around and began to rub her again, his fingers quickly locating her engorged clit.

She moved against him, gave him a look, and struggled to speak into the phone. "No, no idea what happened, it just stopped." Her voice sounded sexy and breathy. Marc swirled his middle finger in wet circles over her sensitive little nub, the look on her face teetering precariously between pleasure and torture.

"Uh-huh," she said into the phone. He could hear the repair guy explaining to her something about pulleys and cables. Her ass was mostly dry now, just sticky, which couldn't be avoided. He kept rubbing, both in front and in back. She met the pressure of his finger in a hot, perfect rhythm, flicking her gaze away only when she had to attempt a response to the repairman. "Yeah, uh-huh, I understand."

She shut her eyes in passion and grew wetter and wetter against his touch. "Yes, you're right, it was very frightening." Her sweet pussy thrust, thrust, thrust against his hand. "Thank you. Please hurry."

The second she hung up, she braced herself against the wall, pumping rougher and rougher against his fingers, until she said, "God, now," and bucked even harder. Pure pleasure washed over her face as she leaned back and moaned her release, long and complete, the sound seeming to echo around them.

When she sighed the conclusion of her climax, Marc felt sure she'd berate him for torturing her that way while she was on phone. But instead she only turned and reached for the hand that had stayed busy rubbing his semen into her ass. She lifted it to her mouth and sucked on his sticky fingers for a moment before she purred, "I'm so glad you came on me. This way I'll feel you there all day."

* * * * *

Diana was exhausted. It was no wonder, when she thought about it.

It only hit her when, late that afternoon, she left the catalog team with her laptop and sought out a quiet conference room where she could check her e-mail and make sure nothing was falling apart without her in the Baltimore office. Of course, as she'd predicted, she was occasionally reminded of her elevator tryst with Marc whenever she shifted in her chair and felt a little sticky, but she did manage to concentrate on the messages she read, among them, one from her boss back home:

All's well here. As promised, I took over your desk, got Shyla involved, and made sure everything got done, so you don't have to worry. Hope the catalog work is going well. Enjoy Vegas and have a drink for me.

Richard

She couldn't help smiling—not only because it did ease her fears, but because Richard knew her well enough to know she'd be concerned. Although her Sin City adventures had been keeping her quite busy, she had found time to spare a thought for her job in Baltimore from time to time and couldn't believe she'd waited this long to check her e-mail.

After reading all her messages, answering the ones she could, and leaving the ones that would require further action later, she was just about to close her e-mail program when a new message appeared there...from Marc. The subject line read: *Whips and Chains*. Intrigued, she grinned as she double-clicked to open it.

Now that I've got your attention...I don't really own any whips and chains, but I'm still aching to see you in Sinsuous leather. How about a little "master and slave" tonight in your room?

Yes, she was exhausted, but how could a girl turn down such a hot invitation? Besides, she didn't want to waste even one night with Marc, because who knew how long she'd be here. She couldn't stay more than a week or two, given her usual job responsibilities. Richard couldn't keep up with her tasks forever, after all. She typed a reply:

Who's the master and who's the slave?

She hit Send and a moment later had another message from the man sitting just down the hall.

Ever since we had that conversation about you feeling submissive, I've been in the mood to show you how dominant I can be. Can you handle it if I promise to be gentle?

She replied:

I can handle it even if you promise not *to be gentle :)*

Chapter Seven

Marc was late leaving the office that night. In addition to his responsibilities on the catalog team, he was still part of the marketing department, and the time spent working on the catalog the last few weeks had left little time for other tasks.

So as other people began trickling out at five, including Diana—who pulled him into a dark corner at one of the coffee stations to kiss him goodbye—he stayed behind and dealt with a few items that had gathered on his desk.

As he turned out the last lights in his area of the office, stepping through the door that led to the lobby, he saw Adrianna coming from her office in the other direction. As usual, his employer was impeccably groomed, looking sophisticated yet feminine in a fitted black suit with a simple white blouse underneath.

"Marc, how's the catalog work progressing?"

"Great, actually. Diana's input has really made us all see that we need another woman to replace Kelly."

Adrianna offered her usual solemn, thin-lipped smile. "Yes, I suspected Diana would be gifted at understanding how to entice our customers." She pushed the button for the elevator.

And Marc knew he should probably bite his tongue, but he couldn't resist. "I hear she enticed you, too," he said with a warm grin.

He'd never seen Adrianna blush and he didn't see it now, either. However, her smile widened as she said, "To be frank, I'm surprised to hear she told anyone about our little...business meeting."

Marc laughed. "Well, she and I are close."

Adrianna raised her eyebrows. "Really? I didn't realize." The elevator arrived and as they both stepped inside, she asked, "Sexually? Or otherwise?"

Both, he thought, but then reminded himself that Diana couldn't be as crazy about him as he was about her or she wouldn't be so set on going back home to Bradley and the good girl lifestyle. "Sexually."

As the car began to descend, Adrianna said, "My, my, so it would appear we're both quite taken with Miss Marsh."

Again, he chuckled. "Quite."

"I had actually hoped to catch her today before she left. I was going to ask her to dinner."

He looked at his raven-haired superior. "For when?"

"Tonight."

Now it was his turn to raise his eyebrows. "That's not like you, Adrianna. Wasting time on a possible second strike-out." It felt odd to suddenly be having this conversation with her, and now he wondered why he'd even started it. After all, he and Adrianna hadn't discussed sex or anything that had to do with either of their personal lives since the day she'd hired him. It hadn't been a stipulation of employment, just a routine they'd fallen into that had always worked. Why was he suddenly risking that?

She cast him an amused sideways glance. "Given that Miss Marsh's assignment here is temporary, and that my briefcase is unusually light this evening, it seemed as if it were an opportunity presenting itself. Perhaps I'll call her at her hotel."

"Sorry," he said with a matter-of-fact smile, "but she's already busy tonight."

As the elevator reached the ground floor, Adrianna stayed quiet, but let her gaze slide up and down his body in a way he recognized from long ago. His dick was already half-hard from continued thoughts of Diana, but Adrianna's predatory look turned it even stiffer.

"You know, Marc, you and I haven't played for a very long while…"

They both exited the elevator and proceeded across the building's large lobby toward the revolving door that would lead them out into the Las Vegas heat. "And you're suggesting?"

"A lovely ménage a trois, of course."

Although Marc couldn't quite believe it, he was actually almost ménage a trois-ed out. He'd really wanted to keep Diana to himself tonight, really wanted to share the whole evening — the talking, the laughing, the touching, the fucking — with her alone.

But Adrianna was a beautiful woman with a beautiful body, and no encounter he'd ever had with her had disappointed. It had been years now, but past liaisons returned fresh to his mind. And when Diana had told him about Adrianna's attempted seduction — ah, the visions of two lovely female bodies in expensive lingerie that had danced through his head. Diana had seemed curious, and he'd sensed her almost prodding him to encourage her toward Adrianna.

As he'd told Diana last night regarding Carter, there would be other chances for them to be alone, but this particular moment, this particular opportunity, might not ever come back to them. And if he knew his hot, hungry little Diana, she wouldn't object to another partner in the mix so long as she knew it got him hot.

"Well?" Adrianna said just before they stepped, one by one, into the revolving door.

The desert heat hit him squarely in the face on the other side and he shielded his eyes from the setting sun as he stopped to look at Adrianna. "Nine o'clock, at the Venetian. I'll leave a note at the front desk with her room number."

Adrianna looked pleased, but didn't bother smiling — it was the same reaction she gave when a business deal came off just as successfully as she'd expected.

As Marc started up the sidewalk, leaving Adrianna to head in the other direction, he stopped and turned back. "Oh, and one more thing."

His too casual words halted her steps and he strolled back toward her.

"She'll be in Sinsuous leather tonight, so you should dress similarly. I'll be the master, you two will be my sex slaves, doing whatever I say."

Now she let her mouth curve into a small smile. "Be certain you enjoy this, Marc. Rarely does a man get to dominate me."

* * * * *

When Diana got dressed for the evening, she felt positively wicked. She started with her favorite Sinsuous item, a black leather waist cincher that defined her curves, binding her from below her breasts to her hips. It was the perfect accoutrement for a night of sexual discipline since it hugged her so tightly and made her feel so confined. The woven leather choker she hooked around her neck served the same purpose, as did the leather g-string below when her flesh swelled within the fabric. Finally, she fastened a Sinsuous leather garter belt around her waist, up under the corset and panties, and attached black fishnet stockings. Looking in the mirror, she smiled, thinking she'd be the perfect little submissive tonight for her man.

Next she put on a simple but fitted strapless black leather dress, which zipped tightly enough up the side to support her boobs without a bra, sporting a hem that just concealed the tops of her stockings. Tall black boots, silver bangle bracelets, and large silver hoops at her earlobes completed the look. She felt so sinful by the time she was ready to go that she knew she was creaming her little black g-string.

Like the other night when she'd been going to meet Marc in her sexy red dress, this outfit garnered numerous masculine stares on the elevator and passing through the casino into the lobby.

At six-thirty on the dot, Marc was waiting at the door. She hopped in his car and they set off for a restaurant on the outskirts of town. "Started out strictly a biker bar," he'd told her earlier, "but now it caters to both bikers and the local S&M crowd."

She'd raised her eyebrows and grinned. "I've played a few leather games in the past, but I've never been in a real S&M bar."

He'd grinned back. "Don't worry, I'm not planning on being *too* rough on you tonight, but I thought this might…get us in the mood."

Now, as they traveled toward this mysterious destination, she wondered what exactly her master *did* have in mind for tonight.

"I like this look on you," she told him, taking in his black leather pants and snug black t-shirt. She didn't like those kinds of clothes on just every guy, but Marc was masculine enough to pull them off with ease and he looked very sexy.

He smiled across the car at her. "You, sweetheart, look like a total dominatrix tonight."

"Is that a good thing?"

"So long as you remember your place," he said with a wicked little grin that reminded her he was in charge tonight. And given the pleasures this man had shown her over the last few erotic days, she figured giving herself over to him completely for a night was the least she could do. She still worried that before her visit to Vegas was done she'd be way too attached to him, but she was beginning to think avoiding that was impossible. In fact, maybe it was *already* too late. After all, when she went back to Baltimore—when this spectacular trip of passionate debauchery ended—wouldn't she always look back on it as a time of total freedom, total lack of inhibition, total fulfillment, all given to her by Marc?

"Speaking of which," he said, drawing her thoughts back to the present, "I've got a little surprise for you."

"Am I supposed to ask what it is, or do I just have to wait and see?"

"It's about Adrianna."

She lifted her gaze, a little surprised their boss would come into their conversation about submission and domination.

"When we get back to your room tonight, she's going to join us."

Even as Diana raised her eyebrows in shock, she wasn't sure how she felt about his announcement. Equal parts aversion and anticipation traveled through her veins. She'd thought their master and slave game would be something private, just between them, and wasn't sure she was comfortable sharing something like that with Adrianna. On the other hand, she hadn't forgotten her recent curiosity about the pleasures of feminine flesh. Adrianna was beautiful and shapely and sexy and if, as she'd claimed, she was using this "last fling" to soak up every sexual encounter she could, shouldn't she welcome an attractive, exciting woman to their little game tonight?

"You don't look happy," he said. On either side of them, the landscape was becoming less urban, with brown rock and desert-like stretches of highway appearing between populated areas.

"I'm just surprised," she said, "but it's all right."

His grin held a promise of the night to come. "That's good, since you have to submit to whatever I want anyway."

She flashed a wry smile, a hint of arousal tweaking her pussy even as she tried to get used to this game and the fact that, apparently, it had already started. "How did this come about?"

"We both worked a little late tonight and she told me she was going to call you and ask you to dinner."

Although never in her life, even after Adrianna's pass at her the other day, had it occurred to Diana that she might go on a "date" with another woman, she felt strangely flattered to hear their boss was still thinking about her that way.

Marc went on. "I told her you already had plans tonight and…well, you know how frank Adrianna is, and I'm equally as honest with her, so it came out that we both had the hots for you and she invited herself along for a ménage a trois. I told her we were indulging in a little domination this evening and she didn't have any complaints."

Diana let out her breath as the ramifications of this hit her fully. Not only was Adrianna joining them for sex tonight, but she'd be in leather, and Marc would be controlling their actions. As before, she was struck with an odd mixture of distress and excitement.

Marc pulled into a gravel lot surrounding a wide, flat, one-story building marked with only a small, crude-looking sign that said "The Cave." Despite the early hour, the lot was filled, mostly with motorcycles and older, souped-up sports cars.

"I may as well tell you," he said, "this is where I know Adrianna from — before we worked together."

She looked at the dark building. "This place?"

"And others like it. That's kind of the little secret I wasn't willing to spill in the limo the other night. Thing is, sweetheart…" He turned to her in the parked car. "…I'm into the BDSM scene just a little. Not all the time, just occasionally. And so is Adrianna."

She tried to swallow back her surprise. She was at once stunned and intrigued. Remembering how his "secret" had come up in conversation before, she said, "So you've done a lot of wild BDSM things. And when we were talking about sex with multiple partners—the other encounters you mentioned had to do with that?"

He shrugged, looking uncharacteristically sheepish even as he gave her a matter-of-fact grin. "Yeah, a lot of my wilder experiences occurred through BDSM."

"You once said you knew Adrianna well. So that means you and she got together a lot?"

Another shrug of his shoulders. "We ran with the same crowd back then, so…yeah. It was when I'd first gotten into the lifestyle, the period I was deepest into it. Since that time, it's kind of faded off—it's just an occasional thing for me now. And…something I'm interested in introducing to *you*. I hope none of this…changes anything. Your feelings about me, I mean."

"Why should it?"

He smiled, looking relieved. "Well, other than my sexual appetites, I think of myself as a pretty conventional guy. And I know most conventional people think this stuff is pretty weird. Even people who really dig sex."

"Color me…fascinated," she said, tilting her head and flashing her best sensual grin.

He looked satisfied. "And color your master well-pleased by that."

Marc placed his hand at the small of her back as they stepped inside. Diana quickly discovered that the restaurant's name was apt—the interior was dark and cavern-like. Most of the patrons, including the bartender and waitresses, wore black leather or vinyl, although a few biker types wore blue jeans and bandannas, with black biker gear or Harley Davidson t-shirts.

She was surprised to find that a hostess was employed to show them to their table—a buxom redhead in a black bustier who sported a writhing snake tattooed down the length of her right arm. She led them down a hallway to another dark room with black walls and ceilings, lit only by a few candles jutting from medieval-looking sconces. The room was small and tables for two lined the four walls, the middle area left open for people to get through. The snake lady escorted them to the last empty table, the others filled with a variety of twenty and thirty-somethings like themselves, decked out in goth-wear and leather. Diana felt like she'd stepped into an alternate universe, and she liked being a part of something so foreign to her.

After perusing the small black menu, she ordered light, thinking of the constricting corset under her dress, which was a constant reminder of what was to come.

"So, what exactly are your plans for Adrianna and me?" She leaned forward just enough to treat him to a little cleavage.

He grinned. "Let me put it like this, sweetheart. You might think you and I have already traveled a pretty damn exciting road together these past few days—but you should brace yourself, because the scenery's about to change, and you won't even recognize it."

* * * * *

By the time they'd finished eating, the crowd in The Cave had started to grow and the mood had begun growing a little more hedonistic. Diana nearly lost her breath when she realized that a girl a few tables away from them wore a low-cut black vinyl vest that revealed her small breasts entirely, and by the time they'd paid the bill and left the table, she was sitting on her big, bald companion's lap having one of them suckled while she nibbled on the chocolate cake she'd ordered for dessert.

The goth and metal music that had played through the meal had been turned up slightly, beginning to make conversation more difficult. Marc took Diana's hand and led her down the corridor they'd traveled to reach the dining room and back into the main area, which she now realized was more of a club.

Numerous people stood around in outfits of black, some drinking, some dancing to the music. In the middle of the room, two goth queens stood making out, one of them fondling the other girl's breast through fabric that looked thin and mesh-like. As they wove through the crowd, Diana began to realize that a number of women wore outfits that revealed their breasts or that rose scandalously high on their thighs, revealing the lower curves of their asses. As sexy as Diana had felt getting dressed earlier, she was beginning to feel utterly conservative in The Cave.

Making their way to the bar, Marc ordered them both the house specialty drink, called Sex Potion #9, promising she'd like it. The drink he handed her a moment later was blood red and the only tastes she recognized were strawberry and lots of rum, and Marc was right—it went down as easy as fruit punch.

"What now?" she asked over the pounding music. "Or is this it? Is this what goes on in your average BDSM place?"

Marc's throaty laugh made her feel—once again—naïve. Sin City, she'd discovered, had a way of making her feel like a total innocent in a strange land. "Not even close," he told her, pointing to a number of doorways across the room.

Signs painted in red and black hung above each door. One said "Wheel of Torture" and another said, "Torture ala Carte."

"Uh…care to explain further?" she asked.

"In the Wheel of Torture room, you spin a wheel and a guy or girl—your pick—in a black mask administers whatever sort of torture comes up. In the ala Carte room, you choose your own."

Her skin prickled. "Like…?"

"Oh, nipple clamping, having certain parts of your body tied with rope, spankings and beatings with various tools, that sort of thing."

She laughed. "That sort of thing," she repeated. "You name them off like they're flavors of ice cream."

He grinned. "Well, I'm your ice-cream man and I'm also your Wheel of Torture man—if you want me to be."

"So you're into that—the torture part?"

"Very low level, sweetheart. Nothing that would alarm you, I promise." As if to reassure her, he grabbed the back of her head and pulled her close to deliver a kiss to her forehead, and it actually *did* work to relax her concerns. This was Marc, her sweet, sexy lover. The guy who'd seemed scared to death she'd regret their evening in the limo. She knew she had no worries, and that even if he was her master, he'd take care of her.

She spotted two more signs that pointed down a dark hallway. One said "Live Sex—Do It." The other said "Live Sex—Voyeurs." She supposed they were self explanatory, but she said, "Do people really…?"

He nodded. "There's a pane of glass between the two rooms and the voyeur room has chairs for you to sit and watch what's going on through the glass."

She couldn't help a small smile up at him. "And I'm guessing you've frequented the voyeur room? Given your penchant for watching?"

He shrugged, grinned. "Back in the day, yeah, I might have happened in there on occasion. But at the moment..."

"Yes?"

"I'm not really too compelled to watch anyone doing anything except my little slave girl here." He grinned and lowered another soft kiss to the top of her head.

She glanced toward the signs again. "Is this even legal?"

He held his hands out in front of him. "You're in Vegas, baby." Then he closed his fingers around hers. "Almost finished with your drink? Ready to go?"

She took the last sip and set her glass on a nearby table. And she didn't know whether it was the rum talking or something more, but she said, "Not quite."

"Oh?"

"You're right—I'm in Vegas, baby. So before we go, I want to sneak a peek into one of those rooms. I'll feel like I'm leaving here a total BDSM virgin if I don't. Any recommendations?" she asked, peering up into his sexy eyes.

"It's early yet, but let's see if anyone's in the Live Sex room."

Diana's heartbeat kicked up as she made her way down the dark hall, Marc's hand at the small of her back. All the leather she wore seemed to, at once, caress her skin and bind her tighter as she walked. When she reached the room for voyeurs, she turned the doorknob, easing it open just a bit.

Only two people sat watching — a couple of biker guys around their age.

Through the glass panel, she spied two girls making out, clad only in black panties. Both were pretty, even with their starkly dyed black hair and heavy makeup. Like during the gentleman's show, she was immediately intrigued by the softness of their kisses, their touches, the way their pointed breasts jutted into each other. She wondered if that would be her and Adrianna later.

"I expected something much rougher in here," she whispered to Marc, who stood watching over her shoulder.

"You'd usually *get* something much rougher in here. Too early yet, I suspect."

"Darn," she whispered.

He stifled a chuckle behind her. "Well, aren't you just the little sex hound?"

Easing back to close the door on the scene, she turned to Marc in the dark hall, smiling. "I told you, I just didn't want to stay a BDSM virgin."

He gave her a slow, deep kiss, his tongue pressing past her lips, then whispered warm in her ear. "Don't worry, sweetheart. The night is young and your virginity will be long gone before morning."

* * * * *

Upon returning to the hotel, they got more than their fair share of stares, especially considering that Marc was decked out so similarly to Diana. He also carried a mysterious black leather bag.

"What's in there?" she asked.

"Whips and chains."

"I thought you said you didn't really have any of those."

His smile was laced with sin. "I lied."

After stopping at the front desk to leave a note for Adrianna, they made their way back through the casino toward the elevators. Diana drank in the stares that told her it was clear what kind of evening she and Marc had planned—she could only imagine how much the spectators would salivate if Adrianna was with them right now.

In the elevator, he said, "Do you know what a safe word is?"

She'd heard the term. "A way to let you know if I want to stop?"

He nodded. "Pick one."

She thought for a few seconds, then smiled up at him. "Ice-cream man."

He grinned. "Got it."

The moment they stepped through the door into her room, the mood between them changed. She sensed immediately that enclosing themselves there meant the game had officially begun, full force. She knew it for sure when he said in a smooth, authoritative voice, "Walk across the room."

It caught her off guard. "What?" She looked up at him.

"Walk across the room, over by the windows. Go slowly."

Swallowing, suddenly feeling nervous, she followed the instruction. Yet as she strolled—slowly, as he'd ordered—she again became as aware of her clothing as when she'd first put it on. She felt the leather moving against her soft skin, the garter belt pulling the fishnets tight on her thighs. Once she reached the window, she stood still, waiting, conscious of how heavy her pussy was beginning to feel within the tight bit of leather stretched over it.

"Now turn around."

She did so and found Marc, still standing across the room, but he was transformed. Gone was his shirt, replaced by a black leather harness. A thick silver ring lay just below his chest; four black straps extended from it—crossing over his shoulders, around his back. She was even more surprised to see him wearing a small black leather mask. It was just enough to make him seem...like someone else...like her *master*. The sexy leather pants still hugged the lower half of his body, although a large bulge rose from his groin. It all served to make her cunt still heavier, tingling within its leather covering.

"Take off your dress."

"Already?" She'd thought they'd wait until Adrianna arrived.

"I said take it off, damn it." His voice was low, gruff, threatening...exhilarating.

Reaching up to the black zipper under her arm, she slowly eased it down, all the way, to the hem. The leather sheath opened around her and fell away, to the carpet. She stood before him, breasts exposed, her corset, garters, stockings and high-heeled boots there for his perusal. She felt almost as excited as if he were a stranger, someone who'd never seen her before. Her nipples turned rock-hard under his masked gaze.

"Your master is pleased," he said. "You look like the perfect little sex slave."

She smiled softly, satisfied.

When a knock came, she flinched, jiggling her breasts. He stood near the door, but moved away from it, sitting down in a chair. "Open the door," he told her. "And don't look through the peephole first."

That last part made her heart flutter nervously—it would surely be Adrianna, but what if it wasn't? Still, she didn't think he'd like it if she questioned him, so she took a deep breath and pulled the door open.

Adrianna gasped when she saw Diana's state of undress. "Miss Marsh, you look delicious—but don't tell me you started without me."

Diana looked over her shoulder to Marc. "*He* did." It was in that moment that a sense of the surreal struck her. She'd known Adrianna was on her way, of course, and she'd thought she was mentally prepared for it. But truly being face to face with her in this situation seemed wholly unreal and, for a few seconds, Diana couldn't quite believe it was truly happening.

"I see my other little fuck slave has arrived," Marc said. "You're late, Adrianna. You'll be punished for that later."

Diana sensed how difficult it was for Adrianna, who was always so in control, to hold her tongue, especially considering that Marc had been her employee for a number of years now. Finally, her eyes ablaze with something that bordered between irritation and arousal, she said, "I'm sorry. Forgive me."

"Maybe if you're a good girl."

"I...will be. And I brought you something." She walked over to him to deliver a small shopping bag. He looked inside and smiled. "Very nice, Adrianna. You get a gold star. Now, Diana, take her dress off."

Adrianna wore a simple black sleeveless dress that buttoned up the front, something suitable for a casual cocktail party. Only her very high, pointy-heeled black shoes gave any hint as to what might be under the stylish dress.

Diana bit her lip, her pussy swelling as she gingerly reached up to the first button, nestled in the valley between Adrianna's breasts. She undid it, and though the glimpse of vinyl she caught underneath tantalized her, she kept going, afraid Marc would think she wasn't following his instructions. He suddenly seemed like another person to her, in manner and action—even in voice.

When she'd undone the last button, she pushed open the dress at Adrianna's waist to reveal a shiny black vinyl bra that outlined her large, beautiful breasts, the nipples rosy and erect. The bra featured a square silver buckle where the fabric met below her breasts, and two smaller buckles up above, on each strap. Her vinyl thong featured three more matching buckles, revealing patches of skin and pubic hair in between, until the bottom one, where her pussy was fully revealed. Despite the pubic hair above, her cunt itself was as smooth and bare as Diana's.

Seeing Adrianna's lovely breasts and pussy for the first time, in bondage-wear no less, set Diana's own pussy nearly ablaze. *These* were not items offered by Adrianna, Inc.

Diana walked around behind the taller woman to remove the dress from her arms.

Marc gave his head a speculative tilt. "Crotchless vinyl, Adrianna? Very nice. Your punishment is hereby revoked. In fact, I think you'll get a reward."

"I'm glad you approve," she said, her voice dry and devoid of tone, as usual.

"Put your pretty ass in this chair," he said to her, motioning to an upholstered seat that set perpendicular to his own.

Adrianna did as she was told.

"Spread your legs."

She did, and Diana couldn't help studying her pale, lovely slit, held tight by the surrounding vinyl.

"Diana, kneel between her thighs."

Crossing the room to where they sat, Diana dropped to her knees as instructed. The hair on her arms stood on end with nervous anticipation.

"Adrianna, I know you want to kiss Diana's pretty mouth. So go ahead. Kiss her for me."

Adrianna leaned forward, cupping Diana's face in her hands. Diana trembled as she met her boss's regal yet desire-filled gaze. This was it—what she had wondered about and dared to wish for.

Their tongues met before their lips, gently, in a slow but potent rhythm of sensuality that made Diana fear her pussy would burst through the leather. Kissing Adrianna was so tenderly arousing that she could have melted there, and having Marc watch her intensified the sensation tenfold.

The second kiss was even better because Diana was ready for it, growing more comfortable, able to appreciate the pleasure of Adrianna's gentle, feminine mouth touching hers. The kisses were softer than anything she'd ever experienced and she was soon getting lost in them, surprised at how different it felt from kissing a man, and what a unique sort of pleasure it sent echoing through her body. As they kissed, Adrianna's hands began to slowly explore Diana's shoulders, skim down her arms. Like her kiss, her hands were soft, and so small compared to a man's—it was impossible to forget she was being touched by another female, all for Marc's enjoyment, and the very knowledge that he watched, that he even dictated their moves, sent spiraling waves of heat into her pussy.

Diana's bared breasts perched on Adrianna's thighs as the other woman's tender mouth continued to sweetly assault hers in kiss after stirring kiss, until finally Marc said, "That's enough," and they reluctantly parted.

"Diana, lick Adrianna's nipples."

So far, Diana didn't mind their little game at all. Adrianna's delicate kisses had tutored her, and now she wanted nothing more than to take her boss's lovely pink crests into her mouth. Leaning forward, she sensually licked one nipple in long, laving strokes several times before delivering the same treatment to the other hard peak. Feeling a woman's taut nipple on her tongue was incredibly arousing and she suddenly understood exactly why men enjoyed it so much.

"May I suck them, too?" she dared ask without looking up.

"Whatever your hot little mouth wants to do to them, sweetheart," he said, and for a moment he sounded just like her Marc again.

Loving that he watched her every move, she suckled one of Adrianna's large breasts, pulling the pretty nipple between her lips as she caressed her other ripe globe, squeezing and molding it in her hand. Above her, Adrianna released dreamy-sounding sighs of pleasure that spurred Diana on. She liked knowing she was pleasing both of them at the same time.

"Now lick her cunt," he said.

Allowing herself the indulgence of raking one last lick over Adrianna's nipple, she backed away, her eyes still on the other woman's breasts, enjoying the wet sheen on the one she'd just been kissing. Then she dropped her gaze to Adrianna's crotch.

Her slit was not open, but her clit and a hint of her pink lips peeked through anyway. As Diana dropped down lower, scooting her knees back slightly, she reveled in the sensation that Marc wanted to watch her eat another woman's pussy.

Was she nervous? Definitely. But as she'd suspected the other day when Adrianna had first made a move on her, having Marc present changed everything, turning trepidation into anticipation. And the delight she'd taken in Adrianna so far made her ready to take that next naughty step.

Using her hands to push Adrianna's shapely legs a little farther apart, she gently caressed her silky inner thighs with gentle fingertips before parting her boss's legs even wider. Leaning slowly in, she drank in the raw, exotic scent of Adrianna's sex, then reached out her tongue and dragged it up the pursed line of her slit, over the lips and clit.

The sensual thrill of having just done the forbidden rushed through Diana like a mini-orgasm as Adrianna sighed prettily up above.

Watching Adrianna's cunt, enticed by the way it seemed to swell, trapped, within the confines of the tight vinyl around it, Diana licked it again, this time pushing her tongue a little deeper.

Adrianna shivered and her pussy lips parted, just enough for a tantalizing glimpse of pink from top to bottom. Diana licked her once more, deep, this time tasting an intense, salty sweetness that added to the excitement racing down her spine. "Ooooh, yes," Adrianna murmured.

Sensing that her boss's cunt was so constrained in the vinyl that it simply couldn't spread very far on its own, she slid her hands down from where they rested at Adrianna's hips and used her thumbs to peel Adrianna's pussy open as if it were a ripe, juicy peach.

All three of them uttered sounds of pleasure when the broad pink expanse of her fleshy cunt was stretched open for visual inspection, the wet passage at the bottom looking deep and open.

Following her instincts, Diana sank her tongue there, into the channel, as far as she could thrust it. Adrianna cried out and Marc growled, "Yes, fuck that pussy with your hot little tongue. Fuck it for your master."

Diana was overwhelmed, surrounded by salty slickness, and his words prodded her. She wanted to do a good job for him, and she had the same urge she'd experienced upon meeting Adrianna for the first time the other day—the urge to please *her*, as well. She knew about getting lost in pleasure, but at the moment, she yearned to lose herself in *giving* pleasure.

She moved her tongue in and out of Adrianna's opening while her boss released sexy moans with each thrust. Diana's own pussy wept, desperately wishing for attention, but she reminded herself this was Marc's night and she was his willing slave, and despite the unmet needs of her body, she was enjoying her role more than she'd ever imagined.

Soon, she used her index fingers to open the top of Adrianna's slit so that she could easily reach her clit. Wrapping her lips around it, treating it exactly as if it were a tiny little cock, she sucked it while Adrianna groaned repeatedly with hot pleasure, caressing her own breasts.

"That's so hot, my little slave girl. You might just get a reward later, too."

After that, Diana delivered long, firm, lapping licks, from the bottom of her boss's pink pussy to the top of her hard little clit, thoroughly absorbed in the giving. Soon, she began to vary her motions, learning what spots and tongue movements seemed to turn Adrianna on the most, finally concentrating on the pretty, swollen nub that emerged above the rest of the slick cleft. Adrianna's hands were down there too now, helping Diana hold it open, and she was rocking her pelvis against Diana's tongue.

"Stop!" Marc said, so forcefully that both women went still and Diana looked up.

He held in his hand a very large black dildo, so big Diana knew Adrianna would never take all of it—it had to be at least twelve inches in length. Even so, Marc said, "No more licking. Fuck her with this."

After taking the mammoth tool from Marc's hand, Diana glanced at Adrianna, who looked far more excited than worried, so Diana decided not to worry, either. Instead she found herself actually enjoying the task of easing the head of the massive rubber cock into

Adrianna's flushed passage. She'd never imagined she would have the ability or power to fuck a woman; she'd never even thought she *wanted* it. Yet here it was, and like all that had come before, it delivered a strange, unexpected thrill to be on the opposite end of sex from what she was accustomed to.

Her lady boss moaned above her, so she didn't hesitate, sliding more of the immense phallus into Adrianna's cunt. It continued gliding through her moisture with relative ease, and Diana remembered how deep and wide Adrianna's channel had looked, even *felt* to her tongue. So maybe Adrianna *could* take this whole colossal dildo. The idea excited Diana on a level she'd never imagined before and she wanted to see it happen. She pushed it farther and when she met a little resistance, drove it deeper still.

"God!" Adrianna cried, and as far as Diana could tell, it was a sound of surprised joy, not pain, so she pushed the black cock in until only a few inches remained, enough that she could wrap her fist around it and work it.

"Fuck her," Marc urged, and Diana began to move it in and out, in and out. Adrianna was moaning, groaning, gritting her teeth, holding her pussy open with her hands and watching, the same as her companions, as the dildo sank deep. Diana was amazed and aroused, her whole body beginning to feel tense, on edge. She experienced another moment of *I-can't-believe-this-is-happening* and an even more shocking moment of *And-I-can't-believe-I'm-enjoying-it*, but she couldn't deny the naughty pleasure that ran through her veins.

"Have you ever had a cock that huge, Adrianna?" Marc asked.

Still moaning, she shook her head.

"Bet you'll be looking for one now."

"Unh...yes, oh yes!"

Diana fucked Adrianna with the gigantic sex toy until her arm began to get tired, but Adrianna showed no signs of wanting to be rid of the massive shaft, and behind his mask, Marc looked mesmerized by the long strokes it made in and out of their boss's pussy.

Finally, just when she was beginning to think she'd be fucking Adrianna forever, Marc said, "Adrianna, take over. Fuck yourself with that big cock for me while I put Diana to work on *my* cock."

Diana waited until Adrianna had taken the tool from her, then turned to Marc, still kneeling. She'd hoped that whenever he was done having her pleasure Adrianna that perhaps he'd ask Adrianna to pleasure *her*. Her breasts ached to be touched, licked, and her pussy had soaked her leather panties eons ago. Instead, it appeared she was still the worker here, the slave.

Marc leaned back in the chair as she turned toward him, Adrianna's little moans filling the sex-laden air. "Come undo my pants, my little slave girl." He put his hands behind his head, as if leaning back to relax and enjoy.

Scooting up between his knees, Diana saw that the leather pants had two zippers on either side of his cock, like a fly. Reaching up with both hands, she lowered them simultaneously. Underneath, his hard cock was wrapped in a tight sack of black mesh. It looked so good there, so hard and powerful through the sheer fabric, that Diana momentarily forgot her frustrations and felt anxious to play with *this* sex toy.

Placing her palm on his hard steel through the mesh, she stroked it lightly.

"Take it out," he told her.

Using her hands to lower the stretchy mesh covering, she obeyed.

"Do you want it in your mouth, slave girl?"

Without taking her eyes from his large, lovely cock, she nodded.

"Then you may suck it."

Diana licked her lips, still tasting the remnants of Adrianna's salty moisture, then wrapped her fist around the base of his prominent shaft and lowered her mouth over it.

He let out a moan, murmuring, "Good little sex slave."

Liking his praise, she used her hand to deliver firm twisting strokes to the bottom of his rod, delivering the same sort of driving, rhythmic sucking with her mouth. Unlike last night when they'd been with Carter, when she'd worked so hard to relax and get Marc's full length in her mouth, tonight she went for sensation and power, taking only what she could suck with ease, but working his whole cock so vigorously that he had no complaints.

She lifted her gaze as she worked, meeting his eyes, in order to let him see his slave performing on him, her mouth going wide and round with each descent onto his magnificent erection.

Her body still ached and burned for attention, but she felt herself sinking more deeply into the game now, into the pleasures of true submission, of serving her master, of being deprived and neglected while she did his bidding, wanting only to please him.

She paid little attention when he reached down beside his chair, because his controlling gaze never left hers. But when she saw him reach over her with something dark in his hand, then felt the snapping sting on her ass, she jolted, releasing his cock from her mouth to look over her shoulder. She found him holding a rather wonderful and wicked-looking weapon—strips of leather that made her think of a horse's tail, extending from a dark, hard handle. She suspected it must be a cat-o'-nine-tails, and was only thankful that the blow she'd taken had not been as excruciating as what the original medieval weapon could deliver.

"Did I tell you to stop pleasuring me, slave?"

Her eyes were drawn back to his.

"Suck me," he demanded gruffly, and Diana felt compelled to obey.

She lowered her mouth back over his erection and returned to her sensual work, although it wasn't work at all, actually. Being his slave had now become something she was relishing, yearning for nothing more than to show him how deeply she wanted to satisfy and entertain her master.

When he struck her ass again with the leather whip, she cried out lightly as the sting spread pleasantly through her ass, pussy, and beyond. The next lash came a little harder—a little *better*. Her body was so hungry for attention that even this brought a pleasure she couldn't have anticipated.

Each stinging thrash echoed through her like a hot little explosion in her cunt, and still she worked away at her master's commanding cock, loving the way it filled her mouth, stretched it, wearied it. In that moment, she thought she could enjoy pleasuring him this way for hours, if that's what he wanted. In that moment, she didn't care if she never stopped sucking his big, beautiful shaft.

"Stop," he said, with impeccable timing.

And—oh, damn it—she didn't want to. She wanted him in her mouth.

Yet the choice wasn't hers and she knew that, so—with regret—she slowly let his cock slip from the warm confines of her lips. She stared up at him, her magnificent master in leather, his whipping tool in one hand, his majestic cock jutting up from his crotch, and wondered what was next.

"Adrianna, remove that monster cock from your cunt and stand up."

Diana and Marc both watched Adrianna slowly slide the enormous toy from her ultra-deep pussy. She let out a little sound of loss as the tip withdrew. Diana couldn't help noticing the expanded size of her passage before it slowly began to contract.

When Adrianna got to her feet, Marc instructed Diana to sit down where Adrianna had been. He reached into one of the bags at his side and drew out two long, black, strips of leather.

Rising from his chair with the strips in hand, he paused before Adrianna, dipping his head to one of her round breasts, sucking her nipple for a long moment, making Diana's pussy seem to cave in with the need that flowed through it, hot and thick and desperate. Jealous. She was jealous—and aroused, at the same time.

Releasing Adrianna's elongated nipple from his mouth, he walked behind Diana's chair. "Give me your hands."

She wasn't sure exactly what he meant, so she hesitated.

"Put them behind your back," he bit out harshly, sending another wave of lust lashing through her cunt.

Lowering her hands, she did as he said, realizing that the back of the chair was attached to the seat by only two thick pieces of wood connected from its arms, leaving a hollow opening between. So when she obeyed and put her hands behind her, he was easily able to reach them.

He crossed her wrists over one another, then began encircling them with one of the strips of leather. He was tying her up.

Her chest ached at the concept. She'd had the occasional boyfriend who wanted to tie her to the bed with scarves or some such sex play, but given Marc's tone through the game so far, being tied up by *him* made her both nervous and excited. He secured her tightly, leaving not a centimeter of wiggle room and making her feel truly helpless and at his mercy.

Next, he looped the other long leather strap around her shoulders. Pulling it tight across the top of her chest, he tied her securely to the chair. The combined effects of the bindings thrust her breasts forward and made them feel constricted. Her nipples tightened from the sensation and her pussy welled beneath the scrap of leather cupping it.

Returning to the front of her chair, Marc took a good long look at her, seeming to enjoy the sight of her bound.

Then he bent Adrianna over the other chair, which sat directly at a right angle from Diana's. Adrianna braced herself by gripping the arms of the chair, and Marc reached down to spread the vinyl as wide as possible around her pussy and anus.

He looked at Diana. "Now, slave girl, watch me fuck my other slave."

Positioning the head of his cock at Adrianna's ass, he drove his shaft inward in one smooth, slow stroke. Adrianna cried out slightly, but it was clear to Diana that her boss had been fucked in that opening before and that Marc knew it. As he began moving in and out, he reached up with one fist and grabbed a handful of her dark hair, pulling her head back.

"Are you watching, slave girl? Are you watching my cock slide in and out of this tight asshole?"

Diana's breasts were heaving, her whole body longing for...something, anything. "Yes," she said. "Oh, yes, master, I'm watching."

"Fuck me," Adrianna demanded. "Fuck me hard!"

Marc tugged again on her hair as he brought his other palm down with a hard slap across her ass. "You're out of line, slave! I give the orders here! But if you apologize very nicely, I *might* keep fucking you."

He went still inside Adrianna until finally she said—in the softest voice Diana had ever heard from her—"I'm very sorry, master. I didn't mean to give you an order."

"That's better. Now tell me what you want. Nicely."

"I want you to fuck me. I want you to fuck my ass so badly."

"Beg," he said, still holding tight to her hair.

Diana could see Adrianna pull in a hard, deep breath. "Please," she said, in a near-whimper. "Please fuck me. Please fuck my ass."

Slowly, Marc resumed driving his cock in and out of Adrianna while Diana watched, her eyes soaking up his every move. God, her body was on fire. She'd never wanted to touch herself so badly in her life. In total frustration, she pulled against the ties at her wrist, thinking—hoping—perhaps they weren't as strong as they seemed. The move only succeeded in making the tight leather strap slice into her soft skin and caused her breasts to push against the strip above them harder.

Her master cast a wicked grin in her direction as he continued banging his cock into Adrianna. "I knew you'd be tempted to play with your pussy, slave. That's why you're tied."

Diana sucked in her breath in aggravation. Torture, this was torture.

But no—you're his sex slave. Be a good little slave girl.

Her current circumstances gave a whole new, strange sort of meaning to the good girl concept, and she liked this one better. At least she could get into it. When being good meant doing whatever her lover wanted in order to please him sexually, it wasn't so hard.

Sit here and suffer—and enjoy it. Relish pleasuring him with your delicious torment while your pussy burns and your breasts ache. Oh God, what she wouldn't have given to just pinch her nipples, sink her fingers into her soaking cunt.

Watching his big cock slam in and out of Adrianna was wildly exciting, but it added infinitely to Diana's agony. Adrianna cried out with each punishing stroke, and he fucked her so hard and long that Diana almost began to feel solely like a spectator and wonder if he'd even forgotten she was there...until he finally looked over at her with another wanton smile.

"Is your pussy hot, sex slave?"

"Yes."

"Has it gotten hotter while you watched me fuck her?"

She nodded. "Oh yes."

"Well, my little slave girl, I think maybe I'll give *you* a reward now. Would you like that?"

"Oh yes, master, I would."

Extracting his slick hard-on from Adrianna, he said to her, "Kneel between the other slave's knees and take off her panties—slowly."

Adrianna complied, although Diana found lifting her ass off the chair challenging given her bindings. Still, Adrianna peeled down the leather g-string while Marc stood watching, and when she got the panties to Diana's knees, he said, "Use your mouth now."

Without hesitating, Adrianna took the scant leather panties between her teeth and tugged them down over Diana's boots until they were free.

Adrianna rested on her hands and knees, and Marc told her to stay that way until he knelt behind her and reinserted his cock in her ass. As she groaned her acceptance of the shaft, Diana experienced a crushing disappointment—she'd been so sure he would fuck *her* now.

"Lick Diana's pussy," he instructed Adrianna, and Diana sighed with relief. Finally, something for her.

Her hands remained tied, her whole body strapped to the chair, but she eagerly spread her legs up over the arms, inching as close to the edge as her bindings allowed so Adrianna could reach her with ease.

Diana knew her master was watching closely as Adrianna dragged her tongue up Diana's cunt. After what that poor piece of flesh had endured for the last hour, one lick felt like fireworks exploding in her clit.

She let out a cry of pure pleasure and Marc looked at her. "Do you like that, sex slave?"

"Yes, master, yes." She wasn't even thinking about the fact that it was a woman delivering the pleasure—only that it was what she needed.

His next words were directed to Adrianna. "Hold her pussy open as wide as you can so I can see how pink she is."

Adrianna settled her arms across the fishnet clinging to Diana's thighs and used her hands to spread Diana's outer lips. She stretched them so far that Diana moaned—not because it hurt, but because *any* touch on her poor cunt right now signaled pleasure, and because it thrilled her to have the depths of her pink folds so very exposed.

"Now eat her," Marc instructed, and Adrianna obeyed, delivering a barrage of licks and kisses to Diana's needy cunt. He fucked Adrianna with pounding strokes and she applied pressure to Diana's sweet flesh in rhythm with his thrusts. "Ah, yes, slave, eat that pretty pink pussy," he demanded as he pummeled Adrianna.

Diana soaked it all up. Her bindings continued to keep her from moving a great deal, but she lifted herself against Adrianna's mouth as much as possible. After a long, lush series of licks, Adrianna fastened her lips over Diana's clit, then ran her tongue around it, French kissing it. It was one of Diana's favorite techniques to use on a cock and she was nearly overwhelmed by how incredible it felt on her clit. "Yes, yes, suck it, yes," she moaned as she felt what was certain to be the greatest release of all time collecting inside her, pulling tight inside her pussy, gathering strength—

"Stop eating her."

At Marc's command, Adrianna immediately released Diana's clit from her mouth.

Diana let out a long, harsh cry of frustration, gritting her teeth as she glared at Marc. "I was just about to come and you knew it!" she exploded.

At that, Marc ceased moving in and out of Adrianna's ass. Only then, feeling his fierce stare, did she realize what she'd done, remembering she was his slave tonight and not supposed to protest anything.

From the expression on his face—the part she could see, anyway—she knew she'd fucked up. All that was left now was finding out how she was going to pay for it.

"You dare to yell at me, slave?"

Her stomach lurched with added nervousness. "I'm...I'm sorry. I don't know what came over me. Forgive me, master."

But Marc only shook his head. "It's too late for that, Diana. You've been a bad little sex slave and now you'll have to be punished."

Chapter Eight

Diana's heartbeat kicked up with a thrill of fear and rabid curiosity. When she'd agreed to this little game, she'd not realized what she was getting into. She'd not realized how seriously Marc would take it, and she'd certainly never anticipated her own depth of involvement—that she would experience a sense of true submission, that she would call him master and mean it.

Even now, when she begged his forgiveness, she felt true remorse, sorry she'd been so impatient, that she hadn't been a good slave to him. Now, she had no idea what to expect, no idea what sexual punishment this darker side of her lover might create for her.

She thought of the safe word: *ice-cream man.*

She could say it if she wanted, if whatever he proposed was too much for her.

But she didn't think she would.

Even in bondage, she thought that whatever Marc wanted her to do, she would be willing.

Marc withdrew his cock from Adrianna and even now—seeing it so slick with her boss's juices, jutting up from the opening in his leather pants—Diana wanted it. In her mouth, in her cunt, between her breasts, she didn't care.

But she knew she wasn't going to get it, because he knew how much she loved his cock and that she'd never consider it punishment. Instead, he walked over to the bag

Adrianna had carried into the room and drew something out. When he turned to face them, Diana saw the big strap-on shaft he held.

Her heart nearly stopped, her pussy froze. The flesh-colored dildo was not as big as the black one she'd used on Adrianna, but was still ominously large. It served as the centerpiece for a number of black leather straps that appeared to buckle closed.

Keeping a stern gaze on Diana, he held the apparatus out to Adrianna, who'd stood up next to him. "Put this on and fuck her with it."

Diana's heart resumed beating at about triple speed as she watched her boss strap on the sizable rubber phallus. The straps circled Adrianna's waist and thighs so that the dildo stood erect on her in exactly the same spot as if she were a man. The cock itself appeared longer than Marc's, and thicker. It looked downright threatening rising above Adrianna's pussy.

"Do you wish me to fuck her where she is, tied up?"

Marc walked to the bed and retrieved the pillows. "Yes, slave," he said, placing them on the floor in front of Diana so that Adrianna could kneel on them, bringing her strapped-on dildo to the right height. After that, he settled back in his original chair for a close-up view.

Diana trembled as Adrianna leaned in, pressing the head of the dildo against her cunt. What would this be like? Would the thickness rip her apart? Would the size make her scream in pain?

Ice-cream man. Should she say it? Should she end the game?

She glanced over at her master, and even as he watched her pussy with anticipation, she remembered—

this was Marc, her lover, her friend. He was playing a role tonight, as was she. And he was playing it seriously, but he wouldn't really hurt her. She knew that.

And as she shifted her eyes to Adrianna's, which were filled with heat as she slowly drove her pseudo-cock into Diana's passage, she knew this would be all right.

Even if it hurt.

Because she was his sex slave tonight. His wish was her command.

To her complete surprise, her cunt was so needy that it swallowed the strap-on dick without problems. Certainly the phallus filled her deeply — to a degree which she'd never been filled before — but she was experiencing far more pleasure than pain. Adrianna pushed it in all the way to the hilt, their pussies nearly touching, and the utter fullness made Diana emit a dirty little moan.

"Does that feel good, Miss Marsh?" Adrianna asked in her usual, more refined voice.

"God, yes."

Adrianna leaned in and gently kissed her lips, then slowly began to fuck her with the strap-on.

"This is my very favorite sex toy, Miss Marsh," she purred, their lips barely parted as she delivered short but pleasant thrusts. "I love having the ability to fuck a woman."

Of course she did, Diana thought. Because until Marc did something to change the tempo again, he'd given Adrianna what she cherished most, power. Perhaps Diana had even *understood* that kind of power when she'd wielded the other massive toy inside her boss. But she didn't mind — in fact, she'd almost missed the powerful side of Adrianna she'd so quickly come to know. As

Adrianna's strokes became longer, more intense, Diana drank it in, enjoying Adrianna's control over her. She moaned at each stroke of Adrianna's false cock. This felt much closer to being fucked by a real cock than she'd expected, and seeing Adrianna behind the mighty phallus, with her high, full breasts and her long, voluminous hair, added to Diana's arousal. The obscene vision struck her senses, once again giving her the impression of being part of something surreal and dreamy. What made it even better was having Marc orchestrate this, and now having him watch.

As Adrianna's thrusts filled her again and again, drawing groans of pleasure from her throat, Diana studied every nuance and detail of the scene she was a part of. Her eyes focused on Adrianna's large, lovely breasts held aloft in the bra, then dropped to the tight black straps that held her fucking tool so securely in place over her revealing skintight vinyl undies. She looked down at her own body—her breasts straining against the tight leather strap above them, her rosy nipples, distended and wanting, the snug black corset that made her look and feel like a sex toy, her naked pussy underneath, accepting that big rod jutting from Adrianna's pelvis over and over again.

As she cried out, pushing against it, her eyes went to Adrianna's face, taking in the slender woman's piercing eyes, the pale patrician features contorted with lusty exertion. Then she shifted her gaze to Marc—her master. He sat in the chair next to her, watching with a quiet hunger that somehow leaked through his mask. His tremendous cock remained at full attention between his legs.

His eyes slowly rose to meet hers.

"Oooh," she cried out at Adrianna's next thrust.

A slow, wicked smile crept onto his face. "You're being a good little slave again, letting my other slave put that big cock in you."

"Thank you, master," she said just before giving another mewling cry of pleasure.

"Mmm, yes, a good little slave," he said, beginning to fondle his dick.

He rose from his chair and began to meander slowly around the two women, studying them from different angles, views. As Diana sank deeper into her role, taking more and more pleasure from Adrianna's fucking, Marc made his way back behind her chair.

Diana nearly died from unexpected pleasure as his strong hands eased down her shoulders, over the leather tie, and onto her breasts. She moaned nonstop as he caressed them, seeming to multiply the sensations echoing through her flesh. He lightly pinched her nipples between his caressing fingers, and she let her eyes fall shut, soaking up any and all sensations that reverberated outward. He'd teased her for so long that now each touch, each thrust, held ten times its normal power.

"Does this feel good, slave girl?"

"Mmm, yes, master." Her voice was a mere whimper.

He let his hands slide upward, his fingers toying with the strap that bound her to the chair even as he continued delivering light touches to her nipples. "Do you like being tied up?"

She turned her head to look at him. "For you, master."

He smiled. "That will earn you more rewards, slave."

"Oh, thank you, master."

He withdrew his hands, and she sensed him working at the tie that crossed her breasts until it fell away, giving her a freedom that felt strange and unreal. Next he worked at the binding around her wrists until it, too, loosened and slipped off. When she began to pull her arms back around to the front, her shoulders ached, her muscles felt tired and abused—but in a good way. Because she was in such a submissive mindset, she truly didn't mind experiencing a little pain if it brought him pleasure.

His voice was a hot whisper in her ear. "Can you take more, slave girl?"

"More of what?" Now that her hands were free, she took the opportunity to indulge her urges—she reached up to cup the outer side of Adrianna's vinyl-surrounded breasts, stroking her thumbs over the lovely nipples.

"More of that big strap-on cock."

Her hands froze as she looked at him. "How could there be more? She's fucking me to the hilt with it already." She cried out as the shaft rammed into her, proving her point.

"Just tell me if you can take more."

Diana's body was assailed with a strange, hard pleasure—pleasure she wanted more of. "For you, master, yes. Whatever you like."

His satisfied little smile reappeared. "Good girl."

With that, he instructed Adrianna to go lie down on Diana's bed. When she withdrew her big tool, Diana felt empty.

Marc propped the fluffy pillows up for Adrianna to lay her head on, and with her vinyl bondage-wear and her strap-on, the boss looked deliciously obscene.

Lying next to Adrianna on the bed, Marc lifted a hand, motioning for Diana to stand up. Her legs felt weak upon rising.

"Go into the bathroom," he instructed her, "and come back with a soapy wash cloth."

She did as he said and when she returned, he told her, "Now, slave, wash my cock."

She met his eyes as she stood next to the bed cleaning him, pleased to feel his hardness through the terrycloth. She wrapped the soapy cloth around him and moved it up and down, making him release a light moan as he lay propped on his elbows, watching her toil. She supposed it was because he'd been in Adrianna's ass and planned to be someplace else soon. She could only hope it was her pussy he had in mind. Maybe he was only teasing her about taking more of the strap-on—maybe he'd only been priming her for his perfect cock.

When she'd thoroughly cleaned him, he said, "Good. Now, go get another wet cloth and rinse off the soap."

She hurried, anxious to leave him completely clean and fresh for her.

Once she'd carefully removed all the soap suds from his shaft as they all three watched, she lay the wet cloth aside and said, "What next?"

"Ride her cock," he instructed, pointing at Adrianna, speaking in a soft, sexy, but deliberate tone that reminded her more of the man she'd come to know these past few exciting days.

That's what he'd meant by taking more. To ride it would be to put her weight on it, to make herself feel it even more deeply. He hadn't just been teasing her.

One part of her couldn't help being disappointed, but her submissive self didn't even hesitate—she simply climbed onto the bed to straddle the beautiful and kinky Adrianna, balanced her pussy at the head of the strap-on, and lowered herself onto it.

Down, down, all the way, slow and sure and deep, until she rested on Adrianna's hips, suffering a sensation she'd only felt in small doses before—pleasure/pain. Forcing the big dildo so deeply into her cunt made her cry out, and for a fraction of a second she feared she *couldn't* take it because the cock pressed into her so hard and unrelenting. Yet the pain came with a strange, thick pleasure so intense she felt attacked by it. She felt the intrusion of the too-big cock vibrate out through every part of her body, sensation echoing through her fingers and toes.

"Is it okay, baby?"

The voice—Marc's, not her master's—drew her eyes to his. Even through the mask, she understood instantly that he wasn't in game mode now, that he was afraid she was suffering.

"It…It…" Her breath came hard. "It hurts and feels good at the same time."

"You can stop if you want."

Without even weighing it, though, she shook her head. She was his slave tonight and he was taking her places so new that they hurt, but she still wanted to experience them, wanted to understand the satisfaction she sensed this could bring.

"Are you sure?"

"Yes. I want it. I want to feel everything. With you. For you. I'm your slave."

Her heartfelt declaration brought Marc to his knees next to her. He lifted his hands to her face, turning her to meet his butterfly-soft kiss. "So fucking sweet," he whispered, then kissed her deeper, their tongues twining.

Without quite planning it, she reached out one hand, gripping his thigh through his leather pants. Then she moved it higher, closing it around his marvelous erection, still solid and huge in her fist.

His voice emerged ragged, impassioned, when they stopped kissing. "Such a good, sweet little sex slave. So submissive. So giving. So fucking hot."

He glanced down to where Adrianna's body met hers, the strap-on cock still buried deep inside Diana. With his eyes there, and with his sexy kisses and words still filling her senses, she instinctively began to move in small little circles that rubbed every part of her pussy just the right way as she rode the enormous dildo. In that moment, wanting to do this for him was the biggest part of her, all she could see or feel.

"God, baby, you're so good," Marc murmured.

Diana bit her lip, the pleasure/pain still warring inside her, but pleasure was slowly winning.

"How is it, baby?"

She couldn't speak, just moaned, trying to let him know she was all right. Reaching down, she closed both her hands over Adrianna's superb breasts, the ultra-soft flesh urging her to knead it as the hard nipples jutted up into her palms like pebbles. Adrianna gasped and smiled at her, gingerly lifting her pelvis to meet Diana's hot, slow movements. Diana clenched her teeth at the added pressure, tension. The pain persisted, yet somehow it was so good, still arousing her, still making her cunt respond.

"Do you like my big cock in your tight little pussy, Miss Marsh?" Diana would never have believed such a question could sound at once so dirty and so dignified, but Adrianna made it that way.

"Yes," she gritted out.

Adrianna's hands found Diana's breasts and began to caress them, as well. The pleasure, added to what she felt below, was positively searing.

"Do you like how big it is?" Adrianna asked.

Diana groaned as a particularly punishing stroke pummeled her depths. "So big I almost can't stand it," she managed to say roughly, "but yes. Yes."

Next to Adrianna, Marc was watching, clearly entranced, but now he put his arm around Adrianna's shoulder and softly instructed her, "Sit up. Sit up so you can kiss each other while you fuck." With that, he helped Adrianna gain an upright position while Diana stayed mounted on her.

Diana immediately began kissing Adrianna's lovely, aristocratic mouth, and fondling her large, pointed breasts. She'd been starved for sexual attention for so long earlier, tortured by Marc's little game, that she was still hot and hungry for satiation. The pleasure in her body blocked out the pain more each second until soon she was riding Adrianna's big strap-on just as eagerly as she would have if it had been Marc's cock.

The two women abandoned touching each other's breasts and instead just rubbed them together—although Diana's chest hovered slightly above Adrianna's, their new position allowed them to brush and press their breasts against each other with arousing ease.

"That's right, my two hot fuck slaves. Rub those beautiful nipples together for your master."

His words made Diana even more excited as she fucked and kissed and caressed their boss. His eyes on her as she obeyed his every command multiplied her pleasure exponentially.

Next to them, Marc began to rise up onto his feet on the bed until his cock was level with Diana's face. She bit her lip and smiled up at him.

He smiled back. "Suck on it, slave."

"My *extreme* pleasure, master," she cooed, passion gathering in her chest.

He moved a little closer so that she was able to reach out with her open mouth and capture the head without using her hands. As she rode Adrianna's big toy, he slid his cock gently in and out of her hungry mouth.

Adrianna clearly wanted to be part of this, too, and her slightly lower position allowed her to lick his round balls.

Marc growled his satisfaction as they worked their mouths on him, and Diana knew she would come soon. Every part of her body was now involved in some form of fucking, and the sensations were building fast and strong inside her. Her entire being seemed on the brink of sexual explosion, but of course the hard crux of her pleasure centered in her pussy, which now rode Adrianna's dildo with fervent delight.

"Your master wants you both to come," Marc said through clenched teeth. "I want you to come hard and furious, and when you're both done, I'm gonna come all over your hot, pretty nipples."

All he had to do was ask—the mere words pushed Diana over the edge of pleasure into a deep, all-consuming, very naughty and satisfying bliss. She didn't release her master's cock from her mouth, though; she simply cried out around it as she pressed hard—her pussy, her breasts—into Adrianna. Just as Marc had wanted, it was a harsh, grueling orgasm that seemed to batter her entire body with the intensity of its force.

Just as the demanding waves receded, Adrianna began crying out as well. "I'm coming, I'm coming! Oh yes, I'm coming for you both!"

Diana enjoyed being so very near to her as she climaxed, her body rocking, breasts bouncing, that incredible strap-on dick thrusting even deeper into Diana's pussy—but she was so wet, and opened so deep now, that pain had diminished completely and all she felt was the incredible fullness.

She concentrated on sucking her master's lovely cock while Adrianna returned her mouth to the two tight globes below.

"So soon, so fucking soon, I'm gonna come on you both."

Diana sucked harder and listened to him groan and curse beneath his breath, as he pulled back from her lips. "Beg me for it, slaves."

Both of them held up their breasts, pushing them together to create a bounty of soft flesh for him to shoot on. "Master, please come on us! Please come, master!" Diana implored, as Adrianna said, "Come on our breasts!"

He groaned with the first spurt of fluid, which spattered diagonally across one of Adrianna's breasts and onto Diana's. The second and third bursts showered mainly Diana's round curves, so he eked out a few more drops on Adrianna, using his hand.

Kneeling next to them on the bed, he helped both women rub his semen into their breasts as they massaged and kneaded each other, as well.

When they were both shiny and sticky, Diana sensually licked her lips and looked up at Marc. "Did we please you, master?"

He leaned over to give her a firm, passionate kiss, then delivered another to Adrianna. "Perfect slaves," he said with a wicked, satisfied grin.

* * * * *

Marc watched as Adrianna slipped on the dress she'd arrived in, dropped her strap-on in the bag, then said, "Thank you both for a lovely evening," before sashaying out the door.

Marc slid off his mask, turning to Diana, who lay next to him in bed. "Never much of a cuddler," he said of Adrianna with a laugh, before turning more serious. "I'm glad, though. Glad to be alone with you for awhile."

Lifting his hand to Diana's cheek, he lowered a kiss to her slightly swollen lips. Nuzzling her afterward, he said, "Did you enjoy it?"

Lying back on her pillow, she looked introspective. "It went in waves for me," she began. "At first I was enjoying it, but then I got so frustrated. Even as I was frustrated, though, I really wanted to submit and pleasure you, really wanted to be your slave."

Her words drew a sensual smile from him, even as they managed to get his cock to perk back to life. "Domination is about trust, and you trusted me not to make you do anything that wouldn't bring you pleasure. You also trusted me to bring you pleasure in the end. It...touches me that you trusted me, and that you wanted to give yourself over to me so completely before it was through."

Her hazel eyes looked incredibly green tonight, seeming to sparkle with tiny gold diamonds as she spoke so softly that she sounded like a young girl. "I don't think I could have fucked that big strap-on if I hadn't been so inspired to please you."

Her sentiments were so open, so earnest, that Marc's chest tightened with emotion. "Was it okay? I mean..." He felt like a shit now, thinking he'd made her do something that *hadn't* been entirely pleasurable. "Is your beautiful pussy okay? Does it hurt?" On instinct, he reached down beneath the covers they'd pulled up and began to gently stroke the smooth flesh between her legs.

"It's fine now," she promised with a smile. "And like I said, I wanted to do it for you. For me, too. To see if I could. And because it made me feel incredibly gratified to be a good slave girl to you."

Damn, it was like there was a physical line between her mouth and his cock—every word she said pulled it more taut. "My only regret is that I let us all come before I got to fuck you." He leaned over to drop a tender kiss high on one breast. "Do you have any idea how incredibly hot you looked, sweetheart?" He ran his hand up onto the boning of her waist cincher. "I love this. And the fishnet stockings and boots." He released a small growling sound to express exactly how much he'd enjoyed her Sinsuous leather and other accoutrements. "Your breasts are so lovely," he told her, lowering a kiss to one beaded pink nipple. "And your sweet little pussy makes me hard just to think of it. Are you sure it's okay? It doesn't hurt?"

She shrugged. "Not really. It might be a little sore later, but..."

"Maybe I should kiss it and make it feel better." He couldn't stop himself from kissing his way down her delectable curves until finally his lips were on the cleft of her cunt. He'd helped take off her boots and stockings before crawling under the covers, and now her legs curled around his upper back as he licked her moist, welcoming flesh.

She released small, pretty moans with each lick, and he found himself hoping his ministrations truly might soothe any discomfort he'd caused her to feel. Although she hadn't complained, he thought now that he'd gotten too deep into his own game, perhaps been too confident that he knew what would bring her the most pleasure in the end. Of course, it seemed to have worked, but still...he'd played such games with women in the past and never before had he felt so strange afterward, at once thrilled by her acquiescence and dismayed by his insensitivity. All his feelings for her were coming on so damn strong he barely knew what to make of it.

Not that it mattered. Seemed he was constantly having to remind himself of that. This was just pre-settling-down play for her and he was just a guy she might remember fondly someday.

That stung a little, but he pushed it aside and forced himself back into the moment, where he was laving her sweet, wet pussy with all the passion he possessed.

Crawling back up her body, he began feeling playful, so he reached over beside the pillow where he'd discarded her stockings and picked one up. Easing her arms up over her head, he kissed her lush mouth and slid the fishnet around her wrists. He didn't tie her tightly this time, just loosely confined her.

Raining kisses across her cheeks, neck, shoulders, he grinned and whispered, "I want inside your cunt, slave girl."

She returned the teasing smile. "Mmm, fuck me, master."

"I'll be gentle," he promised, and he meant it. Slowly he nudged his cock into the warm cave of her pussy until he was snug inside.

Beneath him, she bit her lip in that sexy way of hers and lifted her head slightly to kiss him. As he moved tenderly in and out of her wetness, he lowered more kisses to her mouth, her breasts, and then —

God, he came. It struck without warning and was unstoppable — he was suddenly groaning as he emptied into her sweet body and wondering what the hell had happened. He'd never come so fast in his life, not even his first time when he'd been sixteen and horny as hell.

He laid his head on her breast. "I'm sorry. I don't know why I…"

"That's okay," she said, stroking his hair. "I'll take it as a compliment."

He exchanged a playful smile with her, even laughed. This woman was…doing things to him. Things he didn't want to admit or think about. She was making him want to do way more than fuck her, way more than even hang out talking and laughing with her.

"I wish I could stay with you tonight," he said. He wanted to fall asleep like this, his head nestled on her soft breast. He wanted to wake up next to her tomorrow morning.

She lifted her head slightly, jarring his rest. "You can't?"

He propped himself on one elbow next to her. "I'm expecting a call from Paris at six a.m., which is noon there. I have to be sure I'm home to take it, and I'm afraid if I fall asleep here, I might not be." He cringed. It was the truth, yet it sounded weak. "I'm sorry, sweetheart, but it's important."

She nodded easily. "You don't have to apologize. I understand."

Of course she did, he thought. He'd told her getting this job in Paris was the biggest thing in his life right now; he'd made her believe it was as significant to *him* as marrying Bradley and making her parents happy seemed to *her*. And he'd meant it.

But if Paris was so damn important, why was it so difficult for him to get up out of her bed, put his clothes on, and leave?

"Can I ask you something?" Diana said.

"Anything."

She looked shockingly innocent peering into his eyes. "Why did you only fuck Adrianna in the ass?"

He blinked, a little surprised she'd noticed. "Well, I guess, for some reason...I don't know...I just didn't want to be inside her pussy." He let out a sigh, then a confession. "I guess I just wanted to save doing that with you." He shook his head. "Does that make any sense at all?"

She smiled. "Mmm hmm, and I'm glad. I kind of...didn't actively encourage Carter in that direction, either…for the same reason. But I didn't know if it made any sense, either, so I didn't mention it to you."

He gave her a soft grin and fought down the emotion filling him. "We'd better watch out, sweetheart, or we might just get attached to each other and then all of our plans will be ruined." Bradley for her. Paris for him.

She looked as uncertain as he felt when she smiled tightly and said in a small voice, "Well, we'll just have to make sure that doesn't happen."

As he drove home a few minutes later, a strange melancholy overtook him. Even the bright lights of the Vegas strip couldn't break through it—he barely saw them, or heard the traffic. His mind was back at the Venetian with a certain incredibly "sinuous" brunette who, at moments, made Paris feel like it would be the most boring place on earth if she wasn't there to share it with him.

* * * * *

The next day, Diana arrived at the Adrianna, Inc. offices early. Funny, after the previous nights' activities, she'd have expected to feel exhausted, but instead she'd awakened at dawn, showered and dressed quickly, and even partaken of the large buffet at one of the hotel restaurants. Apparently she'd worked up an appetite last night.

She felt rather sheepish about the idea of bumping into Adrianna, but she was looking forward to seeing Marc. He'd been so wild and forceful early in the evening, but later he'd become soft and sweet and loving, reinforcing for her that the master and slave game was only that—a game, one which she just happened to play very well.

Stepping off the elevator, she found Holly's desk empty, and was walking down the hall toward the conference room where the catalog team spent time brainstorming when the bathroom door opened directly in front of her. Adrianna walked out, looking as prim and proper as ever in a plum Christian Dior suit, a small pair of glasses balanced on her nose, her hair pulled back in a low bun.

Studying the papers she carried, she barely glanced up at Diana. "Good morning, Miss Marsh."

"Good morning," Diana returned, but her boss was already past her and still immersed in her work.

Well, *that* had been easier than she'd anticipated. Not much of a cuddler, to say the least, she thought, bemused with her mysterious employer. She was relieved Adrianna had handled it so...well, so much as if it hadn't even happened.

Although she was glad to have had the experience, glad to have played Marc's sexually daring game, Diana had also awakened thinking maybe she'd found the one aspect of sex that wasn't really *her*. Yes, she'd come to enjoy calling Marc "master" and submitting to his will, and she'd even enjoyed Adrianna's softness, but if they had occasion to do that again, she planned to request it be a party for two. She still found Adrianna wildly attractive and alluring in her power, but something inside Diana was beginning to feel there were certain things she wanted to share only with Marc.

She pulled up short just outside the conference room, realizing what an asinine thought she'd just had. *Things she wanted to share only with Marc?*

Whenever the catalog was put to bed, she'd share nothing more with Marc than an occasional phone call at work, and if he moved to Paris, not even that. It was hard for her to imagine him suddenly not being in her life.

But that was how things were going to be. She was going home to be a good girl, and he was going overseas to seek excitement.

Letting out a sigh, she continued on her way into the room, sinking into the nearest chair. Opening her briefcase, she pulled out her laptop and began checking e-mail, answering a few of the more important ones.

"Hey."

She looked up to see Marc come in. He carried his briefcase and a white bakery bag.

"Donut?" he asked with a smile, holding up the bag in an offer to share.

"No thanks." As usual lately, seeing him made her heart do a little flip-flop as she gently patted her stomach. "I just stuffed myself on the buffet at the Venetian."

He leaned his head back in understanding. "I usually skip breakfast, but was hungrier than usual today, too." He concluded with a wink.

"Did you get your call from Paris?"

He nodded, but didn't offer any information.

"And?" she prodded.

He sat down across from her. "Well, things look good. I'm their top choice. They have two other guys yet to interview, but my contact there said in all likelihood they'll offer me the job." He'd relayed it all in a matter-of-fact voice, as if they were discussing day-to-day business.

She raised her eyebrows slightly. "You don't sound very excited about it."

He blinked, suddenly seeming to come awake, his eyes taking on the spark she was used to. "I am," he said. "Definitely. But I don't like to count my chickens before they're hatched, or my jobs before they're offered, know what I mean?"

She nodded, but she still didn't think he seemed as enthused as he should.

"So," he said, flashing a smile, "what's up for tonight? Or have I so totally exhausted you that you're gonna kick me out of your life for an evening?"

"Well, it's true you've totally worn me out, but...I have way too much fun with you to turn you down."

His grin widened. "That's what I like to hear. So, any ideas on what you'd like to do?"

"What, you don't have a plan for us? Even if I end up calling the shots sometimes, you usually have a plan to at least start us out."

His smile turned slightly sheepish. "That's why I'm asking *you*. I thought after last night, it might be considerate of me to let *you* decide what we do tonight."

She tilted her head, thinking, but it didn't take long before she came up with something. "You know what I'd really enjoy?"

"What?"

"This will probably sound boring to you, especially since you live here, but...I would really love to tour the strip tonight. You know, look around some of the big hotels, do a little gambling, that sort of thing." Her nose wrinkled into a doubtful sneer. "Would that be a total drag?"

Across the table, he bit into a glazed donut and laughed. "Actually, it sounds like fun."

His response made her smile. "Really?"

He leaned slightly forward. "I would *love* to spend a night on the town with you."

* * * * *

Marc couldn't have been more pleased at the prospect of spending an evening alone with Diana—*finally*. When he knocked on the door of her room at the Venetian, she answered in a simple but elegant short black cocktail dress that hugged every curve on her gorgeous body. Although she usually wore her tawny hair straight, tonight it was curled into sexy spirals that gave her a whole new look.

"Have I mentioned that every time I look at you my cock gets hard?" he asked, flashing a seductive grin without even planning to.

She laughed, twining her slender arms loosely about his neck. "I thought that's what happened when you thought about my pussy."

He met her gaze and hoped she saw the fire mixed in with his amusement. "That, too. Sweetheart, pretty much everything about you gets me hot, fast."

She drew one hand down, flattening her palm against the bulge in his pants, which he was pretty sure had become the equivalent of a marble pillar. "Oooh," she purred, her hazel eyes looking sexy as sin.

"Like what you feel?" he asked teasingly.

"*So* much." As if to prove it, she pressed her body flush against his, crushing her soft, lovely cunt against his hard-on before she delivered a provocative tongue kiss.

It took all the strength he possessed to gently separate them to arm's length as he cast a warning look her way. "We can't start that this early or we'll never get out of the room."

He loved that she looked disappointed.

"But later," he promised, lowering his voice to a raspy whisper, "I'm gonna fuck you so good you'll never forget it."

She licked her lips in reply.

"Which reminds me," he said, "did you happen to pack a swimsuit?"

She glanced over her shoulder toward the armoire. "Yes, but given the hours we've been keeping, I haven't had a chance to even think about going to the pool. Why?"

"Toss it in a bag or in your purse. As for why, that's a little surprise for later." When she planted her hands on her hip in mock scolding, he laughed. "I know, I know, I told you tonight was yours to plan, but when an opportunity came up for me to add something at the end, I couldn't resist."

"That's okay," she said. "I love your surprises."

Chapter Nine

After putting her white bikini in her purse at Marc's request, Diana took his arm and they headed toward the elevator. He admitted then that he actually had a *few* surprises in mind for her. "Nothing too shocking," he promised with a grin, "but just a few fun things for your night on the strip."

His first surprise was only steps away, an elegant Italian restaurant called Canaletti, right in the Venetian, overlooking the Grand Canal. The ceilings seemed to rise a mile above the shiny hardwood floors, and the ornate setting was accented with arched windows reminiscent of European cathedrals. They were shown to a luxurious booth that seemed to envelop them and gave off an intense feeling of intimacy.

Over dinner, they talked—about the catalog, about the enigmatic Adrianna, about the wild, glorious sex they'd shared since her arrival, but also about other things, as well. Marc told her a little about his family, who resided in Scottsdale, where he'd been born and raised. His father was a retired cop who'd come west from New York in his twenties after meeting Marc's mother while she was visiting her Italian grandparents in Little Italy.

"That makes you, what—one-eighth Italian?"

He shook his head. "A full half, actually. My mother was the first girl in her family to break ranks and marry a non-Italian. My father is lucky, though. Unlike me, he can cook. He makes a mean risotto," he added on a laugh, "and that's about the only hope he had of proving himself worthy of my mother's family."

He went on to tell her he was the oldest of four children, two boys and two girls, "which meant I got away with the most. By the time my brother and sisters became teenagers, my parents were wise to my tricks. I wasn't a *bad* kid," he went on, "but…well, I guess I was kind of the same as I am today. I was a good enough kid, but I liked to party, experiment, have fun, so I was definitely the wild one in my family."

Diana laughed, feeling a whole new kinship with him. "As I've told you before, I'm definitely the official Marsh family wild child, too."

He gazed deeply into her eyes, and even though she knew he'd done that before, somehow it affected her more profoundly now. "That must explain why we fit so well together."

She smiled, reminded once more of Holly's similar remark on her first day in the office. The more time they spent in each other's company, both at work and at play, the less she could deny the truth of it.

After dinner, they strolled along the Grand Canal and Marc surprised her with the gondola ride she'd requested days earlier. They drifted along beneath the faux Venetian sky, their gondolier crooning a quaint Italian song while other gondolas floated past. Wrapped up in the romantic experience, Diana found herself enraptured with the man whose arm she clung to.

"What's next on my evening of surprises?" she asked as they finally exited the hotel.

He raised his eyebrows playfully. "That's for me to know…"

She grinned. "And me to find out."

They grabbed a taxi and Marc instructed the driver to take them to the Stratosphere.

"Is that the tall, needle-like building?" she asked, almost embarrassed by her ignorance of the town.

He pointed as they approached it. "Yeah, and we're going all the way to the top, sweetheart."

Luckily, Diana was as fearless about heights as she was about sex. So much so that when she found out there was a rollercoaster atop the Stratosphere, she insisted they ride it before even taking in the view from the observation deck.

It was a tame coaster compared to most, but admittedly, being propelled around the tower on the narrow, winding track elevated nearly a thousand feet above the Las Vegas Strip was breathtaking both in terms of the view and her heart rate.

As they came off the ride, Diana adjusted her clingy "little black dress" and said to Marc with a sexy smile, "That ride got me a little excited." Indeed, her pussy was humming as much as the rest of her body—something about the dark and the rush of wind on the coaster, maybe the way it had jostled her body, maybe the way she and her lover had sat crushed so tightly together in the tiny car, had her sense of adventure high and her body buzzing with anticipation. "What next?" she asked.

"Next," he said, his smile telling her he was enjoying her enthusiasm, "we visit the observation deck and take in the view."

"Oh yeah, I almost forgot." It sounded a little too serene for her at the moment, but romantic, too, so she let Marc take her hand and lead her there.

As she stepped up to the wired fence at the edge, Marc settled behind her, easing his arms around her waist. Like on the coaster, the wind was that same dry, warm breeze she'd already become accustomed to in Vegas. The strip stretched below them in the distance like a winding neon river, each side battling to be more ablaze with lights and excitement than the other. Up here, she felt almost disconnected from it, but also as if she could almost see the magic emanating up from this place that so filled her senses. She had the urge to get back to the ground, to sink into the city's wondrous offerings, yet she also liked viewing it this way, from a distance, where, even though the hotels looked so small she felt as though she could hold them in her hand, she could still feel the life pulsing collectively from the illuminated boulevard below. Marc's warm caresses—his fingers moving lazily over her stomach, hips, and waist—only intensified her sense of somehow coming alive in this place in a way she never truly had before.

It was only when one of his hands began to inch downward onto her thigh, toward the hem of her dress, that she realized they were alone, the only people in sight on the dimly lit deck.

Since the thrill of the rollercoaster still echoed through her cunt, she bit her lip, looked out over the city of lights, and parted her legs just enough that once he'd reached under her dress, he could feel her pussy with ease.

His fingers first met the silk of the tiny thong she wore, but he used them to pull the fabric aside. The warm breeze blew over her mound at the same moment his fingers pressed into her slit.

"Mmm," she purred hotly as his touch reverberated through her body.

"Wet," he breathed in her ear. "So wet on my fingertips."

She began to move against them without thought, to undulate in the hot, tight circles that brought her the greatest pleasure. Within moments, she heard his fingers sliding in her juices, adding to her arousal.

His free hand rose to her breast, cupping and fondling it through her dress. The dress's thin straps didn't allow for a bra, so the light squeeze of her nipple between his fingers spread through her as hotly as if she'd been wearing nothing at all.

She turned her head, looped her arm up around his neck to pull him down, and delivered a heated kiss to his mouth. He leaned in to her as they kissed, as his hands worked magic on her body, pressing his hard cock against the crack of her ass.

Turning her eyes back on the glowing cityscape below, Diana grabbed onto the wire railing in front of her, clutching tight with both hands, and simply relished her lover's hot hands on her body. She thrust her heat-filled cunt against his fingers, fucking them, taking herself closer and closer to a sweet bliss that—oh yes, finally broke over her like a huge match igniting, sending flames of pleasure shooting through her entire being. She moaned and whimpered her joy as she continued driving her crotch against his fingers, letting herself burn up in the scorching blaze of pleasure his touch delivered.

* * * * *

After descending from the Stratosphere, her body still alive and in sync with Marc and the night, they taxied back up the strip, exiting at the Paris Hotel.

"Are you ready for some more of Sin City, sweetheart?" he asked, taking her hand and leading her past the replica of the Eiffel Tower that stood only feet away from the boulevard.

"Oh yes," she said. "Bring it on."

The next ninety minutes were a whirlwind.

First they toured the Paris, where both the shopping area and the casino were designed to give the feel of a walk through the real French city. They stopped at a patisserie where they playfully fed each other small chocolate éclairs, and Diana said, "Just think, soon you'll be doing this for real."

"Doing what for real?"

She laughed and held out her arms, motioning around them. "Walking the streets of Paris. Eating true French éclairs."

"Oh. Yeah," he said, smiling—but in the dim lighting of the dusky faux Parisian street, she thought it didn't quite reach his eyes.

Next, they cut through Bally's and headed into the Aladdin, where the interior made her feel she was strolling through a Moroccan bazaar. After that, they traveled up the street into the MGM Grand, a huge shining metropolis, its exterior changing colors from green to gold to red every few seconds.

Entering the casino, Diana played a few slot machines and actually hit a small ten-dollar jackpot when three ripe cherries lined up on the display before her. After collecting her winnings, they crossed the elevated walkway to New York, New York, where they both ordered frozen daiquiris from the Coyote Ugly bar inside. Marc then took her on a short walking tour of the shopping and restaurant area, saying, "My mother swears this is as close as you can get to her grandparents' old New York neighborhood west of the Mississippi."

Departing the hotel, they strolled the replica of the Brooklyn Bridge outside while sipping their drinks, then caught another taxi. This time Marc told the driver, "Caesar's Palace."

As the cab left the curb, he turned to Diana. "Caesar's, sweetheart, is where we'll do a little *real* gambling."

"Real?"

"Roulette, blackjack, whatever you like."

She smiled. "And why at Caesar's?"

"It's quintessential Las Vegas, baby. My favorite place to lose money," he concluded with a wink.

Within minutes, Diana found herself seated next to Marc at a roulette table. She learned the game quickly and found it fun and easy to play. She liked the sound of the spinning roulette wheel and enjoyed the anticipation of waiting for the little ball to drop into a red or black slot, determining the winning number. Although she stuck mostly with safe bets, she put a handful of chips on number eleven for one spin of the wheel, and raked in a bundle when her number came up.

Marc, who was nearly out of chips to her right, laughed and said, "Either you're having terrific beginner's luck or you've totally hustled me and you've been playing this game all your life."

Next, they moved on to blackjack. The pace was fast, forcing quick decisions, but Diana held her own, and by the time they left the crescent-shaped table, she had a few more chips than when she'd sat down.

They were just about to cash in their chips when a male voice behind Diana said, "Excuse me, I'm in need of a lovely lady for a few minutes if you'd be so kind to oblige."

She turned, surprised to find Rick from the catalog team. He seemed just as surprised to see her. "Diana—hey! I didn't recognize you. You changed your hair."

She reached up to finger one of her curls, laughing. "Yeah, I'm incognito tonight."

"Well, this is even better. I'm on a roll at craps and I've got this superstition that when you're doing good at craps, you find a beautiful woman to start rolling the dice. That way, no matter how things turn out, you've got a good view." The blondish man she'd come to know at the office this week quirked a smile.

"Sir, you're holding up the game." They both turned to see the bow-tied, vested man running the craps table looking impatient.

"Do I have to know how to play?" Diana asked Rick.

He shook his head. "No—just roll the dice."

Glancing up at Marc, who smiled and said, "Roll the man's dice for him," she let Rick lead her to the head of the table, where she also found Blaine and Holly placing bets on her upcoming roll.

"Seven," the bowtie announced after her first throw, and Rick kissed her on the cheek.

"Way to go, honey—keep 'em coming."

Her next roll produced an eleven, which had everyone at the table besides Rick sulking as he, conversely, punched a triumphant fist through the air, shouting, "Let it ride."

Diana still had no idea how the game worked or even how much money Rick was betting—although his stack of chips was impressive—but the excitement was infectious as she leaned over the table and gave the dice another hard toss.

"Seven," she heard the bowtie say, and this time Rick threw his arms around her in celebration. She hugged him back and he announced he was quitting, taking his winnings—which she learned were over seven hundred dollars.

Holly and Blaine chose to leave the game, too, and insisted Rick buy them a drink, considering how much he'd won and how much they'd lost.

Diana found Holly striking in a slim, sexy lavender dress. She'd worn it to work today, but with a jacket. Shedding the jacket had turned professional to hot and, for some reason, the very idea had Diana envisioning Holly getting naked with Adrianna in her office.

"I can't believe we ran into you," Marc said to Rick, and Diana easily understood his surprise—the Vegas strip was crowded, in the hotels and out on the street, with countless thousands of people. "What brings you guys out?"

Rick glanced at Holly and grinned. "Today is Holly's twenty-fifth birthday."

Marc's jaw dropped and Diana was surprised, too. "How were we at work with her all day without knowing that?" she asked.

Rick shrugged. "She didn't tell anybody, didn't want people making a fuss over her…until her girlfriends bailed on her. They were supposed to take her out tonight to one of the male reviews, but they both cancelled at the last minute. We were on our way out the door and I happened to see her looking down and asked why. When she told us, well…hell, you know how sweet Holly is. What else could we do besides take her out for some fun?"

Diana withdrew herself from the guys' conversation and stepped over to where Holly stood talking to Blaine. "Happy birthday," she said with a smile, reaching to give Holly a hug.

"Thanks, Diana. You're sweet."

"I can't believe you kept it a secret all day. And twenty-five is a big one, too."

Holly shrugged and laughed. "Well, even if I kept it a secret at work, these guys have got me in a partying mood *now*." She slid her arm warmly around Diana's waist and leaned in close. "So, you and Marc, huh? Just like I said on your first day."

Diana felt her face color, only because she'd originally told Holly so emphatically that nothing could happen between her and Marc because of Bradley. That had been back when she was still trying to turn things around, still trying to resist losing control of herself with Marc over and over again. In the ensuing days, she'd nearly forgotten she'd come out here with the intention of being a good girl, since Marc and Sin City had made it so easy for her to be bad. "Well, we…" Oh hell—she gave up the pretense. "Yes, it's just like you said. We fit together really well."

"But you have this broken-up-but-we're-getting-back-together boyfriend at home, right?"

She nodded uncertainly. "That's the plan. Although I have to admit that, as it's worked out, I picked an excellent time to take a vacation from him."

Holly tossed a glance toward Diana's lover. "Marc's an excellent reason to indulge yourself."

Diana chuckled. "I agree, wholeheartedly."

Having caught the glance, Marc extracted himself from talking to Rick to join the two girls. "Sorry to break up the party, ladies," he said, glancing down at how close they stood, their arms still around each other's backs, "but I've got plans for Diana this evening."

Holly laughed. "Sure, ditch me on my birthday."

They all laughed, and Holly leaned in to kiss Diana on the cheek. "Have fun, you guys!" she said.

"You, too," Diana told her, pulling away from her warmth.

"Don't worry, I plan on it. A girl only turns twenty-five once."

As Marc dragged her away, Diana asked, "Where are we going in such a hurry?"

"To your last surprise," he said as they approached the crosswalk that led back to the Venetian, where he'd valet-parked his car.

"Hmm, that would have something to do with the bathing suit in my purse, right?"

He grinned. "Yes, and it would also have to do with spending some more time alone with you."

She couldn't deny liking the idea of that. Whereas, a couple of days ago, that sounded almost dangerous to her heart, she now didn't care, and knew it was too late to worry about, anyway.

* * * * *

Once Marc got her back to his place, he told Diana to slip into her suit. A moment later, she returned from the bathroom in a stunning — and delightfully skimpy — white thong bikini. Her skin appeared tan against the bright white and her body looked killer in it. Her nipples jutted at the thin white triangles, showing dark rosy shadows through the fabric. He'd changed into swim trunks while waiting for her, and now he felt his cock beginning to make a tent in them.

He took her hand and led her from the condo. "Come with me."

She didn't ask where he was taking her, just smiled and followed. He loved that about her — that infinite trust she put in him, that total lack of fear. Even given his stint in the world of BDSM, he'd never been with such a truly devil-may-care woman, but he'd quickly learned it was a trait that excited the hell out of him.

Leading her on a short stroll on the walkways that led through his condo complex, he finally approached the gated entry to the pool. Reaching in his zippered pocket, he extracted the key Carter had gotten for him earlier today after Marc had told him what a hard time he was having getting Diana *alone* for sex. "It's not that I haven't enjoyed every minute of everything she and I have done with other people," he'd explained to his friend, "but I want a night for just her and I, with no distractions." The urge for that sort of private union with her had grown in him more and more, and when Carter had suggested the idea of some midnight sex in the complex's lush pool area, Marc had been unable to resist.

As he unlocked the gate, she caught sight of the sign that said pool hours were strictly nine a.m. to nine p.m.

"Are we cheating?" she asked, her eyes alight with mischief.

He grinned, nodded. "Since Carter helps out with some of the maintenance around here, he was able to get the key. Which means," he said, drawing her along the path leading inside the pool area, "I finally get you all to myself, completely, with no interruptions, no distractions, no sharing."

They came upon the curving edge of the pool, its banks partially hung with verdant green plants from above. The water sparkled in the moonlight and he could barely wait to get her in it.

"I thought you liked sharing me," she said, wearing a typically coquettish smile.

He returned it as he gently pulled her toward the steps that led down into the cool blue pool. "I've loved sharing you, sweetheart. But tonight I want it to be just you and me." *Making love*, he almost said, but stopped. Shit, when had he started using—even *thinking*—terms like that? He certainly couldn't tell her that even as fun as their little threesomes and more had been, that over their days and nights together, he'd started to feel more and more jealous. Hell, maybe that was why he'd kept letting those liaisons happen—in hopes of proving to himself that he *could* keep sharing her and that he *didn't* feel jealous. Except that he did.

It wasn't an emotion he was accustomed to, so it hadn't been easy to recognize, but even last night, while one part of him had reveled in watching her with Adrianna, another deeper, more hidden part of him had wanted to be the only person pleasuring her, wanted to be the only thing she could see. And now, tonight, he would have that.

Diana followed him willingly into the pool. The water was refreshing, but still warm enough that she could walk in right behind him. When she was immersed up to her waist, he turned to face her, sliding his arms around her. Wrapping her own arms about his neck, she engaged him in a hot, sexy open-mouthed kiss, licking delicately at his tongue. Beneath the water's surface, his hard cock pressed warmly into the low cut front of her bikini bottom, making her ready for more.

He seemed to read her mind, leaning back and pulling her with him to create a small splash as he took them plunging into slightly deeper water. Diana took the opportunity to make a small dive under that brought her up with wet hair laying smoothly back over her head, her curls relaxing into soft waves. Marc followed suit, and when he resurfaced, he pinned her to the wall of the pool, the water hitting just below her breasts, and delivered another kiss, this one rough enough to elicit a little moan from her as its effects traveled her veins like a sweetly electrifying shock.

Their kisses grew longer, deeper, and Diana almost thought she'd be content to stand there and make out with him forever — his lips were so firm, the kisses they traded so heated and sexy. She understood why he'd brought her here; the atmosphere was conducive to seduction. The abundant greenery jutting out over the water, the palm trees sprinkling the landscape, and the vibrant flowering bushes all made the pool seem like a tiny oasis in the midst of this desert city. She took in the sweet scent of thriving foliage mixed with the perfume of blooming hibiscus as his hands made their way to her breasts.

Continuing to kiss her, he massaged her ever-sensitive mounds of flesh as she arched, pushing them more firmly into his kneading hands. Their lush surroundings made her want to soak up every ounce of sensation available to her.

Soon, he was pushing the narrow white triangles of her top aside, baring her breasts to his eyes, his hands, and the lovely breeze that wafted down through the palm fronds. Watching him gaze upon her, she bit her lip. "Why don't you show them how much you like them?" she whispered.

Casting a quick, hot grin into her eyes, he molded her rounded flesh in his hands while bending to tenderly lick one protruding nipple. Diana released a joyful sigh as the tingling heat he delivered to her breast raced through the rest of her body. Moving to her other mound, he licked it, as well, this time more firmly, vigorously, finally attaching his mouth around her nipple, sucking her so thoroughly she felt it directly in her cunt.

"Hey, guys, surprise!"

Stunned, they both looked up to see Holly entering the pool area.

"What the hell...?" Marc began, still holding Diana in a loose embrace.

Holly only smiled. "Rick told us you had the key to your pool, so we thought we'd come join you."

"Damn it," he bit off, under his breath. "I had to make the mistake of mentioning where we were going."

Diana couldn't contain her light laugh. Every time they attempted to be alone, other people ended up intruding in their plans. While she, too, had really wanted to have some privacy with Marc, something about the situation struck her as almost comical. "I guess you *didn't* mention wanting to be alone, though," she said.

He grinned down at her. "I'm glad you're so damned amused at my plan falling through."

She smiled. "We'll make the best of it. And…maybe if we're nice to them, they'll go away soon."

He rolled his eyes and laughed. "I doubt that."

"Hey, hey, we're here, the party can start," Blaine's voice sounded.

"D'you find them, Holly?" Rick inquired before his eyes landed on Diana and Marc as he asked. "Looks like you did. Mmm, mmm, mmm, Diana—*very nice.*"

"Oh!" He was talking about her boobs, so she lifted her palms to cover them, although they were much more than she could hide with her small hands. When Holly had spoken to her and Marc without even alluding to the fact that Diana's breasts were fully exposed, she'd forgotten to be modest.

"Don't worry," Rick said easily, "we're all friends here—no big deal."

Just then, she spied Holly freeing herself from the shoulder straps of her clingy lavender dress, letting it drop to the tiling that surrounded the pool, revealing that she hadn't worn a bra or panties under it. Her breasts were pretty, medium-sized with pale pink nipples that turned slightly upward; her pussy was shaved except for a small thatch of pale brown above her slit.

When Diana realized the guys were getting naked, too, she didn't bother putting her top back into place. Instead, she simply went ahead and took it off completely, tossing it up on the edge of the pool.

"I don't suppose," Marc said, turning to the guys where they stripped off their shirts, ties, and suits, "it ever occurred to you jerks that I was taking Diana out of the casino and into the pool for some *privacy*." She could tell he wasn't really angry, just irritated.

Blaine stood at the edge of the pool in a pair of black underwear. Next to him, Rick struggled with his shoestrings, and Holly was gliding down the steps into the water, looking slightly drunk, very merry, and considerably sexy in her nudity.

"Sorry, dude," Blaine said. "I, for one, did figure that out, but once it came up, these two were set on going swimming."

"And hey, it *is* Holly's birthday," Rick chimed in, finally freeing himself of his shoes and dropping his suit pants. "You don't want to disappoint a girl on her birthday, do you?"

Marc just looked at Diana, shook his head, rolled his eyes, and laughed—then turned back to his friends. "No, far be it from me to spoil someone's birthday."

Holly approached Diana in the water, addressing both her and Marc. "I decided I'd had enough gambling—I was sick of losing on my birthday, so Rick was sweet enough to buy me a couple of Long Island iced teas, and when he mentioned what you guys were doing, I suggested a skinny dip." She came to lean up against the wall of the pool where Diana stood, lowering her voice slightly and speaking directly to her now. "I'm sorry if my timing was bad, though. I didn't even think about this being a romantic thing for you guys or I wouldn't have suggested it. I just wanted to have some more fun on my birthday."

Diana couldn't hold the ill-timed arrival against Holly—she was too fun and guileless and well-meaning. "I want you to have fun on your birthday, too, Holly, so forget about it. It's perfectly fine. I'm glad you guys came."

That last part was a bit of a stretch, but she didn't want Holly to feel bad.

Holly leaned over to give Diana another hug, this one a lot more intimate than the one at the casino, given that Holly was naked and Diana wore only bikini bottoms. Diana couldn't help enjoying the soft, warm collision of their bodies, and she quickly became aware that they were both prolonging it. When they finally parted, Diana missed having Holly's pretty breasts pressed up against hers.

"Thanks for being so sweet," Holly said, then gave her a warm kiss on the lips. Diana instinctually kissed her back and when their soft lips separated, Holly backed away from her with a smile.

She turned it on Marc, who was approaching Diana from across the pool. "Lucky guy, Marc. Diana's hot."

He flashed a grin. "Don't I know it."

Diana caught a glimpse of the other two guys wading into the pool naked as Marc's arms closed around her in a warm, wet embrace. A sensual light sparkled in his gaze. "You and Holly looked good together, sweetheart. If you want to play with her for a while, I don't mind watching."

She smiled into his warm brown eyes. "She's very cute and attractive, but...tonight the only person I really want to play with is you." To accentuate her words, she reached beneath the water's surface and stroked his hard cock through his trunks.

Marc drew her into a series of long, warm kisses that thrilled her from the top of her head to the soles of her feet. His erection pressed against her cunt and she wanted to fuck him so badly she could almost taste it—alone or not. Beyond them, she was vaguely aware of light laughter, some splashing sounds, the words, "Come here and let me tell you happy birthday the right way," but her world centered on Marc.

"Tomorrow night," she whispered, "you and me, alone. Doesn't matter where—my place or yours. We won't even go out. We'll order room service or a pizza and we'll fuck each other's brains out all night long."

He was nuzzling her neck, a soft chuckle escaping him. "That sounds *so* good, baby. I can't wait."

He kissed her again, a slow, deep meeting of tongues that nearly buried her alive.

When she happened to glance over Marc's muscled shoulder, she caught sight of Holly making out with Rick in the pool. Blaine stood behind Holly, reaching around to caress her breasts. Drawing in her breath slightly, Diana looked at Marc and pointed. "It's your lucky day," she whispered teasingly, "since you like to watch so much."

He cast a grin that seemed to say, *Very funny*, but that didn't stop him from wrapping around Diana from behind as they both took in the scene.

The moment Holly's lips broke away from Rick's, Blaine said, "My turn," and spun her around to face him. "Happy birthday, Holly." As his kiss enveloped her, Holly put her arms around his neck and from what Diana could tell, Rick was rubbing against her in back, probably sliding his cock up and down her ass.

Backing up into a spot where the pool rounded sharply, almost creating a corner, Holly leaned against the wall and kissed Blaine some more while Rick took one of her perky breasts into his mouth. A few minutes later, Rick resumed kissing her mouth and Blaine dropped to feast upon her nipple.

"Do they taste good?" she asked a few minutes later.

"Mmm, yeah," Rick said, as Blaine replied, "Delicious, baby."

At that, Holly easily boosted herself up onto the tiled edge of the pool, lithely spreading her legs so wide that Diana knew she must have been a cheerleader in high school. The lips of her cunt parted, revealing the moist pink flesh inside. She situated her crotch so that it was elevated above the near right angle the pool's rounded walls formed. "I bet my pussy tastes even better. Why don't you boys give the birthday girl a special treat and find out?"

As they watched the two guys take turns eating Holly's cunt, Marc began lowering sensual kisses to Diana's neck, gently squeezing her breasts, and rubbing his enormous cock against her ass. She sighed as his kisses and caresses sent ribbons of desire spiraling through her. If she'd wanted to fuck him badly a few minutes ago, now she was craving him.

Holly moaned and pinched her nipples while *she* watched her pussy get eaten, too. "That's so good," she was saying to Rick as he worked his mouth on her. Rick kneaded Holly's inner thighs as he dragged his tongue deeply through her slit, and she lifted in a slow, hot rhythm against his mouth. Blaine stood by, caressing Holly's leg, lowering kisses to wherever he could reach as he patiently waited his turn.

Diana wasn't sure how much more she could take before she spun and yanked Marc's trunks down. She yearned to suck his cock, take him deep inside her, everything—she wanted him in every way and Holly's birthday show was increasing her heat and *de*creasing her patience.

When Blaine took Rick's place between Holly's thighs, she told him, "Suck on my clit. Suck on it and I'll come."

Blaine's head lowered to her pussy and she responded by lifting her ass from the tile for slow undulations. "Come on, baby," Rick prodded her. He reached around Blaine to close his hand over one of her breasts, flicking his thumb across her hardened nipple.

Holly had apparently known exactly what her body needed, because it wasn't long before she was panting and gasping and whimpering, finally saying, "Yes, now, now, now—I'm coming!" Diana watched with excitement as Holly drove her cunt against Blaine's face again and again as she cried out her ecstasy, eventually slowing, settling back into place to murmur, "Mmm, happy birthday to me."

But the guys weren't done with her just because she'd orgasmed. Moving her to the steps and reclining her in the shallow water, Blaine parted her thighs and eased his erection inside her. At the same time, Rick knelt by her head. She reached out, wrapping one hand around his sturdy-looking cock, and drew it to her lips. Holly looked as skilled as Diana in the art of pleasuring a man with her mouth, and Rick let out a groan of pleasure as Blaine pumped into her below. The girl appeared ravenous and enraptured at having two guys at once, a sensation Diana could relate to given her recent experiences.

Marc's hand had slid down into the front of Diana's bathing suit by now, fingering her pussy while they continued taking in Holly's pleasure. Watching Holly enjoy the two stiff cocks made Diana wonder what she looked like in similar positions, and she almost understood about Marc's "weakness", as he'd called it, of wanting to watch. She wondered what she looked like when she grew as excited and impassioned as Holly was now. Thinking about it, she let out a sensual sigh, moving softly against Marc's stroking fingers.

"I'm gonna come on you soon, honey," Rick warned Holly. "I'm gonna come all over your sexy body."

"You want me to come in you or on you?" Blaine panted as he drove into her.

She loosed her mouth from Rick's cock to say, "On me. I want your come all over me."

When both guys announced they were ready to explode, Blaine pulled out and, as promised, they emptied themselves onto Holly in quick shooting bursts of white. Their target lay stretched out across the pool steps, watching with delight as it spattered her breasts and torso.

When they were done, she lay rubbing it in and peering languidly up at both guys. "Mmm, I think this will be a birthday to remember."

Diana turned into Marc's embrace. "Maybe they'll leave now."

He shook his head. "That would be too convenient for us."

"I think I get it now," she told him.

"Get what?"

"About why you like to watch. I mean, I guess I've never really just *watched* someone before this, outside of a movie. It's...incredibly arousing, isn't it?"

He grinned uncertainly. "Odd you should say that."

"Oh?"

He ran his hands up her sides, raking his thumbs gently across her nipples. "Because I'm experiencing a weird little phenomenon—I'm starting to think it only excites me now if I'm watching *you*."

She drew in her breath, surprised, shockingly moved.

"Which is a problem," he said teasingly. "Since I also keep wanting to get you totally alone, with nobody else. Kind of hard to watch then."

She smiled. "Perhaps if we incorporated a mirror? Like in the elevator. That worked nicely."

He brushed his thumbs across the sensitive pink peaks once more, a sensation that shot straight to her pussy. "You're right, it did. I'll have to get a mirror mounted on the ceiling above my bed. Like...tomorrow. Or maybe tonight. Definitely as soon as humanly possible."

They laughed over his urgency, but at the same time, frustration mounted inside Diana. She'd enjoyed watching Holly get her birthday present, but now she really wanted their visitors gone. She wanted Marc. And she didn't want it to be a group activity this time.

"Want to forget the pool and go inside?" she whispered.

His thumbs continued tenderly stroking her nipples, turning them harder and harder. "No. I don't think I could make it that far right now."

Indeed, his cock was huge between his legs. They weren't even standing flush against each other and it jutted firmly into her abdomen.

"I want you," she pleaded. "What can we do?"

Marc took a deep breath and peered over her shoulder. She looked to see that he was right—the trio of lovers now played in the water, swimming, hugging, splashing. They weren't going anywhere.

"I have an idea," Marc said, leading her deeper into the water, farther away from the others.

She let him pull her along, curious where he was taking her.

As the pool narrowed into a stream, the overhead greenery even more lush here, he released her and they swam, side by side. The pool widened again, leading to a waterfall she'd caught a glimpse of upon her arrival. Smiling, Marc said, "In here," and drew her beneath the curtain of spilling water.

Putting her feet down, she found the water shallow enough that she was only chest deep. They were enveloped in a private enclave with rocks on one side; on the other a semi-circle of water fell so smoothly it reminded her of liquid glass. The only sound in the private spot was the crash of water all around them.

Reaching beneath the surface, Marc began to push her bottoms down to her thighs, and Diana soon had them off. Marc looped them over one wrist before pushing down his trunks and breathing, "Finally, I get to have you—just you, just me. Come here, sweetheart."

Marc's hands found her ass and lifted her until she locked her legs around his hips and he entered her. "Oh God," she whimpered. It seemed like so long since his perfect cock had been inside her. Had it been only twenty-four hours?

She almost couldn't believe she'd let him invite Adrianna to their private slave party last night and proceed *not* to fuck her. He had afterward, of course, after Adrianna had gone. But she wished he'd done it *during* the threesome, too. He felt so glorious inside her that missing even one opportunity to have this seemed tragic. "You're so big in me, baby," she whispered.

"And you're so good and tight. So hot and sweet."

Wrapping her arms around his neck, she rode him, thrusting her pussy against him beneath the water's surface. Her breasts were level with his mouth and he took turns kissing and sucking them, making her moan with each delectable ministration.

"I'd trade a hundred nights with Adrianna...or any other woman," he breathed, his voice ragged, as they crashed against each other over and over, "for just ten minutes...like this...with you."

His affectionate words were the last thing she heard before her orgasm broke. The wild sensations seemed to split her in two as she rode out the pleasure, hard, against his cock, crying, "Baby, oh baby, oh baby. yesssss."

"Don't stop," he said, "Me, too," so she kept pumping against him as hard as she could, wringing the come from his magnificent cock and listening to him groan as he held her tight against him.

When it was done, they both went still, stayed quiet, their bodies remaining connected behind their private waterfall. Marc leaned forward, letting his forehead come to rest on her shoulder, and Diana basked in the simple joy and contentment of the moment, until he raised his head and gave her a small, satiated grin. "Well, not exactly the private seduction I'd planned, but..."

She smiled and rocked her cunt against him one last time. "Don't worry, baby. I'll take you any way I can get you."

* * * * *

Like the previous morning, Diana bounced into work early, ready to get a good start on the day. She and the guys were making very healthy progress on the catalog, given the brief time she'd been here. It was Saturday, so most of the office would be quiet, but as Marc had informed her earlier in the week, Adrianna expected them to be there every day until the catalog was put to bed.

The one perk of working on the weekend was dressing down a bit, so Diana had opted for crop pants and a sleeveless sweater. She entered the conference room feeling chipper and energetic, no doubt from her romantic, if brief, tryst with Marc beneath the waterfall last night.

Part of her wondered if she should feel sheepish about working with Blaine and Rick after last night's little party, but she was beginning to understand that in Sin City, what happened socially stayed in that realm and didn't interfere with work relationships. As she and Marc had already discussed, even *they* had maintained a comfortable professionalism that pleased her. She liked being able to work with him so easily and productively, and then turn around and be a bad girl with him at night.

Marc walked in a few minutes later wearing blue jeans, today carrying a whole *box* of donuts. "Can I tempt you, sweetheart, or did you do the buffet on me again?"

Actually, she *hadn't* eaten, so she peered hungrily at the box. "What kind do you have?"

He grinned teasingly. "What kind do you want?"

"Mmm, something chocolate-covered?" she asked hopefully.

"You're in luck."

Taking the box, she opened it to see an array of breakfast confections, but her eyes were drawn to the long narrow yeast donut drenched with chocolate frosting. "My favorite," she said, plucking it out.

He laughed. "Now that I know you like those, we can put chocolate on my cock and let you pretend."

"Mmm, mmm, sounds delicious," she said, licking a bit of chocolate icing off her oblong treat with a playful smile.

A few minutes later, the rest of the team straggled in. Like Marc and Diana, they were dressed down, and Blaine and Rick, in particular, looked a little worse for wear. Dave, the only married guy in the bunch, who'd been notably absent last night, said, "Late night, guys?"

As Rick exchanged an amused glance with Diana, Blaine said, "We took Holly out. It was her birthday and her friends ditched her at the last minute."

"Hope you showed the lady a good time," Dave said absently, studying his laptop.

Diana bit her lip and the rest of the guys had to stifle a laugh, but Dave was oblivious.

"Yeah, I think she went home in a happy mood," Blaine concluded.

"Today," Diana announced with a smile, thinking they'd best get down to business, "we're going to tackle the Cozy Panties pages. The real challenge here will be to make them sound exciting while at the same time touting them for their main purpose—the comfort they provide." The panties in this line were all made of a soft cotton that truly was top of the line in comfort, but they weren't Adrianna's best sellers, likely because women figured they could buy their cotton undies anywhere.

Just as Marc was laying out the current mock-ups in the center of the table, Adrianna walked in the door.

Unlike the rest of them, she wore her professional attire—an olive green suit with a cream-colored blouse beneath.

After exchanging brief good mornings, she said she had an announcement that would affect everyone in this room, "but mainly Miss Marsh."

Diana sat up a little straighter, wondering what it could be.

"Late yesterday evening, I got a call at home from Richard Watkins, Miss Marsh's supervisor in Baltimore." She honed her gaze in on Diana. "You're needed there right away, I'm afraid. We've made arrangements for you to fly back this afternoon."

Chapter Ten

Diana's jaw dropped.

"Baltimore experienced a computer crash yesterday and everything specific to East Coast advertising was lost," Adrianna went on. "I've officially reamed out everyone in IT who did not have proper back-ups of this material, and I apologize, Miss Marsh, that the brunt of rebuilding it will fall on you and the rest of your department in Baltimore. Richard tells me the department has multiple upcoming deadlines with a number of fashion magazines and relevant newspapers and they need you back if they hope to get the material in place on time for fall advertising. I apologize, too, for putting you in the position of around-the-clock work, first on this project and now on the ad retrieval, but I'll personally see to it that your hard work and dedication is rewarded."

Diana barely knew what to say as the ramifications — both professional and personal — began to sink in. The only thing that came to her mind to utter was, "What about the catalog? It's not done yet."

"I've been following your progress and it's my belief that you've gotten the team back on track. Although I wish you could finish the project you've done such excellent work on these past days, you're simply needed more in Baltimore. And I have faith in our team here to complete the revisions using what they've learned since your arrival."

"All right," she said, feeling rather adrift and helpless, considering how valuable Adrianna was telling her she was. "Um...when do I leave?"

"I have your plane ticket right here." Adrianna handed her an envelope. "Your flight is at two, but given that you'll need time to pack and also get to the airport early because it's a weekend, I'd recommend you return to the hotel within the hour."

The whirlwind news had literally left Diana breathless. "Uh...okay."

"And if you don't mind, Miss Marsh, I'd like to see you in the hallway for a moment."

Diana drew in her breath and, without a chance to even contemplate what else Adrianna might have to say to her, she got up and followed her out into the hall, pulling the conference room door shut behind her.

Turning, she found Adrianna peering into her eyes, her blue gaze thoughtful and penetrating. She took both of Diana's hands in hers. Glancing down, Diana noticed they were as perfectly manicured as usual. "I just want to tell you, Miss Marsh, that I've sincerely enjoyed having you here these past few days—both professionally and socially—and I'm sorry you'll be leaving us so soon. I meant what I said about the quality of your work and how much I appreciate your dedication. You *will* be compensated."

Still, Diana remained flabbergasted. "Well, thank you, Adrianna. I've enjoyed it, too, on both levels. It's been a pleasure to spend time with the woman who built Adrianna, Inc. into the company it is today."

Adrianna's smile was one of the warmest Diana had ever witnessed from her. "Thank you...Diana," she said, finally using her first name. Something in the gesture touched Diana, making her feel that perhaps she'd advanced beyond mere employee to Adrianna, even past mere sexual liaison, into a place of mutual respect. "And should you ever need anything, don't hesitate to call me personally. I mean that."

Before Diana could summon a response, her boss turned and walked down the carpeted corridor, away from her.

Exhaustion from the action-packed week finally caught up with her, and she turned to lean back against the wall, releasing a huge breath. She was leaving. Going home. Leaving Marc. Already.

He was the best, most giving, and at the same time most powerful lover she'd ever had. And more than being her lover, their extreme intimacies had also made him something else to her, something she couldn't exactly put a name on, but she cared for him, and leaving him—now, today—sounded like impossible, heartbreaking torture.

Of course, it was her own fault—she'd known from the start she shouldn't let herself get too close to him, and she'd done it anyway. She'd let him inside her soul. And now she would pay for it.

Taking a deep breath, she turned the doorknob and peeked inside. "Marc, can I see you out here?" Damn it, she felt like she was going to cry.

Stop it, she commanded herself. *You're a strong, capable woman, and you do not cry over a man you only met in person five days ago.*

By the time he stepped out into the hall, she had hold of her emotions.

"So," he said softly, "this is it. Already."

She tried for a smile. "My thoughts exactly. I'm not really, um, ready to go."

He looked into her eyes, his brown gaze deep and intense. "I'm not ready to *let* you go, sweetheart."

She bit her lip, glanced down at her shoes, forced her eyes back to his dark, handsome face. "Unfortunately, I don't think it's up to us. I know you're probably headed to Paris, but me, I'm a company woman. I intend to have a long, thriving career at Adrianna, Inc., so…that means I do what I have to do to make that happen."

He took her hands. "Do you know how much I admire that about you?"

She shook her head, swallowed back her emotions.

"It's something I noticed about you right away, the first few times we spoke on the phone. I could tell you felt passionately about Adrianna, Inc., and…well, I supposed I wished *I* felt that passionately about something. Maybe that's why I'm going to Paris. To find that one thing, that special something that makes me want to sacrifice myself for it. You inspire me that way."

She simply gazed up into his eyes, amazed at all he saw in her.

"So even though there's a part of me that's tempted to ask you to stay, to even ask you to blow off Bradley and quit caring what your parents think of you, I can't do it. Because you're a determined woman and you always know what you want and you always go after it. I'd hate myself if I tried to change that in you."

Diana couldn't keep from throwing her arms around his neck and drawing him into a hard kiss. His arms closed around her waist and after the kiss ended, they held each other, long and firm and intense, a hug she never wanted to end.

"Let me take you to the airport," he said softly in her ear.

But she shook her head. "It'll be easier if we say goodbye here."

He didn't argue, apparently recognizing the truth in her statement.

"Will you tell the guys, and on Monday, Holly, that I said bye? I...just don't think I'm up for going back in that room right now."

He nodded, pulling her tight against him again, and she wondered if he was feeling the finality of their relationship the same way she was. A few minutes ago, they were teasing each other about sex, laughing about the idea of putting chocolate on his cock for her, and now she was never going to see him again? It seemed impossible, but it was true.

"I'll miss you," she said, thinking it was the understatement of the century. "And...you'll let me know about Paris, right?"

"Of course. I mean, we'll still talk on the phone. I'm sure I'll still have a million questions for you about the catalog and other marketing issues."

She nodded, yet said, "This coming couple of weeks, though, I'll be swamped with putting our ad material back together, so...I might not be able to chat, you know?"

He nodded, looking sad.

"God, I hate this," she told him.

"Me, too."

And she knew if she stood there much longer, she'd give up everything—her parents, her career, everything that was important to her—just to stay in this man's arms and bed for a little while longer. So she took his face between her hands, gave him a firm, sweet kiss, and said, "I have to go. Now. I'm sorry," then turned and practically sprinted up the hallway.

* * * * *

Marc ambled to the refrigerator, only to find that his milk had gone bad. Great. One more little annoyance to add to his fluctuating emotions. God, he was tired. Physically. In his head. In his heart. He swallowed back the pain, but couldn't deny his sense of devastation after having Diana walk out of his life as quickly as she'd walked into it. He couldn't believe he was suddenly without her.

He wasn't sure how the hell such feelings had grabbed hold of him. He'd been having fun with her, a good time, enjoying her company and the sex, and somehow it had turned into this searing pain in his chest now that she was gone.

What day was it? Damn it, with all this work—and play—he'd lost track.

Sunday, he remembered. It was Sunday morning, and one of the reasons he felt so disjointed and out of it was that he hadn't slept at all, tossing and turning all night. He'd spent last night lying on the couch, watching nothing in particular on TV. There were women he could have called, or guys he could have gotten together and gone out with, but he just hadn't wanted to. He couldn't remember a time in his adulthood when he'd felt that way without being physically ill. He was a party guy and it took a lot to keep him down. Guess that meant Diana qualified as "a lot". To say the least. She was everything he wanted.

When the phone rang, he flinched. Who the hell was calling him this early on a Sunday morning?

Then it hit him. Could it be her? He snatched it up. "Hello."

"Marc, zis iz Jacques." His contact in Paris.

He cleared his throat, tried to wake up, or at least sound like it. "Jacques, it's good to hear from you."

"Even better, I'll wager, when I give you ze news. Ze job is yours."

He felt his eyes bolt open, his skin prickling. He'd practically forgotten about Paris, about the reality of it. It had become like a long series of phone calls that had no end, but now, here it was—and he felt surprisingly empty, blank. He struggled for something to say. "Oh. Wow."

"We're very pleased to have you on ze Briolet International team." Jacques went on to say that Briolet owned a corporate apartment on the West Bank where he could reside until he found his own place. He asked Marc to call him back with an arrival date once he got his affairs in the States in order, adding, "Ze sooner ze better."

Marc hung up the phone with a knot in his stomach.

What the hell...?

This was what he'd wanted. Wasn't it?

Lowering himself into a chair at his kitchen table, he couldn't shake the melancholy surrounding him. He was supposed to be excited about this, yet he wasn't, not at all.

He couldn't help thinking that Paris sounded a world away from Diana.

But then again, so was Vegas, now.

He ran his hands back through sleep-rumpled hair, then pushed to his feet. Hell, what was he hesitating for? This *was* what he'd wanted, after all—what he'd wanted for a long while now. As he'd told her yesterday, it was a chance for him to find something he felt passionately about, and what single guy wouldn't want the chance to live in Paris for a while? It truly *was* a dream come true.

And it was just what he needed to get his mind off Diana.

* * * * *

Diana yawned, wiped her tired eyes, and tried to focus on the notes she was making—what the hell had that ad copy said before it was lost? Something about Adrianna, Inc. being for every woman...*every woman you are*...?

Damn it, she couldn't remember. Then again, it was Sunday night, darkness had just fallen outside her office window, and that meant she'd spent nearly twenty-four hours, minus one little catnap on the couch in Richard's office, silently toiling away to rebuild files and reconstruct ad copy and graphics.

But her energy was fading fast. And she was painfully conscious of missing Marc. Despite the strength she'd been so determined to show when they'd said goodbye, she'd cried before ever getting to the airport, and she'd cried again on the plane.

She could barely understand it herself. He was a great guy, sure, but how had she fallen so hard for him so fast? Of course, they'd been getting to know each other for months on the phone, but...God, he understood her so well. He let her be who she was and he seemed to accept the real her—the bad her, the good her, whichever *her* happened to be on display at any particular moment. There was no pretense with him. No trying to be something she wasn't, like with Bradley.

Maybe he was right and she was making a huge mistake by planning to marry Bradley in order to please her parents. She'd barely thought of Bradley while she'd been in Sin City fucking another man, not to mention a number of the man's friends. And she hadn't even bothered to call him to say she was back.

She'd told herself that was because she was so rushed and would be so busy for the next week or two, and also because they were officially broken up at the moment, but she knew in her heart it was really because she'd enjoyed being away from him and just hadn't wanted to hear his chipper, yuppie voice, the very sound of which somehow urged her to put on an act, be someone she wasn't.

And maybe...maybe she'd also made a big mistake leaving Marc if she felt this strongly about him.

Maybe...she should call him, tell him—tell him she'd ditch Adrianna, Inc. and come back to him this very minute if he wanted her to.

Taking a deep breath and reminding herself that someone as exhausted as she was couldn't make rational decisions, she decided she needed a distraction. From Adrianna, Inc. *and* Marc. And what better distraction existed than e-mail? Laying down her pencil, she turned to her laptop and clicked to check it.

When she saw Marc's name in her inbox, her stomach did a somersault. And her heart lifted. Crazy, but it made him seem so much closer, already.

She opened it without delay.

Hey sweetheart, good news. I got the job in Paris. No word on when I'll be leaving, but soon — I'm giving Adrianna my notice in the morning. Wish me luck. Guess this means no more phone calls for us, but at least there's always e-mail, right? Take care, and hope you're not too snowed under at the office. M

She let out a huge sigh. So much for going back to him this very second. His message was at once so comfortable-sounding, so at ease, and yet…was that all they would have now? E-mail?

She typed a reply.

Congratulations on the wonderful news! I hope you find your heart's desire, the thing you feel passionate about, in Paris.

Here, well, snowed under is putting it lightly. It's more like an avalanche.

That said, I should get back to work. Keep in touch, and when you get to Paris, eat an éclair for me. D

After hitting Send, she closed her eyes for a moment to blink back a tear. Then she picked her pencil back up, determined to return to work, deciding she simply couldn't think about this anymore. Rebuilding an entire ad campaign and computer system from scratch suddenly sounded much easier.

* * * * *

A week later, Diana sat at home in her condo in a pair of flannel pajama shorts and a thin tank top. Yesterday Richard had officially sent her home with orders to sleep for two or three days. So she'd slept for over twenty-four hours straight, not counting short breaks to eat something or go to the bathroom, and she was beginning to feel human again. Not human enough to put on real clothes or leave the house, but human enough that she'd gotten up, made herself some eggs and bacon, even though it was officially evening, and was now watching a sitcom on TV.

But she couldn't relax completely, she realized, because something was weighing on her, something she knew now that she must do, only she hadn't done it *yet*.

Taking a deep breath, she used the remote to turn down the sound on the TV, then picked up the cordless phone next to her and dialed Bradley's number.

When he answered, he sounded so glad to hear from her that she almost chickened out—but then she remembered that she was doing what would be best for him in the end, too. So she forced herself to begin. "Bradley, you remember how I wanted some time to think about us and decide if we should continue our relationship?"

"Of course I do. It's killed me to let you have that time, but I didn't want to pressure you."

To *let* her have time? As if it were his to give? She brushed aside her annoyance and forged on. "Well, I've made a decision. I *don't* wish to continue. I've decided it's best if we go our separate ways."

"Wh-what? Diana, why?"

Poor Bradley was obviously dumbfounded and she felt like a heel, but Diana knew now that she could never be the good girl he needed and that her family wanted. She totally understood Shyla's little analogy now. When you took the feathers off a chicken, it *was* still a chicken. And she was still a bad girl. "You and I are...different," she said. "More different than you could possibly know. And even though you won't believe me, trust me when I tell you that we could never make each other happy in a long-term relationship."

Even if she was alone forever, she was a bad girl to the core and knew she couldn't change it—didn't even want to. Now that Marc had opened her up to so many new, exciting experiences, she understood that deep inside she wanted more than Bradley. She wanted the kind of exciting, sensual life she'd found with Marc in Vegas.

Of course, she no longer had Marc to *share* that sensual life with, but she'd come to accept that it was part of her soul and it wasn't going to change. It had been a waste of her time, and Bradley's, to pretend it could.

"I'm just sorry I kept you waiting. I want you to move on and find the *right* woman for yourself and have a nice life, okay?"

It took some convincing for Bradley to accept their breakup, but fifteen minutes after she'd called him, she finally hung up, feeling an immense sense of relief. Her life was hardly in order, but this was definitely a step in the right direction, and one less concern to be plagued with. And now Bradley could get over her and move on with his search for the real Mrs. Right.

Her next call was to Shyla. Her girlfriend had been working just as hard as she had, but Richard had sent her home for mandatory rest yesterday, too, promising that the worst of the crisis was over and they could all resume normal hours from this point forward. Diana hoped Shyla was feeling rested now, as well, because she needed someone to talk to.

Fortunately, Shyla sounded even more awake than Diana and agreed to come right over.

When Diana opened the door to her friend twenty minutes later, Shyla looked dressed to kill, even just wearing a simple pair of fitted black pants and a clingy, sleeveless top that showed off her curves.

Shyla put her hands on her hips at the sight of Diana. "You're still wearin' your pajamas, girl? Not that you don't look hot, sugar, 'cause that skimpy little top is doin' fine things to your breasts, but I thought maybe we'd go out, get a drink, drown your sorrows, find you a new man."

Diana glanced down to see that her nipples were jutting through her thin cotton top. She hadn't given it a thought when she'd called Shyla. "I was thinking more of a girl's night in," Diana explained. "Popcorn, confessions, that sort of thing."

Shyla planted herself on Diana's sofa, patting the spot next to her. "All right, girlfriend. Come tell Shyla all about it."

Diana sat down next to her friend and gave Shyla the short version of what had happened in Vegas. "I couldn't say no to anything he wanted. Although I'll admit I didn't try very hard. I thought I was going to come back home and talk myself into marrying Bradley and that Vegas would be my last chance to have fun, and good sex, so I went for it, a hundred percent. And somewhere along the way, while I was trying to have this wild, no-holds-barred fun, I ended up falling for Marc. I've just never been with a guy who was so totally acceptant of the real me, who seemed to want something...real, something that mattered, even after I was a wild woman with his friends, maybe even *because* of that. But now he's going to Paris for a job, and I'm stuck here in Baltimore anyway, and...I just feel so lost. Lonely. Empty."

"Come here," Shyla said, holding out her arms, "and let Shyla make it all better."

Diana leaned into her friend, accepting the hug. Although when it went on longer than she expected, one of Shyla's hands lightly caressing her back, the other her hair, she realized Shyla wanted more than just a hug.

Diana had always thought Shyla attractive, and now that she'd come to know the joys of being with another woman, she thought she should feel tempted. Shyla was beautiful and sexy with her pale bronze skin, her almond-shaped eyes, her tall, thin model's body...and maybe getting lost in a little physical pleasure was just what Diana needed.

She let her own hands begin to slowly roam Shyla's back and she pressed her thinly covered breasts against her girlfriend's.

"That's right, sugar," Shyla murmured in her ear. "Just let it all go."

Part of her *was* tempted...but a much bigger part of her just wasn't into it. Despite herself, the only person she wanted to be with sexually was Marc.

Finally, she pulled away, out of Shyla's embrace. "I'm sorry, I can't."

A slow smile of understanding grew on Shyla's coral lips.

"It's not you," Diana said, "it's me. It's...Marc."

Shyla patted her knee. "That's okay, sugar. I thought maybe I could interest you in *another* kind of comfort, but I can dish the girl talk with you just as easy," she concluded with a wink that put Diana at ease.

Diana smiled. "Thanks for understanding." Then she glanced toward the kitchen, deciding she was hungry again. "Want some popcorn?"

"What I really want, looks like I ain't gonna get," Shyla replied with a mischievous grin. "But popcorn sounds like a decent substitute."

* * * * *

Still not quite recovered from her around-the-clock work, Diana slept in late on Monday, arriving at the office around ten. To her relief, the whole mood of the place seemed calmer than when she'd last left it, reassuring her that the crisis truly was over and nothing bad had happened since her last departure.

As soon as she sat down behind her desk, coffee cup in hand, Shyla appeared in the doorway, decked out in a fuchsia skirt and coordinating blouse that — as usual — only she could pull off with ease.

"Morning, girlfriend."

Diana cast a tired smile. "Morning."

"Don't get your pretty ass too comfortable in that chair. Richard wants to see you right away."

Diana sighed. Was there no rest for the weary? The last time Richard had summoned her like this, he'd sent her dashing off to Las Vegas — and a week of sinful pleasures that had turned her world upside down. What could he want *now*? "If he thinks he's going to send me jetting off to some other Adrianna's office or boutique with no notice, he's in for a surprise."

Shyla wiggled her hips and gave her fingers a dramatic snap. "You tell him, girl."

Taking her coffee with her so it wouldn't get cold, Diana trudged down the hall to Richard's office. The door was open, so she didn't bother knocking, just walked in, set her cup down on his desk, and took a seat across from him. "What now?"

A Cheshire cat's smile spread across Richard's face. He looked like a man who had a secret.

"What is it?" she demanded. "Spill."

"Diana," he said very calmly, resting his hands atop his blotter and lacing his fingers together, "you've been offered a new position."

Diana blinked. "What?"

"You've been offered a job as head of marketing at corporate. Adrianna just called."

Diana still couldn't quite absorb what he was telling her. Maybe she *still* hadn't had enough sleep. She shook her head lightly. "What are you talking about?"

Richard continued smiling at her. "Marc put in his notice recently, and now that he and Kelly are both gone, Adrianna thinks it's a good time to reconfigure. She wants you to reorganize the department, to centralize our national and international marketing efforts, to run the whole show in terms of marketing Adrianna, Inc. to the world." His smile faded just slightly. "So, we'll miss you if you choose to go, but it's a big step up in the organization, and just to put in my two cents, you'd be crazy not to take it."

Diana's first thought was how ironic it was that this would happen *now*, now that she was free from Bradley but Marc was leaving the country.

Yet it still sounded like a great opportunity, a huge leap in her career, and...well, whenever she finally got over Marc and started wanting to party again, where better to do it than Vegas? Not to mention that she already knew much of the department and thought she'd be happy working with them. It took less than a minute for her to make up her mind. "Tell Adrianna I accept and will be happy to start as soon as I can make relocation arrangements."

"The expenses of which will be covered by the company, of course," he added.

"Of course," she said, and for some reason it reminded her of Adrianna's promise to compensate her for her dedication. This job must have been what she meant.

Her head was spinning by the time she left Richard's office. She was excited about this change. It would be a whole new chapter in her life, a whole new beginning, something she desperately needed right now.

Returning to her desk, she realized she was too keyed up to dive into work just yet. But on a lark, she decided to e-mail Marc.

Guess what? Adrianna has offered me a job...as Head of Marketing! I'll be relocating to Vegas as soon as possible. What timing, huh? You'll probably be in Paris before I arrive, but if you're still there, I'd love to see you at least one last time before you go. No travel plans yet – this is brand new news! – but I'll call you as soon as I arrive. D

A few minutes later, she got a reply.

Wow, congratulations! Head of Marketing! I can't think of a more worthy person for the job – you deserve it. My travel plans still aren't completely set, either, and I may not know exactly when I'm leaving until almost the last minute, but yes – try calling me as soon as you get here. I miss you and would love to see you again. M

Of course, seeing Marc one last time, all the while knowing they'd soon be parted, would be nothing short of torture. Yet *that* was a temptation she *couldn't* resist. Torture, yes, but of the sweetest kind.

* * * * *

The next two weeks were nonstop work for Diana. In addition to packing up her home, putting her condo on the market, and saying goodbye to friends and family, she'd also been trying to wrap up her old job and help Shyla—who'd been promoted to take her place—transition into it.

The night before she left, she'd had dinner with her parents and her younger sister, Carrie. Of course, they'd been upset to hear she'd broken things off with Bradley, but the job transfer had helped smooth things out with them. Although they'd miss having her nearby, they were proud of her career achievements and they seemed proud of this promotion, too.

Even so, she'd firmly decided she had no intentions of living a lie with them, so she made it clear over dinner that she'd parted ways with Bradley not because of the relocation, but because they had so little in common and, "Face it, Mom, Bradley is just too straight of an arrow for me. I need fun, excitement. And if I *ever* get married, I need a man who appreciates that about me."

She'd been surprised at how well they took it, and she supposed her older sister Liz, had sort of paved the way for her with her recent "break from ranks" down in New Orleans.

"Besides," Diana added with a wink, "you guys have always got Carrie to fall back on." The most conservative sister of the three, Carrie would definitely always serve as the good girl her parents needed at least *one* of their daughters to be.

"Maybe now would be a good time to tell you," Carrie had chimed in. "Jon and I have finally set a date." A wedding date, she meant.

And given how long it had been in coming, their mother's face had instantly lit up as she said, "Oh my, we'll have so much work to do! What's the date? Tell me everything."

Carrie looked sheepish. "Uh, don't have a total cow, but we've only got a couple of months to plan the wedding."

"A couple of months! What's the hurry? The boy takes years getting around to this and suddenly we're in a mad rush?"

"Well, I guess we're both feeling like we've waited long enough, so why wait any longer?"

It had taken the emphasis *off* Diana—thank goodness—and when she'd been congratulating her little sister privately after the meal, she'd also thanked her for her impeccable timing.

Carrie had shrugged and smiled. "What are little sisters for?"

Now, Diana was stepping into a lavish suite in The Four Seasons, a complex connected to Mandalay Bay at one end of the Las Vegas Strip. Although she hadn't spoken to Marc again by phone or e-mail, she'd decided to go out on a limb and book a luxury room for the weekend, in case she was fortunate enough to find him still in town and wanting to get together.

The amazing suite was the most incredible hotel room she'd ever seen, offering a spacious living room and bedroom, each featuring a wall of windows overlooking the strip, and the *piece de resistance*, an enormous Jacuzzi on an elevated platform that jutted outward, surrounded on three sides by a stunning view of the strip and the mountains far beyond. Night was falling and soon the view would be filled with dazzling neon of all colors, the street of sinful dreams stretching out before her like a magical, modern-day Yellow Brick Road. This, she thought, was a place for a truly fitting goodbye to her lover.

Now she only had to pray he was still here, in Vegas, to share the extravagant bathtub with her.

Her heart pounded against her chest as she picked up the phone and dialed his number.

After the first ring, she was nervous. By the second, she was catching her breath, anticipating the sound of his deep, masculine voice. After the third, she became worried that she was too late and he was already gone. Her chest tightened and her hopes for a wonderful weekend of sex and companionship plummeted.

By ring number six, she was ready to hang up the phone, cut her losses, and try to at least enjoy her lavish surroundings, even if she was alone.

"Hello?" said an out-of-breath voice.

She gasped lightly. "Marc? It's me. Diana."

"Thank God I got to the phone—I was out on the balcony, hanging with Carter. Are you here?"

"Yeah."

"Can I come see you?"

"Definitely."

"Where are you?"

"The Four Seasons." She gave him the room number.

"Give me an hour," he said. "And put on something way too skimpy to go out in, because once I get there, we're not leaving the room."

Her thoughts exactly.

Chapter Eleven

"She's here, I have to go," Marc said, sticking his head out the French door to where Carter sat, drinking a beer.

His friend raised his eyebrows and cast a smile. "Good luck, buddy. And hey, enjoy!"

As Marc left the condo, he thought that enjoying her wouldn't be a problem, but he *might* need some luck when she heard what he had to say. Had he gone too far? Taken things between them too seriously? He'd only find out once he got there and told her what he'd done.

It was all he could do to drive the car—he wanted to see her so badly his chest burned. He couldn't wait to look into her beautiful hazel eyes, kiss her luscious lips, take her sumptuous body in his arms.

When he turned on to Las Vegas Boulevard as night began to fall, the lights and energy of the place seemed to beckon to him in a whole new way. He wanted to speed to the Four Seasons as fast as his four wheels would carry him, but he had a stop to make first. At the Paris Hotel.

After that, his night, his world, was all about Diana.

* * * * *

Diana's chest ached with anticipation as she dressed for her reunion with Marc. She put on her most extravagant piece of Adrianna, Inc. lingerie, from the Champagne and Diamonds collection, and stepped in front of the mirror.

The champagne-colored lace teddy hugged her from crotch to breasts. It featured a thong back, and a satin lace-up front that fit so tight it barely concealed her nipples. Her thigh-high stockings were nude and their lace tops had tiny bits of gold thread spun through for a shimmer effect. To finish the outfit, she added diamond earrings and a matching rhinestone choker, as well as champagne-colored strappy heels. She wanted him to remember this night, wanted him to have to compare every lover he took in Paris to her *and* decide they didn't measure up.

She'd ordered a bottle of champagne from room service as soon as she'd hung up with him — along with a few other choice items to make their evening deliciously memorable — and now she poured herself a glass of the bubbly to calm her nerves.

Before she even took a sip, though, a knock came on her door. And, like magic, when she looked through the peephole and saw Marc on the other side, any nervousness fled. It was her sweet, exciting lover, the man who fulfilled all her desires and put her at ease in every way. Why had she been nervous at all?

When she opened the door, she found him wearing black jeans and a silky, short-sleeved, button-up shirt that hugged his broad shoulders and lay pleasantly over his muscular chest. He looked even more handsome than she remembered as his eyes took in her sexy ensemble.

"Sweetheart, you did it again," he told her as easily as if they'd seen each other yesterday.

"Did what?"

"Made me hard with just one glimpse of you."

She smiled and drew him in the door with her free hand, then passed him a glass of champagne. "Let's toast."

He grinned, lifting his glass. "All right. To this night, and whatever it may hold."

The warm words he'd echoed on their very first night together seemed to burst apart into tiny shimmery lights that wafted down through Diana's body. Clinking her glass with his, she took a drink.

He did, too. "Mmm, you got the good stuff."

"I wanted to make this night special. A little expense and room service seemed in order."

"Well, I have something for you, too." With that, he opened a small bakery bag she hadn't even noticed him holding, and drew out a fancy scallop-edged paper cup containing two mini-éclairs like the ones they'd shared at the Paris Hotel.

Holding one of them up, he fed it to her. The sweet confection filled her mouth with cream and chocolate. Swallowing, she said, "Yum. Thank you."

Finishing his own éclair, he licked his lips and looked long and deep into her eyes. "I'm glad you liked it, sweetheart, because that's as close as I'm going to get to a real Parisian éclair."

Diana blinked, confused. "What do you mean?"

Taking her hands, he pulled her over to sit down on a plush divan. "It means that...well, after I heard you were coming back here, to stay, I decided to stay, too. I decided I want to soak up all the sin in Sin City with you.

"You're so wild and fun and unapologetic about your sensuality...getting to know your beautiful free spirit has made me realize you're exactly the kind of woman I need in my life, and that...well, *you're* the thing I've been looking for, Diana, the one thing I truly feel passionate about. I figured out I couldn't find that in Paris—I can only find it here, at your side."

Diana's heart filled nearly to bursting with emotion. He was staying? To be with her? Somehow this whole crazy mess had worked out so that she could have her dream job in a dream city with her dream *man*? It seemed impossible, but he was telling her it was so, and Marc was always honest with her, so it must be true.

"I...love the way you accept me for me," she told him. "I've never been so happy in my life as I was with you those few days I was here. And I've never been so miserable as I was at home, without you."

"You're beautiful and exciting and I could never want to change you, baby."

"And your job?"

He grinned. "Adrianna was happy to give it back to me. Hope you don't mind being my boss."

She finally kissed him then. It wasn't a choice, but a thing her body was simply driven to do. She took his beautifully handsome face in her hands and lifted her mouth to his, just basking in the joy of being back in his presence.

His arms closed around her and he held her tight for a few long moments, until finally he resumed kissing her— her mouth, her neck, her breasts. He let his palms slide over the champagne lace that hugged her curves, molding warmly to her hips, ass, breasts, before finally untying the satin string that held the fabric closed over her chest.

Pushing it aside to free her breasts, he laid her back on the bed to caress them with both hands and mouth. "Mmm, I've missed these, sweetheart. So damn much."

"They've missed you, too," she promised, adding, "*only* you."

He lowered another kiss to her puckered nipple, which hummed its way through her body, then looked up. "Hmm?"

"They've…I've…" She shook her head lightly against the bed. "I just haven't wanted anyone since you."

He flashed his sexy grin. "No Bradley?"

"Bradley's out of the picture—completely. I told him I didn't want to get back together, that we both needed to move on."

"What about your big plan?"

She smiled. "Sometimes plans change."

Marc leaned his head back slightly. "Thank God." Then he looked back at her. "And no one else, either?"

She shook her head. "As much as I loved the experiences I had with you and your friends, I've figured out that I loved fucking you alone the very best. And since we haven't had much practice at that, well…how would you feel about getting a little more? Or maybe a *lot* more?"

"Sweetheart, that would be my deepest pleasure—for now, and for always."

She arched one eyebrow. "You won't miss watching me with someone else?"

He hesitated, then grinned. "I was going to let this be a surprise, but I just had a big mirror installed above my bed. And on my closet doors. And on the opposite wall. So I can watch and *do* at the same time."

She grinned. "Naughty boy."

"Inspired by my naughty girl."

Diana's body tingled with the pure joy of having him back, just the way she wanted, knowing this was real, lasting, between them. It was a dream come true. And now that they'd said everything important to one another, she began to feel like the more aggressive woman he'd come to know.

Pushing past him to rise off the bed, she reached down for his hand, pulling him up to his feet. Leading him across the lavish suite with her breasts exposed somehow added to her feeling of sensual power.

Once they reached the Jacuzzi, where she'd drawn a hot bubble bath before he'd arrived, she instructed him to get undressed.

He grinned. "Am I the slave tonight?"

She laughed. "Nothing quite so serious as that, but...I have plans for you, so just be a good boy and do what I say."

Keeping his sexy gaze on her, he stripped out of his shoes, shirt, and jeans, then pushed down his underwear, stepping free while she watched. His cock was just as magnificently large as she recalled, and it stood at complete attention for her. She couldn't wait for a taste of it.

"Now," she said, "step into the tub, but not *all the way* in — just sit on the edge."

Following her order, he descended carefully into the Jacuzzi, resting on the upper rim, awaiting her. Behind his lovely naked body, the Las Vegas strip was coming alive, the neon glow providing the perfect, exciting backdrop for her perfect, exciting man.

Slowly, she too undressed as he took in every move with hungry eyes. After easing free of the shoulder straps, she ran her hands over her plump breasts, then toyed lightly with her nipples.

"I want to taste them again," he said from his place at the edge of the tub.

"Soon," she promised, "and the next time they're in your mouth, I promise they'll taste extra good."

Next, she wiggled her hips a little as she slowly pushed the champagne teddy over them and down. It dropped to the carpet in a rush of lace, and she stepped free of it, naked but for her shoes, stockings, and jewelry.

Sitting down on the tub platform across from where he waited, Diana spread her legs for his viewing pleasure, stroking one long finger up the center of her pussy and putting it in her mouth to suck it clean.

She saw Marc pull in his breath and could have sworn his cock swelled even bigger in response.

Reaching one slender leg out across the expanse of the tub, she said, "Take off my shoe."

He did as she asked, gently caressing her foot in the process.

"Now, slowly remove my stocking."

He used both hands, caressing both inner and outer thigh as he rolled it down with painstaking thoroughness that had her cunt practically dripping.

After he finally completed the task, she pulled back her leg and offered the other one. His shoe and stocking removal was just as lingering and sexy this time, and she liked that he was willing to go as slow as she requested, given how badly she knew they both wanted to just leap on each other.

Finally, Diana stepped down into the tub and knelt before him. "Spread your legs."

He did as she asked and she took his big, hard cock in her fist, drawing it downward, toward her face. She used her other hand to reach up on the edge of the tub next to her lover and remove the linen tablecloth she'd used to hide her little tray of delights. It contained the open bottle of champagne resting in an ice bucket, a bowl of strawberries, and another bowl filled with melted chocolate.

He laughed when he saw the chocolate, pointing. "*That* wasn't on the room service menu."

She shook her head, agreeing. "A special request I relayed to the very nice lady on the phone."

He stopped laughing, though, when Diana dipped a soup spoon in the bowl, using it to dribble warm chocolate on his erection.

"Oh God," he murmured, looking down at her as she licked the dark chocolate off the tip of his cock.

A naughty smile grew on his face. "You want more than that, don't you, sweetheart?"

Flashing a playful expression, she gave an enthusiastic nod before easing her mouth over his nice, chocolaty cock. The chocolate filled her senses with delectable taste as his dick filled her mouth with heat and desire. She sucked him, enjoying both sensations more than she could have predicted. And when she had sucked him nearly clean of all the chocolate, she released his slightly messy hard-on from her mouth and smiled up at him.

"How was that?" he asked.

"Delicious, of course."

"Want some more?"

"Mmm, yes. Chocolate-covered cock is one of my favorite treats."

He laughed and said, "Well, baby, we'll just have to make sure you get to have it all the time." He reached for the spoon, adding, "I love what a bad girl you are for me," just before spreading another thick glaze of melted chocolate over his length.

She didn't hesitate to close her lips over his sweet, tasty erection. This time she sucked him harder, swallowing the chocolate and any pre-come she might be drawing from his ever-so-stiff shaft. They covered his thick cock with chocolate three more times before they decided to move on to something else.

Marc announced he wanted some chocolate-covered breasts, so he eased down into the bubbles next to her, spooning the chocolate onto one of her nipples. "Mmm," she moaned, not only at the sensation but at how scrumptious it looked. "Lick it off."

Bending his head, Marc obeyed her, thoroughly cleaning her breast of the liquid chocolate.

"Now the other," she said.

He continued, dribbling chocolate on her, licking and sucking her clean, until finally he said, "I don't know about you, but I need something to wash all this chocolate down."

Diana reached for the strawberries and Marc extracted the champagne bottle from the ice. They took turns then, feeding each other the luscious red fruit and drinking champagne from the bottle.

Eventually, Marc spilled the champagne down her chest, licking and suckling her clean. She did the same with his cock before she perched on the side of the tub and playfully nestled strawberry after strawberry in the pink folds of her pussy, letting him extract them with his tongue.

After nearly an hour of food play, Marc leaned close to her ear and said, "This has been so incredibly erotic and fun, baby, that part of me never wants to stop, but another part of me is dying to fuck you so bad that I can hardly breathe."

"Mmm, I bet I know the particular part," she cooed, reaching into the bubbles until her hand was wrapped firmly around his enormous cock.

Setting all the food aside, they washed each other with the soap and soft sponges provided before Diana straddled him in the Jacuzzi, balancing her pussy on the head of his big, strong shaft. Biting her lip, looking into his eyes, she lowered herself, smoothly taking him inside.

"Oh, baby," he moaned. "This is like coming home."

"Mmm," she sighed, "Yes. Home."

And it was. She'd thought she might never have him inside her again, and that moment of being filled with him truly *was* like going back to someplace she missed, someplace she cherished. "So big," she whispered. "So hard."

"All for you, baby. All for you."

She rode him, soft at first, and then with more power—she just wanted to feel him in her, penetrating deeper, fucking her harder than ever before. "Fuck me," she whispered. "Fuck me, baby."

"I'm going to fuck you forever, sweetheart. Every day and every night."

His hands roamed her body, her breasts, her ass, until finally he inserted one finger into her tight little asshole, said, "I love you," and made her come with a fury she'd never experienced before.

"Oh God, yes, yes, yes, yes," she panted, riding it out for all it was worth, realizing he was there, too—pumping hard and deep and furious into her, letting out a deep, satiated sigh, then resting his head on her shoulder.

"I love you, too," she whispered in his ear. "I'm so glad I'm here with you, Marc. I suddenly can't imagine being with any other man in any other place in the world."

Slowly, he lifted his head, and flashed a wicked smile. "Welcome to Sin City, sweetheart."

Enjoy this excerpt from

HOT FOR SANTA

© Copyright Lacey Alexander 2003

"Would you like to sit on Santa's lap, little girl?"

Would I ever! thought Amy Finnegan.

But, of course, he wasn't talking to her. Forcing a smile, she reached up to straighten her green elf hat, then took the hand of the child in question. Leading the little blonde girl to Santa's throne-like chair, situated in the middle of the mall, she watched the child climb onto one red-clad thigh.

Oh, to be able to lower *her* ass onto that sexy thigh. She wanted to moan at the mere thought. Her breasts tingled against her elf costume just imagining that the man with the fake white beard had summoned *her*.

She bit her lip, envisioning what it would be like if the two of them were alone here, if her sexy Santa invited her to sit on his lap, and if she chose to straddle him in his big red chair instead. Her pussy went damp when she pictured him running his hands up under her little green dress, all the way to her hips to discover she hadn't worn any panties.

Of course, she *had* worn panties, every single day they'd worked together, but since everything else about the vision was pure fantasy, why not go all the way?

When Santa lifted her dress in front, spying her bare slit, all open and ready for him, he'd immediately reach into those fur-trimmed pants of his, pull out his hard cock, and watch as she lowered her hungry little cunt down on it, taking it deep inside.

"You know what?" Santa's deep voice boomed.

Amy flinched as she was yanked from her fantasy, only to find he was still addressing the little girl.

"You're the very last child to tell me what she wants for Christmas this year before I hop in my sleigh tonight and start delivering toys."

The tow-headed girl looked uncertain. "Will you have time to make mine?"

Santa smiled. "Of course I will, with the help of my trusty elf, Amy." He pointed in her direction. "She's my favorite little helper." He sent her a quick wink, and dear God, even *that* made her pussy pulse.

After convincing the little girl she'd get everything on her list, he lowered her to the floor, told her to be good, and—flashing a grin that looked sexy as hell even behind his snowy beard—told her not to forget the cookies, since he'd need a snack by the time he got to her house.

As the child ran off to her waiting mother, Amy saw him glance to the large, ornate clock suspended from the mall's ceiling. Pushing to his booted feet, he took a few steps toward her. When he spoke, it came out a little less hale and hearty than his Santa voice, but the warm tenor of his tone still heated her up inside. "Well, that's the last one. Looks like I can hang up my beard for good."

She tried to sound just as cheerful. "And I can take off my pointy elf shoes for the last time."

She knew she should be happy about that, but she wasn't. She'd never dreamed she could lust so hard for a man in a Santa suit, but now that it was Christmas Eve and their charity work was drawing to a close, a heavy shroud of disappointment settled over her. She'd looked forward to seeing him every day after work for the few hours they did the Santa gig together in the evening. And during the last month, Saturdays and Sundays had become her very favorite days of the week, even if it meant elf detail from ten to ten. Now, as the final last-minute shoppers dashed past and storekeepers began to lower their steel link doors, she couldn't help thinking how boring her nights would seem from this point on, without even the *hope* he would make a move on her. It was going to be a long, cold winter.

About the author:

Lacey Alexander's books have been called deliciously decadent, unbelievably erotic, exceptionally arousing, blazingly sexual, and downright sinful. In each book, Lacey strives to take her readers on the ultimate erotic adventure and hopes her books will encourage women to embrace their sexual fantasies. Lacey resides in the Midwest with her husband, and when not penning romantic erotica, she enjoys history and traveling, often incorporating favorite travel destinations into her work.

Lacey welcomes mail from readers. You can write to her c/o Ellora's Cave Publishing at 1337 Commerce Drive, Suite 13, Stow OH 44224.

Why an electronic book?

We live in the Information Age—an exciting time in the history of human civilization in which technology rules supreme and continues to progress in leaps and bounds every minute of every hour of every day. For a multitude of reasons, more and more avid literary fans are opting to purchase e-books instead of paperbacks. The question to those not yet initiated to the world of electronic reading is simply: *why?*

1. *Price.* An electronic title at Ellora's Cave Publishing runs anywhere from 40-75% less than the cover price of the <u>exact same title</u> in paperback format. Why? Cold mathematics. It is less expensive to publish an e-book than it is to publish a paperback, so the savings are passed along to the consumer.

2. *Space.* Running out of room to house your paperback books? That is one worry you will never have with electronic novels. For a low one-time cost, you can purchase a handheld computer designed specifically for e-reading purposes. Many e-readers are larger than the average handheld, giving you plenty of screen room. Better yet, hundreds of titles can be stored within your new library—a single microchip. (Please note that Ellora's Cave does not endorse any specific brands. You can check our website at www.ellorascave.com for customer recommendations we make available to new consumers.)

3. *Mobility.* Because your new library now consists of only a microchip, your entire cache of books can be taken with you wherever you go.

4. *Personal preferences are accounted for.* Are the words you are currently reading too small? Too large? Too...**ANNOYING**? Paperback books cannot be modified according to personal preferences, but e-books can.

5. *Innovation.* The way you read a book is not the only advancement the Information Age has gifted the literary community with. There is also the factor of what you can read. Ellora's Cave Publishing will be introducing a new line of interactive titles that are available in e-book format only.

6. *Instant gratification.* Is it the middle of the night and all the bookstores are closed? Are you tired of waiting days—sometimes weeks—for online and offline bookstores to ship the novels you bought? Ellora's Cave Publishing sells instantaneous downloads 24 hours a day, 7 days a week, 365 days a year. Our e-book delivery system is 100% automated, meaning your order is filled as soon as you pay for it.

Those are a few of the top reasons why electronic novels are displacing paperbacks for many an avid reader. As always, Ellora's Cave Publishing welcomes your questions and comments. We invite you to email us at service@ellorascave.com or write to us directly at: 1337 Commerce Drive, Suite 13, Stow OH 44224.

Discover for yourself why readers can't get enough of the multiple award-winning publisher Ellora's Cave. Whether you prefer e-books or paperbacks, be sure to visit EC on the web at www.ellorascave.com for an erotic reading experience that will leave you breathless.

WWW.ELLORASCAVE.COM

Printed in the United States
38647LVS00001B/50

9 781419 951695